Buried in Shamrocks

Also available by Lisa Q. Mathews

The Irish Bed & Breakfast Mysteries

The Jig is Up

The Ladies Smythe & Westin Series

Fashionably Late
Permanently Booked
Cardiac Arrest

Buried in Shamrocks

AN IRISH BED & BREAKFAST MYSTERY

Lisa Q. Mathews

NEW YORK

Published in the United States by Crooked Lane Books, an imprint of The Quick Brown Fox & Company LLC.

Library of Congress Catalog-in-Publication data available upon request.

ISBN (hardcover): 979-8-89242-107-2
ISBN (paperback): 979-8-89242-241-3
ISBN (ebook): 979-8-89242-108-9

Cover design by Rob Fiore

Printed in the United States.

www.crookedlanebooks.com

Crooked Lane Books
34 West 27th St., 10th Floor
New York, NY 10001

First Edition: February 2026

The authorized representative in the EU for product safety and compliance is eucomply OÜPärnu mnt 139b-14, 11317 Tallinn, Estonia, hello@eucompliancepartner.com, +33757690241

10 9 8 7 6 5 4 3 2 1

With love to "The Chief" in our family,
John Thomas Quinn.
This one's for you, Daddy.

Chapter One

"Saint Anthony, Saint Anthony, come around. Something's lost and can't be found."

My seven-year-old daughter Bliz, occasionally known as Mary Elizabeth, squeezed her eyes shut in concentration, rocking in her green jelly sandals as she repeated her singsong chant.

"Don't think that's going to work, Blizzie B." Maeve shaded her eyes and frowned from the driveway into the open Buckley family garage. Well, it used to be my parents' garage. The entire space was now even more stuffed to the rafters with boxes and bags and assorted junk. On either side of the rusty basketball hoop above the garage door, Irish and American flags drooped in the late-June, midday heat.

At least it wasn't lashing rain like the last time we arrived here in Shamrock, Massachusetts. Not yet anyway. Gray thunderclouds were already starting to move across the robin's-egg blue sky.

"Don't discourage her, honey," I murmured to Maeve. "She's praying. Sort of."

Maeve, my doppelganger with her slender build and shoulder-length auburn hair, gave me the fourteen-year-old eye roll behind Bliz's back and reached down to give her little sister a squeeze. "Saint Anthony is really busy right now," she explained. "He has to help lots of other people find super important things. Like wedding rings and wills and actual missing persons. Not Barbies."

Sparks instantly replaced the tears in Bliz's bright blue eyes. "Ciara is *not* a Barbie. Well, not anymore. She's my Irish dancer doll. Gram made special dresses for her and everything."

I brushed away a long blond curl plastered to my younger daughter's cheek by humidity and tears. "Sweetie, we'll find Ciara soon, I promise." I gestured vaguely toward the garage. "When we unpack all of this. But that may take a while."

Little green lie number ten-thousand-and-one today. Who knew if we'd ever completely unpack.

The dinged and dented, cheapest-available moving van was still parked here in the driveway of the Buckley House, my parents' B&B. The vacancy sign, I noticed, leaned perilously close to the sidewalk. Had we somehow hit it with the van?

I jogged over to straighten the sign. When it didn't budge, I pulled harder, and the whole thing came all the way out of the ground. Rotten wood from the recent rains, probably. And was that a bug? No, *three* bugs. Ugh. I decided against hauling the sign to the trash can next to the garage and stuck it back as best I could in the soggy lawn. The trash was already full anyway.

I'd mention the sign rot to my dad later. And I knew exactly what he'd say: "Fetch my hammer there from the garage, will you, Kathleen? Or maybe you'd want to give it a go yourself."

When the Chief was mildly annoyed, he called me "Kathleen." When he was in a more jovial or sentimental mood, I was "Katie Margaret." As if I were ten. To everyone else, I was mostly "Kate."

Of course I didn't mind helping out with home maintenance. But again . . . *bugs.*

Brushing dirt from my T-shirt, I glanced down Galway Court, with its parade of neat homes: triple-deckers, small Victorians, duplexes, and the occasional Craftsman with cozy porch glider. In keeping with the town's Irish theme, practically every front yard on the block boasted some festive offering of summer décor in green, white, and orange. Lawn leprechauns, gazing balls, limp windsocks and balloons, fairy bird baths, you name it—with Boston sports team paraphernalia thrown in for good measure.

Oh, how nice. The Sheehans had put out a plastic bucket filled with multi-colored chalk sticks, so passers-by could draw pictures or leave messages on the sidewalk.

I squinted. Yikes. Maybe not the best idea. Hopefully some of those ruder messages would be washed out by the rain before any kids saw them. Or the Sheehans.

The sole Buckley House nods to the Celtic craziness usually consisted of an Irish flag or two beside the American ones and the green and gold awning that said, *Céad míle fáilte*—"a hundred thousand welcomes" in Irish. The porch bunting was a new addition this summer. And my dad had placed a fresh Emerald Society sticker in the window next to the front door.

As the beloved former head of the Shamrock PD, Dermot Buckley had to make at least a nod or two to the Green Wave. Even now that he was reluctantly retired after being seriously injured in the line of duty, our family—like everyone else in town—still called him the Chief.

After thirty years of distinguished service on the force, old habits died hard.

My once rough-and-tumble hometown had nearly gone broke about ten years ago. But thanks to the zealous efforts of the mayor, Chamber of Commerce, the Turn Shamrock Green resident coalition, and a slew of determined developers, it was now charmingly—and lucratively—Irish-themed. You didn't have to be Irish—many of the residents and business owners weren't green-blooded in the least—to join in all the fun. And profits. Shamrock's year-round celebrations and festivals—not to mention its trendy restaurants, pubs, concerts, dance shows, and shopping—brought eager tourists by the busloads.

Well, until recently. Mom had reported that things were much quieter so far this summer. There was a sad reason for that. During Saint Patrick's week, when the girls and I last visited, a tragic murder had proven it wasn't always shillelaghs and shenanigans here in Shamrock.

The first homicide in a long while, Deirdre Donnelly's death had hit all of us Buckleys and the whole town especially hard. Deirdre, the Irish Steps star who'd retired early to run her family's dance school, was my sister Colleen's best friend.

Speaking of Colleen, where was she? She hadn't shown up to help us unpack the van. It was her idea for us to come out this summer. Oh well. Too late now.

Even if Shamrock was far from perfect, I loved my hometown. So many people close to my heart lived here. And it was a close-knit community, for better or for worse.

The new Shamrock made people happy. But other than Deirdre's murder, the Chief and I both missed the grittier version, which felt more real sometimes. Recently a miniature version of the Cliffs of Moher was built for tourists to rock climb out by Emerald Lake. No blarney.

The girls and I planned to stay here at the Buckley House at least until September. Our apartment back in the city was sublet through Labor Day when our annual lease was up. I needed to give our landlord a renewal decision by August first. He was itching to jack the rent.

"Hey Kate, we're done here, right?"

My brother Frank stepped out of the garage, wiping his brow with the shoulder of his faded Red Sox tee. The neckline sagged with sweat, revealing his thick gold chain. And I was pretty sure that was a grease stain from the breakfast sandwich he'd wolfed down on the Brooklyn–Queens Expressway.

I felt a twinge of guilt as I also noted a couple of white paint blotches. Over the weekend he had helped me touch up the apartment for the subletters. Part of the deal. My landlord declined to pay for the refresh. No shocker.

"Yup, we're done," I told my brother. "Really appreciate this, Frank. You've gone above and beyond."

He shrugged. "Have to take care of my elderly sis."

Seriously? There were less than three years between us. I was thirty-six, for heaven's sake. We were both more than a decade older than Colleen, though. She'd always be the baby, and next month she'd be twenty-five.

"I owe you, Frank. I'll buy you a new T-shirt." I reached up to pat his ebony hair, still styled perfectly in place. "Whoa, is that another gray hair?" I peered closer. "Hold still, I'll yank it out for you."

He stepped back, scowling. "Get outta here, Kate."

"Hey, some women love the silver fox look. Really." I grinned. "Go get cleaned up. You stink."

"Can't," he said. "Gotta get the truck back to the rental place before I start my tour. I'll grab a shower at the station. McGavin's gonna drop me there," he added, as I pulled my Subaru keys from my jeans pocket.

"Oh." I felt myself flush, and not due to the heat. Garrett McGavin and Frank both worked for the Shamrock PD. My brother didn't need to guess that my high-school boyfriend and I had started to get reacquainted—just a teensy bit—during Paddy's Week. Frank could be completely clueless sometimes, and he might spill the Boston baked beans to the Chief. They both liked Garrett, but I'd never hear the end of it.

The girls didn't need to know either. Because it was no big deal.

And here was Garrett now, pulling up at the curb in his sister Siobhan's heavily decaled SUV. A magnetic sign on the side advertised Shamrock's specialty pet store Paddy's Paws, which Siobhan managed. A single mom, she also managed a large household menagerie of foster fails, plus kids the same ages as mine.

Siobhan leaned out the passenger window, red curls spilling out of her retro-print bandanna. "Hey, Buckley clan!" she called, waving. "Special delivery for you."

Delivery? Had Maeve ordered something on her phone again?

Siobhan, never one to let the clover grow too fast under her Converse, hopped out of the car, followed by a pile of little girls. Yup, she was the ever-upbeat mom of triplets. Garrett was already trying to coax a senior golden retriever to jump down from the SUV's hatchback.

Poor doggo. Last time I'd seen him, walking in the Saint Patrick's Day parade with my sister and the Donnelly School of Irish Dance, he'd seemed fine. Probably a touch of arthritis.

"Rover!" Bliz squealed, her sandals dangerously flopping as she tore toward the newcomers. "You're here! And Brogan and Fiona and Ginger!"

I watched, confused, as Siobhan started tossing bags and boxes from the back of the SUV. Whatever was in them, we needed more stuff like a hole in our heads.

The pile of excited kids became a furious scrum, with the dog somewhere in the middle. Garrett, his dark hair buzzed even shorter for the summer, looked sheepish as he held the end of a leash embroidered with tiny beer mugs. At least his sharp navy polo and khakis, along with the shiny detective badge at his hip, lent him a shred of dignity.

I went over to give him a quick, hey-buddy hug. "Good to see you, Garrett." I gestured toward the blur of gold fur. "And you brought . . . Rover." Aka Irish Rover, like the song. Maeve had fallen in love the minute she'd spotted him at Paddy's Paws in March. Another of Siobhan's many fosters.

"Always room for more, right?" Garrett nodded toward my parents' white Victorian. I tried not to ignore the bright yellow dandelions dotting the grass. The steps up to the porch looked a little splintery, too. "The guests will love him. This guy can be the Buckley House's new mascot."

Wait, *what*? "Rover's, um, here to . . . stay?"

"Yup. Guess I'm off the hook for this ol' guy. Colleen officially adopted him." Siobhan came up and dropped a giant dog food bag at our feet. "For all of you. You know, to help the girls adjust to living here in Shamrock. And Rover already loves you guys. Colleen told us to bring him over right away, so he could be here to greet you."

Instead of her. "Wow, what a nice surprise."

What was my sister thinking? Sure, I'd said yes to Rover coming for visits, even overnights, this summer. But we had Banshee, our cat from the city, who was already somewhere in the house. And what if the girls and I didn't stay past the summer? We couldn't have a dog back in Brooklyn.

I found it hard to believe that Mom and Dad had signed off on another permanent guest for the B&B. We all loved dogs, including me. But the timing was terrible.

As if he'd read my thoughts, Rover peered out from around Garrett's legs and gave a doggy smile, panting with his tongue hanging out.

"Mommy, can we give him my last Munchkin?" Bliz asked. "It's not stale yet. It's wrapped up in your pock-a-book."

"No honey," I said. "Dogs can't eat sugar. And neither should you."

"He needs water," Maeve said. "I'll take him into the house." Even though it was generally uncool for her to show excitement about anything now that she was a rising ninth grader, her flushed face told me she was thrilled. And probably hot.

"See you later, pal." Garrett gave Rover a sendoff pat and handed the leash and one of the bowls to Maeve. Bliz and her friends skipped after them toward the house.

"All this stuff should last you for a while," Siobhan said to me, waving toward the bags. "Just let me know if there's anything else you need. I emailed Colleen a whole list of instructions. Rover's pretty mellow, but he really likes to be outside. You may have to keep an eye on him."

"The backyard is fenced," I said. "Mostly." The latch was loose on the gate last time I'd walked through it. Another item for the summer repair list.

"I'll bring all these up for you." Garrett piled the bags and an overflowing box into his well-muscled arms. He and Frank worked out at the gym off the Square where all the cops hung out.

"Thanks, Garrett." As he walked away, I discreetly peeled my striped Yankees jersey away from my sticky body. I could use a shower as much as Frank—well, almost—and I needed to ditch the shirt ASAP anyway. I wasn't in New York anymore, and doubted all the Sox fans here would give me special dispensation for moving day.

"I'm so glad you and the girls made it," Siobhan said, as Garrett started up the steps. A rawhide bone fell out of the box and bounced into the pachysandra below, but he didn't seem to notice. "I was worried you might change your minds."

A few times I'd come close to nixing the summer plan. But I'd promised Colleen. And Mom could use another set of hands for the B&B. "Oh, no, we're thrilled to be here," I said. "We have all kinds of family projects planned."

Frank emerged from the house, peanut butter and Fluff sandwich in hand. He stopped on the porch to hold the screen door open as Garrett dropped the dog supplies in the foyer. The girls and Rover wove around the bags and boxes and scrambled down the front steps.

"We'd better roll," Garrett said to Frank. My brother nodded with his mouth full.

"Everyone back in the car!" Siobhan called to her girls.

After a chorus of "do-we-have-to"s and farewells to Rover, the triplets scrambled toward the SUV.

"You'd think these kids didn't have enough other animals at home." Siobhan sighed. "Our place is a literal zoo. Conor's cleaning his Komodo dragon's lair right now," she added with a shudder. "My crazy son is obsessed with that thing. But hey, Kate, just give a shout if you need to talk. All the fair drama will be tough on you."

Drama? No, thanks. I had enough of that in my life already.

Each year around the Fourth of July, the town hosted the week-long Great Shamrock Fair, a major Irish-themed fair and music festival. This year it would be an extra-important event, after what happened during Saint Patrick's week. We Buckleys used to be super involved in fair activities—me with music and Colleen with Irish dance, and Shamrock PD overseeing security. Not to mention, my sister always helped out with the Miss Shamrock and Little Miss Shamrock contests, as a former winner of both. At seven, even a reluctant Maeve had worn the Little Miss Shamrock tiara and banner. And Mom was always running back and forth between the B&B and the fairgrounds.

"We're not really doing anything for the fair this year," I said. "Except Colleen, I guess. She's got the dance school and Miss Shamrock stuff."

"Right." Siobhan glanced back at the car.

I frowned. "Is there something going on I should know about?"

My friend hesitated. She was a terrible liar.

"Come on, Siobhan," I said. "Nothing can be worse than what happened in March."

She bit her lip, guilt flooding her face, then said in a rush, "Colleen wants to tell you. I only saw her for a minute, a couple of hours ago."

The thud of deja-vu hit me like a gold bar dropping from the sky.

Not again.

Colleen had a bad habit of keeping problems from me, her big sister and protector since childhood. Then they grew into even bigger headaches, like the gorse blooms in Shamrock Park spreading along every path despite the constant rains. With Colleen, it was better to nip any issues in the bud. Or try to, anyway.

Unfortunately, my sister was a pro at finding trouble—and running away from anyone who tried to help her. Last March, she'd even been a suspect in Deirdre's murder. I'd found myself playing amateur sleuth—alongside the Shamrock PD, the investigator from the County District Attorney's office, and our dad—to help clear her name.

Frank honked the horn and started to back the lumbering rental truck down the driveway, with Garrett checking out the window to make sure they didn't crush Mom's petunias. Maeve and Bliz jumped back onto the lawn, and I pulled Rover safely toward the sidewalk.

Garrett gave a small salute as he and Frank rumbled off, and Siobhan offered a crooked smile. "Sorry, Kate, but I've gotta go, too," she said. "We're headed to visit my mom, and I need to get everyone cleaned up. See you and Bliz at dance practice tonight, right?"

With a waggle of her fingers, she jumped back into the SUV, checked the triplets' seatbelts, and beelined it after the truck. She was gone so fast, I didn't even have a chance to answer.

Siobhan had said there was drama brewing with the fair, not Colleen. I wouldn't rule out either option. That was the way things usually went with my sister. Perfectly manicured fingers in every disaster pie.

But maybe I was being too tough on her. Colleen was still grieving and recovering from the shock of her best friend's death.

So was Shamrock. From what Mom had told me, no one talked about the murder now. Even Deirdre's widowed mom, a friend of hers and Colleen's boss at the Donnelly School of Irish Dance, kept a stiff upper lip. Plus, the town depended on tourist dollars. Enough said.

Was it too late to grab the girls and pets, leave all our worldly possessions in the Buckley House garage, and high-tail it out of Emerald City right now?

I looked down at Rover, chewing on the beer mug leash. He gave a thumping tail wag. "No worries, boyo," I told him, with a pat on the head. "You're an official Buckley now. We're all in this together."

The words had barely left my mouth before a shiny Mercedes squealed up at the curb.

Colleen jumped out in a crisp, short white shift tailored to her curvy figure. With a wave to the driver, her on-again boyfriend Aidan O'Hearne, she clicked up the asphalt in pink flowered heels, her long blond ponytail bouncing behind her. Fresh as a daisy, to match her shoes. "Hi, fam!" she called.

"Aunt Colleeeeen!" As the girls ran toward her, my sister gracefully bent to retrieve an object from the petunias. She held it up with a questioning look.

A frizzy-haired fashion doll. Kitted out in a bright green, homemade Irish dancing dress. Missing one white poodle sock and lace-up black shoe. But otherwise unscathed.

Bliz skidded to a stop in front of Colleen, who handed over the doll. "Ciara," Bliz breathed, accepting the treasure with reverence. "You found her."

Maeve looked back at me and gave a shrug of acknowledged defeat.

Yup. Colleen Buckley: One. Saint Anthony: Zero.

Chapter Two

Of course I didn't have a chance to pull my sister aside as we all trooped into the house. Colleen held Bliz's hand. And between us, Maeve encouraged a slow-moving Rover.

But I'd learned my lesson on our last visit. I wouldn't let Colleen out of my sight until she divulged whatever super-important item she needed to tell me.

We headed straight to Buckley Family Central: Mom's cheerful kitchen. The open shelves displayed decorative plates and Celtic knickknacks. Colorful plaques with amusing Irish quotes were framed on every wall. For once, everything was tidy as a whistle.

Except for the large oak table, where the Chief sat frowning from his wheelchair at a jumble of electronics strewn across the green-and-white checked tablecloth. Broken chunks of Styrofoam stuck out from a sleek white box. At my dad's feet was a brown shipping package from a major online retailer I'd never known him to order from.

His sharp blue eyes crinkled in greeting when we walked in, but otherwise he seemed frustrated.

"What are you up to, Dad?" I asked. The Chief's idea of cutting-edge technology was the old-school police scanner in the living room.

He shook his head. "All these yokes here, they're banjaxed."

Translation: The stuff on the table was broken.

My dad grew up here in Shamrock, in this very house. But sometimes, when he was either really annoyed or extremely excited, he sounded like my late grandfather from Ireland. The way I remembered him, anyway.

Mom was on the corded, moss-green wall phone across the kitchen, listening intently to the person on the other end. Slim and tall even in her flats, she looked like a silver-haired Mary Tyler Moore today, in mint-green linen capris and a sleeveless yellow blouse. It was easy to figure out which of her daughters had inherited her sense of style.

She made a shooing motion with her free hand for the girls to take Rover through the butler's pantry toward the mudroom. The three disappeared in a blur of happy golden retriever tail.

Huh. Mom hadn't missed a beat at our new family member. He'd already been inside the house earlier, though, so I guess his presence wasn't a surprise. Nothing surprised Eileen Buckley much, anyway.

Colleen went straight to the fridge and grabbed herself a lime seltzer. She handed another to me, which I gratefully accepted. I held the bottle to my forehead for a minute, trying to cool myself off before I opened it. The kitchen was stuffy, even with the windows open.

Someday my dad would agree to central AC. Almost all of the guest rooms had small wall units, and there were plenty of ceiling fans throughout the house. But each summer just got hotter in Shamrock.

The Chief always said that Victorian homes weren't designed for AC, and fans were part of the charm of days past. This was an Irish-themed B&B, and few people had AC in Ireland.

Not to mention, it would cost a fortune to install.

"Well, thanks very much for letting us know," we heard Mom say into the phone. "We're sorry you won't be joining us this week, but we do hope you'll consider a stay at the Buckley House in the future." She replaced the receiver with slightly extra oomph.

"Another cancellation?" Colleen asked when our mom didn't elaborate. "Gee, that's too bad." She sighed. "What a waste of all that cleaning."

"That's what we pay you for now, isn't it?" One of the Chief's bushy eyebrows twitched, more with amusement than annoyance. "Along with the room and board."

I hid a grin. My parents were delighted to have their baby still home at age twenty-four, even if she wasn't the perfect B&B employee. I suspected they gave her extra slack now that she was working at the dance school too.

"Sorry, Daddy." Colleen went over to give him a hug. "You know I didn't mean it that way." He smiled and patted her hand on his shoulder.

"The house really does look nice," I said. "I noticed when we took our bags up. All the woodwork gleams. And the fresh flowers are so pretty. Are they from the garden?"

"Nope, I got them on shopper's special from Kilpatrick's," Colleen said. The Buckley House kept the local specialty market, which carried farm-fresh produce as well as food and sundry items imported from Ireland, in business. So did the Smiling Shamrock, the fancy B&B across town.

"Perhaps you girls can work on the gardens this summer," Mom said. "A nice outdoor project for you."

"Um, sure," I said, as Colleen crossed the kitchen and emphatically shook her head behind Mom. Neither of us had green thumbs, exactly. "So what happened, Mom?" I nodded toward the phone.

She joined the Chief at the table. "A party just changed their minds. An hour before the cancellation cut-off, can you believe it? They're going to Maine instead. To the Blueberry Inn or some such. Unfortunately, they'd booked the Connemara Suite and two other rooms with us."

"Wow, we'll be practically empty, then," Colleen said. "And it's fair week, too. That's almost as bad as vacancies during Paddy's Week."

I glanced at Mom, wishing my sister hadn't pointed that out. But she was right. As a professional accountant back in the city, I'd taken over the Buckley House books during tax season this year. March was a disaster, and I knew full well what this last-minute cancellation would cost us.

"Ah now, Colleen, you're exaggerating," the Chief said. "Marty McCleary and the lads are already here."

"Lads as in . . . the Limerick Lads?" I said, with a speck of trepidation. The four white-haired members of a popular Irish music group—who happened to be longtime buddies of the Chief's—headlined the Great Shamrock Fair every year. "They're staying here at the Buckley House again? With us?"

"Of course," the Chief said. "Why not?"

"For free," Mom added, smiling gamely. Every summer, she swore never again. The lads came and went at all hours and enjoyed holding impromptu musical sessions in the living room. They were also big talkers. And ate and drank us out of everything in the house.

"Free, huh?" I looked at my dad, who busied himself with his electronic toys again.

I wasn't surprised by my parents' generous hospitality. But with all the costs involved in keeping the B&B running, we needed paying guests filling practically every room.

Colleen must have been thinking the same. "I'll ask Frank to move the vacancy sign higher up on the hill," she said. "That way people will see it better when they drive by."

"Um, about the sign," I began. "It's not doing so well."

But my sister didn't hear me. She was in action mode. "We'll put something out on social media right away. What awesome deal can we offer to bribe people into making a reservation fast?"

"Bribe?" The Chief said. "The Buckley House is a fine lodging establishment."

"Right," I agreed quickly. "No need for any deals. Not yet, anyway. There was plenty of tourist traffic on the way out here. I bet not everyone booked ahead."

"Maybe," Mom said. "But those short-term rentals are so popular now."

I summoned the sprightly tone I often used to encourage the girls. "Don't worry, Mom. With the Smiling Shamrock closed for renovations—"

Colleen bit her lip. Our parents exchanged glances.

Oops. Ever since the sad events of Paddy's Week, no one in our family mentioned the fancy B&B that was the Buckley House's big competition. And especially not the Shamrock's owners, Una and Nuala McShane. The ban extended to the elderly sisters' great-niece, Moira McShane Kelly, who lived with them. She'd gone to Holy Innocents with Colleen and Deirdre, and even back then she'd been a pain in the butt.

Colleen cleared her throat. "There's a slight update on the Shamrock, Katie. Aidan just told me yesterday."

Colleen's boyfriend, a recent star of the wildly popular dance show Irish Steps—and Deirdre's former dance partner—was in town this summer, creating his own production: Crossroad Dreams with Aidan O'Hearne. His vision was an arty, Riverdance-style show with dance troupes and musicians touring the United States, Ireland, and other international destinations.

"OK, then, what's the deal?" I prompted, as Colleen hesitated. Was this what she had wanted to tell me? Something about the Shamrock? Nothing would surprise me with the McShanes.

Mom got up and started peeling carrots from a metal bowl next to the sink. The Chief rummaged around in one of his boxes.

Colleen took a long swig of her seltzer. "The Shamrock isn't closed anymore. Turns out they never did any renovations. Nothing major, anyway. It was all a big lie. The McShanes just shut everything down and took an extended vacay over the pond."

"Oh. Well, who could blame them, really?" I said. "They wanted to get out of town for a while." I was sure the town had enjoyed their absence, other than the decreased tourist bucks.

"The Shamrock is the number one listing again on Irish B&B Advisor. And Emerald Choice. They got all their shamrock ratings back, too."

I sighed. "We knew they wouldn't be down for long, even with the whole town mad at them for how they acted when Deirdre died. The McShanes are survivors."

"Connivers," the Chief muttered, without looking up.

Colleen twirled a strand of hair on her shoulder. "So remember how Aidan stayed there during Paddy's Week when he was Grand Marshall for the parade? And the McShanes got all that great publicity because of it?"

I nodded. "Sure."

"Well, the preview shows for Crossroad Dreams are supposed to kick off at the fair."

"I know," I said, a bit impatiently. "The ads and trailers have been all over social media for months." I frowned. "Don't tell me Aidan caved and gave Moira a starring role in the show?"

"In her dreams," Colleen said. "He'd never do that, no matter how much she bugs him. She drives everyone nuts." Moira was an excellent dancer, in a technical sense. She'd been fired from Irish Steps for "artistic differences." But mostly because no one could stand her.

Mom turned around from the sink and sighed. "Colleen, just tell your sister, please."

When our mother broke into our conversations, that was bad. I braced myself on the edge of the table with my fingertips.

"The Crossroads cast is staying at the Shamrock now," Colleen said in a rush. "Well, the leads, anyway."

"We couldn't fit them all here," I said. "The Shamrock is a lot bigger than we are."

"Plus, the Chief won't let Aidan stay—quote—'under his roof if we're not married.'" My sister glanced toward our dad and rolled her eyes.

"Exactly right," the Chief said.

"But Aidan wanted the dancers in one place as a group anyway because the show isn't coming together the way he wants it," my sister went on. "It's a mess, he says. And the McShanes luck out because *Shamrock Today* features a profile of one of the stars every morning on WSCK. Filmed at the B&B."

"Why isn't anyone profiling the Limerick Lads?" I said. "They're doing the music, right?"

"Kate, they're *old*," Colleen said, in a low voice. "That's part of the problem."

"I heard that, missy," the Chief said.

"Anyway, bottom line is, the McShanes are getting a ton of press," Colleen finished.

"Not all of it good," the Chief pointed out.

"Dermot, dear, why don't you get this mess cleaned up?" Mom gestured toward the table. "It's almost time for tea, and we need to move around here in the kitchen. You can take everything upstairs to your office and figure out all that smart-house nonsense there."

"The lads won't mind a few bits and bobs lying around," the Chief said. "We can take tea in the front room."

As I continued to absorb the Smiling Shamrock comeback news, Mom and Colleen swiftly swept the tech hardware back into the boxes. The Chief gazed into the smaller one Mom placed on his lap in the wheelchair. "Where is the instruction booklet?" he said. "Those online eejits forgot to include it. I'm going to call them and—"

"Remember, darling, Frank told you," Mom said soothingly, as the two of them headed toward my dad's private elevator at the end of the main hall. "You need to find some code or such and take a picture of it on your phone."

"I'll go help Dad," Colleen said to me. "He'll never figure it out."

"The Chief will be fine," I said. "You can help him later. Can you please finish your story first?"

"Katie, don't act so worried. Things haven't changed that much. We've always had to deal with the McShanes."

"Yeah, but I don't get it." I frowned. "Why on earth would Aidan agree to help those witches? He could have put the whole Crossroads cast up at the Celtic Holidays Inn out on Route One."

"Actually it was my idea." My sister bit her lip.

"Yours?" I almost fell to the linoleum floor.

"Look, Kate, I get it," she said. "No one can stand the McShanes. Especially us. But there are mental health issues in that family." She dropped down at the table. "Maybe we need to cut them some slack. You know . . . move on."

"I'm a little surprised you feel that way," I said slowly. "They were horrible to us—and especially you—when Deirdre died."

"I know." My sister traced the green and white lines in the tablecloth with her finger. "But it's what Dee would have wanted, I think. And her mom agreed. Aidan and I talked to Bernie about it first."

"Oh." That was a surprise, too. Bernadette Donnelly, known to all as Bernie, was a tough cookie. But also a more generous and forgiving person than I was, apparently.

My sister looked really sad right now. And I was making her feel worse. "Hey, Colleen Queen, I understand," I said gently. "If Bernie's on board, and it's that important to you both . . ."

"It's important to the town, too," Colleen said. "Mayor Flanagan made that pretty clear. The Shamrock does a ton of advertising to tourists. They're, like, a destination hotel. We're kind of the overflow choice. Not as fancy, and we charge almost as much."

"We have to," I said, a little defensively. I'd convinced Mom to up the Buckley House room rates when the Shamrock temporarily closed. "It takes plenty of cashola to keep an old house running. This place isn't in as good shape as the Shamrock, and we have fewer rooms."

"And we don't serve meals," Colleen pointed out. "Just Continental breakfast and afternoon tea and an evening snack."

I held up one hand. "OK, OK. You're right. But I've seen our reviews. Plenty of guests find the Buckley House charming and cozy. Because it is."

Colleen's dimple appeared briefly as she smiled. "Five shamrocks for cozy. Three-point-five for service and two for amenities."

"Well, we can work on improving the ratings this summer," I said. "It's the perfect time, especially with the B&B on the less-full side." I cocked my head. "Speaking of amenities, what is the Chief planning to do with all that equipment?"

"Oh, he wants to upgrade the security system again. You know, new wireless smoke detectors and cameras and intercoms and doorbells and who knows what else."

"I'm not sure we can turn this place into a smart house," I said. "It has crazy wiring, and the wi-fi is iffy at best."

"Frank told him everything would be easy to set up, and they could do it together. But the Chief didn't want to wait or bring anyone else in to help, so . . . well, you get the picture."

"Yup." I sighed. Our dad was always in search of a new project, ever since his earlier-than-expected retirement from the force. Usually those projects were directly related to law enforcement, though, and "advising" his buddies at the Shamrock PD. The Buckley House had as many cops as guests trooping through the place. It felt like it sometimes, anyway. "So that was what you wanted to tell me, the news about the Shamrock?"

It could have been something a lot worse.

"Well, not exactly *all* of it," Colleen said.

We both jumped at a sharp knock behind us. A woman about my age, her blond hair cut in a perfect long bob, stood in the kitchen doorway. She wore a black-and-cream, summer-knit top and short black skirt. And a very annoyed expression.

"I need to speak with the proprietor," she said. "Immediately."

Chapter Three

I rose from the table, smoothing my Yankees jersey at the same time, to respond to the stranger who had barged into our kitchen. But Colleen beat me to the punch.

"Oh, hi!" My sister clicked to the doorway in her heels. "We're the proprietors of the Buckley House. Well, technically, our mom is, but she's—"

"The doorbell is broken," the young woman said.

"Really? Gosh." Colleen sounded genuinely surprised. "Sorry, we'll check that out right away."

"How may we help you?" I asked. The new arrival's black Gucci belt perfectly matched her shoes. Even I recognized the distinctive designer logo. "Are you looking for a room?"

"Heavens, no. Not for me, anyway. My fiancé and I have made other arrangements. I'm inquiring about a group of three. Two rooms."

"Wonderful. Let me just take a look at availability first." Colleen pulled up the Buckley House calendar on her phone, tilting the screen away from anyone else's view. "What dates do you have in mind?"

Gripping the strap of her pocketbook, the young woman stepped further into the kitchen, and I glimpsed the serious sparkle from a gorgeous diamond and emerald ring. I used to have one like it. Not quite as flashy, but still. "Arriving this evening," she said. "Staying through the week. Possibly beyond."

"Double-checking." Colleen swiped her phone. "Huh. You're in luck. We just had a cancellation."

"Have you? Grand." The young woman finally smiled. "I'm Fallon O'Malley, by the way." She paused, as if to let that info sink in.

Should we know her? I snuck a look at my sister, whose expression was as blank as mine probably was. Colleen recovered quickly.

"Nice to meet you, Fallon. I'm Colleen Buckley, and this is my sister, Kate. So you're from London?"

"Dublin." Fallon sounded slightly annoyed.

"Oops, sorry. Guess my accent radar is off," Colleen said cheerfully. Mine, too, apparently. "But you do look familiar. Were you at the party the other night down at—?"

"I've been in New York," Fallon cut her in. "On business."

"Oh. Double bad on me, then." My sister, who rarely forgot a face, flashed her dimple. "Why don't we go out to the front desk, and we'll get your party set up?"

"I'd like to see the rooms first, thank you," Fallon said. "To be sure they'll suit."

"No problem." Colleen stepped into the hallway. "I'll get the keys and give you the penny tour, as our mom says. Follow me."

I trailed along, too, but we didn't get far. Fallon stopped and gazed up the main stairs with a slight frown. Then she stuck her head into the parlor. "What is that crackling sound?" She pointed in the direction of the closed drapes.

Colleen waved. "Oh, just the police scanner. Our dad loves to listen to it. Sometimes he forgets to turn it off when he leaves the room."

"Police scanner?" Fallon's eyebrows rose nearly to her black velvet hairband.

"Dad is retired PD," I said. "It's a . . . hobby." More like an obsession, but she didn't need to know that.

"The guests all get used to it," Colleen said. "Most of them don't even notice. You must have great hearing."

"Mm." Fallon wandered further into the parlor, looking around in a nosy way. Fortunately, the room looked especially neat and tidy today. The Limerick Lads, wherever they were at the moment, must not have had a chance to mess things up yet. I did notice that the Waterford crystal bowl on the coffee table in front of the floral couch and striped armchair was only half full of candy today. Usually Mom put out butterscotch, but the sweet du jour was peppermint.

There were a couple of empty wrappers lying right there on the coffee table. I knew who the culprit was, too. Not the Chief's Irish musician buddies.

Frank.

I grabbed them up and stuck them in my jeans pocket for now. Fallon was still circling the room, running one finger over the piano—my old childhood friend, back when I'd wanted to be a professional musician myself. Was she looking for dust?

Well, she wouldn't find much. Colleen looked irritated at the subtle test, after all that alleged extra cleaning. "So, shall we move on to the rooms?" she asked.

"Just a moment, if you don't mind." Now Fallon peered closely at a small group of framed photos on the piano top.

She seemed particularly interested in a shot of me and Maeve at Emerald Lake, the year Bliz was born. You couldn't really see our faces, because our hair was flying everywhere in the wind. My ex-husband, Ian Forde, had taken that one, seconds before the wake from a passing speedboat almost dumped us out of our canoe.

Ian was back in Ireland now with his band, following his music dreams. Not so much any family ones.

Why was Fallon peering like that? Maybe she had bad eyesight.

Mom came up behind me and took my elbow. "Kate, dear, can I please have a word?" she said in a low voice.

"Oh, hi, Mom!" Colleen called from across the room. "This is Fallon. She has a group of friends who want to book rooms for the week. Maybe longer."

"How nice. We'd be happy to host them here at the Buckley House, Fallon." I couldn't help but notice the huge relief behind Mom's smile. Then she added to me, "Shall we go, Kate?"

I excused myself from the rest of the tour, but I couldn't shake the feeling that the snoopy young woman had zeroed in directly on that photo of me and Maeve. It gave me the creeps, to be honest. What was she looking at—or for?

"We have a bit of a situation outside," Mom said, as we walked down the hall together to the main back door. "Nothing serious, but I thought maybe you'd prefer to handle it."

"Is everything OK?" I asked.

"Mostly," Mom said.

I pushed on the screen door handle and stepped outside, ignoring the immediate wall of heat.

Oh no.

The first thing I saw was Maeve throwing dirt into a gaping hole near the side gate with a rusty shovel. She must have gotten it from the oversized, gingerbread style shed at the back of the yard. Bliz was on her hands and knees in a bed of garden mulch, trying to rescue a collection of uprooted pansies, their colorful faces wilted in the hot sun. Half hidden behind the huge permanent rock Frank and I used to climb—and jump from—I spotted the back end of a golden retriever. And a continuing shower of fresh dirt.

"Girls!" I called. "What is going on here?"

Maeve halted her labors and leaned on the shovel. "Nothing."

Bliz looked up and smiled, her face pink and smudged with dirt. "Don't worry, Mommy, we're fixing everything."

Beside me on the stone patio, Mom covered her chuckle with an ill-disguised cough. "Sorry," she said. "Does bring back memories."

I sighed. "OK, grab the dog, and everyone over to the garden hose." I pointed to the side of the shed. "I'll get some beach towels, and you all wait outside. Rover needs to be on his leash for now. Where is it?"

"Umm . . ." Maeve bit her lip. "Here in the grass somewhere. We'll find it." She took Rover by the collar and led him toward the spigot.

"I'll get the towels, Kate," Mom said. "But there's something I want to give you first, between us." She took a folded piece of spiral notepad paper from her pocket and nodded toward the side gate. "We need to get that latch fixed right away and put in stronger fencing. Especially now with the dog. I spoke to Mr. Petrocelli at Shamrock Hardware this morning and took measurements. They're there in the note.

Will you stop by the store before closing and put in the order? Just add whatever we need to the Buckley House tab. And ask how soon we can get everything delivered."

"Sure, Mom."

"I'm happy to take the girls to dance practice. Bernie is running the younger group tonight, so Colleen doesn't need to be at Angels Hall until later. You two can grab a bite and have a chat in town after the store."

Well, that was nice of her. On the other hand, Mom seemed a little eager for my sister and me to spend quality time together—out of the house. Did it have anything to do with what Colleen had been about to tell me before we were interrupted by Fallon's arrival?

Maybe I was reading too much into Mom's gracious offer. "Great, thanks," I said. I glanced over my shoulder to check on my daughters and Rover. Maeve was fiddling with the handle on the spigot and holding on to the dog at the same time. Bliz tried to brush the dirt off Rover, mostly transferring it to her sundress.

"Oh, and honey," Mom added, "no need to mention the fence to your father yet. I've put a wee bit aside from the grocery money." She lowered her voice again, even though there was no one else to hear her. "The pricing is for vinyl fencing. Much more durable than the wood, but you know how your father is about—"

A thunderous shout drowned out Mom's words as the sputter from the hose became a ginormous blast of rushing water.

A slightly built older man stood in front of the lawn glider, sopping wet. That would be Dad's friend and lead Limerick Lad, Marty McCleary.

He looked like a furious Christmas elf.

I hadn't even noticed him earlier. Most likely he'd been taking a nap in the glider. His summer cap lay in the soggy grass at his feet, knocked to the ground by the spray.

"I am really, really sorry, sir," Maeve said, as soon as she'd managed to shut off the water. "Something just flew off the hose."

The dripping man looked even more upset, but not at my daughter. "There she is," he said, pointing past us with an accusing finger. "The divil herself!"

Chapter Four

The devil, right here in Shamrock? Who knew?

Mom hustled the girls and Rover into the mudroom as I turned to see the source of Marty McCleary's agitation.

I could probably rule out my sister. Colleen looked positively angelic as she stood outside the Buckley House garage, listening intently and nodding to whatever the chic young woman beside her was saying. They seemed to be getting on swimmingly.

"Fallon O'Malley?" I said to Marty. "You know her?"

"I do," Marty said. "You'll want to avoid her, that one."

Funny, that had been my first instinct as well. And I'd just met her a few minutes ago.

Mom ran back out, drying her hands on a tea towel. "Marty, come inside and have a nice cup of tea. So sorry about the unexpected shower. We'll get you sorted in no time."

"Dad." A lanky, sandy-haired guy about my age excused himself as he brushed past Mom and jogged across the grass. I hadn't seen Marty's son Noel for a while, but I'd known him for ages. He and Ian had started a band together in New York, and later a new one in Ireland. "Let's go into the house now," he said to Marty. "There's a load of biscuits. With the jam on top."

Marty did love those cookies. Hopefully Kilpatrick's wouldn't run out of them this week.

But the elderly man didn't budge. "What is *she* doing here?" He glared again toward the driveway, as Colleen and Fallon disappeared around the garage. "Nothing but trouble, she is."

Noel glanced over his shoulder, then scooped up his father's muddy cap from the ground. "You're dreamin', Dad," he said, shaking his head. "Fallon's not that bad. Hey Kate, how are ya?" he called up to me.

I smiled and waggled my fingers in greeting.

"She'll be the death of us all, the wagon," Marty muttered as Noel led him to the house. "You'll see."

I felt a little better, to be honest, that I wasn't the only one who didn't care for Fallon. At least she wouldn't be staying at the B&B.

Colleen and the "wagon" were back now from the garage.

How nosy could that woman be? Had she peeked through the side window to check out all our family stuff and assorted rubbish packed in there? No one went in the garage except us Buckleys. And maybe a few mice.

She wasn't even scoping the B&B for herself. Were her friends even pickier?

If so, we didn't need their business that badly. It didn't matter if the Buckley House went into the red. I'd announce to Fallon that those recent guest cancellations had been suddenly uncanceled. The B&B in Maine had sadly and inexplicably burned down to its last blueberry bush. Poof.

The kitchen was empty when I walked in, thank goodness. Other than the Chief, everyone was either having tea in the parlor or getting cleaned up. No sign of Colleen.

Hopefully the Buckley House hadn't met Fallon's high standards, and she'd left. Good riddance.

But after a minute or two of scrubbing extra diligently at a coffee stain in the sink, I regained my composure. We could deal with Fallon's friends for a week. Money was money. We'd dealt with demanding guests before.

I grabbed the Kilpatrick's cookie bag off the counter, dumped the remaining contents into the cookie jar, and stuffed the bag in the trash so no one would see it. Then I slumped into a chair at the table. A muffled protest sounded from somewhere near my feet.

I lifted the green-checked tablecloth. "Rover," I said. "Are you supposed to be in here?"

He slunk out like a muddy golden panther and sat in front of me, wagging his tail.

I had to laugh and dropped him a cookie crumb or two on purpose. "I have your number, buddy. We're signing you up for doggy obedience class. You can learn new tricks. And how to behave nicely, if you're going to live here."

He rested his head on my knees, looking adoringly up at me. And the rest of my cookie.

I popped it into my mouth and took him back to the now-literal mudroom, where I settled him on a nest of old towels. I'd found them stacked in a wicker basket next to the dryer, under a laundry schedule sign that said, *Sort today; Wash later; Fold eventually; Iron? Ha ha*. The towels, edged in raggedy lace, needed to be retired anyway. Why did Mom keep those?

"Hey." Colleen appeared, a little breathless, and gracefully hoisted herself on top of the frontloading washer. "Guess what? We're all set. Rooms filled. Well, almost. The two new guys are sharing one and the girl will take the other. We still have the Connemara Suite left. And your room, if we need it."

"That's great," I said.

"And guess what? They're paying extra!"

I frowned. "Really? Why?"

Colleen clasped her hands with a pretty jingle of bracelets and gave me her most winning smile. The one that said I wouldn't like the answer, but I was the best big sister in the world. "I gave them access to the garage."

I stared at her. "What? We need the garage. There's barely room for Dad's van, with so much junk Mom and Dad don't want to get rid of. And as of this afternoon, the girls and I have all our stuff in there, too."

"Well, we did plan to move the boxes into the basement right away," Colleen helpfully reminded me. "Frank will do most of the heavy lifting. I'll bake him some cookies." She produced her cell from her dress pocket in a flash and tapped the screen. "I have another idea, though. I can get some friends to volunteer, no problem. We'll have that whole garage cleared in, like, an hour. We can pay them in pizza or something."

I threw up my hands. "You're unbelievable." I said, and headed back toward the kitchen.

Rover was happy to remain behind on his new ratty-towel bed, but Colleen jumped off the washer and followed at my heels. "Yeah, but extra money for filling the rooms is a good thing, right? Don't worry, I know I can get people to help move that stuff out fast. You won't have to lift a thing. This plan will work even better."

"But I still don't get it." I whirled around. "Why on earth do those guests want the freaking garage? Do they have a limo that's too fancy to get wet?"

Colleen carefully flicked a tiny, wayward piece of dryer lint from the hem of her white dress. "They have a band. Fallon happens to be their manager. I think she handles all the PR, too. Anyway, they were invited to play the fair last-minute, and she said they're on a deadline for some new music."

I sighed. "So now we have two groups of musicians staying here?"

"Pretty cool, huh?" Colleen said. "They're an indie band, really up and coming. Sort of Irish contemporary folk rock. Like, trad but kind of punk, too."

I raised my brows and waited.

"You'll know them," Colleen assured me. "I guess Mayor Flanagan wanted to add some new blood this year. You know, to bring in younger fans to the fair. The Limerick Lads are getting pretty old."

"Shh!" I glanced toward the hallway. "Stop saying that. They might hear you."

"Nah," Colleen said. "I doubt they hear much at all anymore."

I sighed. "OK, so what's the name of this hot new group?"

Colleen fixed her eyes on the laundry schedule. "Peat."

I literally grabbed at the kitchen doorway to steady myself. "Peat? As in, *Ian's* band Peat? My *ex-husband Ian's* band Peat?"

My brain and stomach swirled at the same time. Of course. Ian and I used to rehearse in that garage, with a few friends in a short-lived, not-so-great band. It was the summer we'd started dating, after Garrett joined the military and before I left for college. The last hurrah for my musical career. I'd played keyboards, mostly. Ian had made a few adjustments to the space so the acoustics were awesome—as in, the sound didn't travel to the house. My parents had been all for us taking over that garage.

"It's OK," Colleen said quickly. "Even if Ian comes by and jams with the rest of the band a few times, it's not like he'll be staying here at the house or anything. And he'll want to see the girls, anyway. Right?"

"Sure." I'd suddenly gotten distracted by an unwelcome image dancing before my eyes. A single diamond, framed by a square of dark green emeralds. It hung in my mind for a second or two, then disappeared like the kaleidoscope close of a retro cartoon show.

My engagement ring.

I'd sold my plain wedding band in the city years ago, but I'd given Ian back his family heirloom. The gemstones had to be faux, because the Fordes weren't wealthy. And the stones had dulled over time. I honestly hadn't cared. I'd loved that ring, with its ornate antique setting.

But the gems in the sparkling near-replica I'd seen on Fallon's finger were clearly real. She and Ian were both involved in Peat.

And with each other.

No doubt about it. My ex had a new fiancée. And her name was Fallon O'Malley.

Chapter Five

"So where do you want to go now?"

Colleen and I stood outside Shamrock Hardware, errand for Mom completed. Behind us, green twinkle lights flashed around a summer window display of motorized leprechauns: manning a grill, dozing in a lounge chair, digging into hot dogs and potato salad at a child's wooden picnic bench. One toasted a marshmallow on a stick over a crinkled orange paper campfire. Another carried a life preserver toward a blue-tarp lake.

Oh, and in a corner a troublemaking leprechaun was about to set off some kind of firework from a vintage box. I hoped he was a licensed operator. Fireworks were illegal in Massachusetts for nonprofessionals, which I knew because the Shamrock PD remained vigilant year-round.

"Earth to Kate." My sister waved in front of my face, creating a welcome breeze. "You didn't answer me. Where do we go next? Gallagher's? Molly's happy hour? Farrell's on the way home?"

"No pubs," I said. "I am still majorly ticked off at you about the Peat thing. One drink, and I might actually kill you."

"Oh, come on," she said, linking my arm in hers as we started down the brick sidewalk. "I told you, everything will be fine. And Fallon already paid for the rooms." She grinned. "Maybe a tiny bit extra."

"Well, that's good," I said, half grudgingly. It was hard to stay mad at my sister for long. She had a way of worming herself back into my—and everyone else's—good graces. No idea how she did it.

"And the girls will get to see Ian more," Colleen added. "Maybe the two of you can call a truce and—"

"Colleen," I broke in, stopping in front of Gifts of Gab and withdrawing my arm. "Ian and I get along fine, OK? We just have completely separate lives, with a whole ocean between us. If Ian ever wants to be more of a dad, there's video calling and Aer Lingus. And even occasional bank transfers."

"I'm sorry." Colleen bit her lip. "You're right."

"It doesn't matter," I said. "Moneywise, I mean. I'm doing fine handling everything myself." For now, anyway. "It's sad for the girls, though. Ian doesn't mean to be a jerk. He's just sort of . . . checked out."

"And charming," Colleen reminded me. "In his own clueless way."

I sighed. "Maybe. But he seems a lot less charming now. Time whizzes by, and he doesn't even realize it."

"His loss," Colleen said.

"And the girls'," I added. "Bliz hardly knows him, so she doesn't talk about him much. Or ask many questions." That was a good thing, I supposed.

"I guess he just focuses on his music," Colleen said. "I mean, he always has, right? But it must be paying off for him, because Peat is starting to get major attention across the pond. Maybe they'll really hit it big, and the girls will grow up to be globe-trotting heiresses. With massive trust funds that kick in at 18. Just in time to pay for college."

I laughed. "Yeah, that'd be great. But Ian can't be that broke right now. Did you get a load of Fallon's ring?"

"I was temporarily blinded." Colleen peered into the window of Gifts of Gab. "Hey, look at all these weird little statue guys. How ugly are they?"

I joined my sister at the display. "Hideous," I agreed. The intricately carved trolls—or whatever they were—looked a lot more ominous than the leprechauns cavorting around in the window at Shamrock Hardware. Different sizes, the tallest about three feet, but they all sported long, clawlike toenails, twisted expressions and carved accessories that would make perfect murder implements. Shovel, pitchfork, knife, hatchet—even a scythe. One carried a sketchy looking bag. I shuddered.

Maybe they seemed extra creepy because they were completely out of place among the other, much cheerier gift items in the window. Flying fairies with gossamer wings. Needlepointed mushroom footstools. Colorful teapots of every shape and size. Adorable stuffed wool sheep. Pricey knitwear from Shamrock Mills. Even an apron that said: *Kiss Me, I'm Your Irish Chef.*

I stepped aside, moving behind Colleen, as the heavy red door to Gifts of Gab opened behind us. And out walked Marty's devil herself, Fallon O'Malley.

Somehow, I wasn't surprised in the least. It was just the way my day was going.

Luckily, Fallon didn't notice my sister or me. She appeared in a hurry to leave Gifts of Gab in the fairy dust as she tossed a store business card into her overstuffed tote. Then she motored down the street, not even looking up as she scrolled her phone.

Colleen blew out a breath as Fallon disappeared around the corner. "Phew. At least we didn't have to talk to her."

"Well, I'm sure we'll run into her again at some point," I said. "Especially with Peat booked at the Buckley House," I couldn't help adding.

"Hey, we can still cancel their reservations," Colleen said. "Want me to run after Fallon and give her the glum news?"

"No, thanks, that's all right." I sighed. "Forget it."

Colleen shrugged. "Well, OK, if you're sure."

"I am. Absolutely. I swear."

Faced with the reality of telling Mom earlier that I wanted to unbook Peat from the Buckley House, I couldn't go through with it. She would be so worried again. Not just about the lost revenue, but about me. I couldn't let my mom know I was upset that Ian might be coming around the B&B. And how could I let my own feelings interfere with more chances for Maeve to see her dad?

That would be selfish and petty of me, not to mention completely unfair to Maeve. I'd simply have to deal with it.

"I don't need to be at Angels Hall until six thirty," Colleen said, checking the time on her phone. "And the guests won't show up til later tonight. Let's go in and say hi to Gabby."

"OK," I said. I hadn't seen Gabby Carroll, the owner of Gifts of Gab and my high-school-era boss, in ages. Plus the shop had stiff, heavenly AC.

Following my sister into the shop, I stooped to pick up a piece of cardboard on the welcome mat. Another business card. It must have fallen from Fallon's tote.

I was just curious. And, as always, I had a weird compulsion to correct things that seemed out of place. Stray pieces of paper drove me nuts.

I should have ignored it. The swirly font engraved on the creamy linen card stock read: *Bridget of Shamrock. Gowns, Lingerie, and Accessories for the Discerning Irish Bride.*

Oh.

Tears pricked behind my eyes. Why had the universe done this to me? Not that I wanted to be a bride again anytime soon. If ever. And the last thing I'd want to do was remarry Ian.

But still.

I took a sharp inhale of Innis candle scent and tucked the card in my back jeans pocket as I stepped further into the store. I'd responsibly recycle it later.

Soft, calming harp music played from speakers somewhere as I negotiated the cluttered shop in search of Colleen. I found her already checking out the sale rack. "Is this cute or what?" She held up a short, velvet dress that could have doubled as an Irish dance costume.

Gabby, a round, fiftyish woman in a drapey green dress with a light crocheted shawl—available for sale in the extensive Irish knitwear section—was busy tidying a stack of striped tank tops. Her apple cheeks glowed pink from her exertions. "Hello, Buckley girls!" she greeted us warmly. "How nice of you to come in. Is there anything I can help you find?"

"Not today, thanks, Gabby." Colleen returned the dress to the rack. "We were just passing by and thought we'd stop in to see how you're doing." I stepped out from behind my sister and waved, inadvertently knocking a pile of T-shirts.

"Sorry," I mumbled in embarrassment, gathering up the tees from the floor. Each had a bright yellow cow on the front mooing, *Butter Visit the Great Shamrock Fair!*

Colleen quickly started refolding, and Gabby hurried over to assist us. The stock tables were crowded together, so it took her a minute.

"No worries at all, Katie." Gabby held up one of the shirts. "Aren't these adorable? Butter, get it?"

I nodded. "Very cute."

One of the fair's biggest highlights every year was the giant butter sculpture. Created by a well-known local artist with a carefully guarded surprise theme each year, the attraction drew crowds of adoring fans. Mayor Flanagan unveiled the sculpture with great fanfare outside the gazebo on the town square. Directly after the ceremony it was rushed back to a refrigerated glass space at the fairgrounds, where butter fans could watch the artist, Nick Sweeney, touch up his masterpiece before it melted.

Technically, the sculpture was supposed to be carved in pure Irish butter, which was extra yellow and melted faster due to its higher fat content. It was rumored Mr. Sweeney cheated a bit, mixing it in with cheaper American butter.

Gabby finished restacking as I clumsily pulled myself up from the floor, taking extra care not to grab onto any tables or knock over new T-shirt piles. "Katie, remember when you helped me here at the store that one summer? Those were fun days."

"Of course I remember. You were such a nice boss." I felt myself flush with shame. That was back in high school, and I'd been possibly the worst employee ever. I never did learn to fold clothes properly.

I was the one who'd given Mom that lazy laundry sign for the mudroom one Christmas.

Colleen, on the other hand, was a pro folder. Other than in her own closet, anyway. "All done!" she announced, restoring the last pile to its proper place and giving it a little pat on top. "So Gabby, how's business? Getting many tourists so far?"

"A few, in and out." The shop owner fanned herself with the edge of her shawl. "It's been quiet for fair week."

"We passed a customer on their way out as we came in," I said. "Was she interested in anything in particular?"

Colleen rolled her eyes at my blatant fishing for info on Fallon, but my old boss didn't seem to notice.

I'll admit, I was curious about my ex's fiancée. And no, I hadn't learned my lesson after picking up the bridal store card.

"It was so odd," Gabby said. "That young woman—straight from Ireland, isn't that nice?—wanted to purchase the entire collection of garden gnomes in my window. But of course I had to tell her no." The shop owner lowered the clingy shawl from her shoulders and tied it around her waist. "I hadn't even had a chance to put up the information sign yet. But those sculptures are all numbered collectibles. Not one the same. They add a certain something to my display, don't you think?"

"Oh, absolutely," I said, as Colleen smiled and bobble-headed in agreement. "They're so . . . intriguing."

"Sadly for my window, the pieces will be auctioned off at the fair," Gabby went on. "For charity, of course. That's why I couldn't sell them to her. But it was the strangest thing. She started picking up every one of those gnomes, even the larger ones, and checking the base. Very odd."

"Maybe she was looking for the artist's signature," I said.

"I suppose," Gabby said. "Those darling critters are Athena Sweeney originals. She's quite the up-and-coming artist. Have you heard of her?"

"I think I met her with Aidan at a party not too long ago," Colleen said. "At her dad's gallery. We didn't hang out with her, though. I mean, she's like forty."

I tried not to cringe, and didn't look at Gabby. I was younger than she was, but in a few years I, too, would be a certified antiquity at forty. Right up there with the Limerick Lads, in my sister's book.

Colleen suddenly seemed to realize she'd been unintentionally rude. "I bet there'll be a bidding war on those statues, Gabby," she said. "And everyone will remember them from your store window."

"Definitely," I said. "They're sure to go fast." *Into a dumpster, maybe.*

"I know the money is for a good cause, but I'll still be sorry to see them go." Gabby sighed. "They'd be perfect for this year's Halloween window contest."

"I can't think of anything scarier," Colleen said.

"Wish I could afford the little guys myself, even as a business write-off." Gabby still sounded sad. "The artist refused to sell me just one. They have to stay a set. But I'm not allowed to bid on auction items, anyway, since I'm a volunteer."

I really did feel sorry for Gabby. Her extreme attachment to the ugly creatures was a little odd—and a bit comical. But as a gift shop owner, she'd always appreciated quirky "treasures."

Gabby tightened the knot on her lacy shawl, which threatened to slide off her hips. "The customer said she might make a significant bid," she said, in a brisker tone. "I wished her luck, of course, and gave her the artist's card. You know, in case she didn't win and wanted to commission similar ones. She didn't seem as interested in that idea, but she took the info."

"Huh," I said. What would Fallon want with a bunch of ugly statues? She'd have to ship them back home over the pond, for heaven's sake.

And Ian would absolutely hate them. I tried to imagine him working on his music surrounded by hideous elves.

Gabby leaned closer to whisper, even though there was no one else in the store. "And this is the best part," she went on. "There's a secret, very valuable prize inside one of those sculptures. No one but Athena knows what the prize is or which gnome it's in. It'll be part of the fun and drive up the bidding even more."

"Everyone loves an extra value surprise," I agreed. "Colleen, you said Athena is related to Nicholas Sweeney?" I asked.

"Yup. The butter sculpture guy," Colleen said.

"Nick is a very prolific artist," Gabby said. "He moved his gallery here in town to a larger location out by the mills. The sign says 'Sweeney & Daughter' now. That's Athena."

"I overheard her telling someone she used to live in Europe," Colleen said. "She studied art there."

"Such a beautiful name, Athena," Gabby said dreamily. "I used to know her mother, may she rest in peace." The shop owner made a quick sign of the cross.

"It's nice Athena's following in her father's footsteps," I said.

Gabby beamed. "A true talent. It's such a shame about Nick, though. The poor man isn't doing well."

"What happened?" Colleen asked.

"He fell from a scaffold a couple of days ago and hurt his back." Gabby shook her head and gave a little tsk-tsk. "He ended up in Shamrock Hospital. Of course that means he won't be able to do the butter sculpture for the fair this year."

"That's terrible," I said.

"Awful," Colleen agreed. "I hadn't even heard about that."

"Well, the mayor and the Chamber of Commerce—I'm on the board of directors, you know—are trying to keep the info quiet until the fair. With all the bad press Shamrock has had lately after Deirdre—" Gabby clapped her hands to her mouth as she looked at Colleen. "Oh, my dear, I am so sorry. I didn't mean to bring up what happened to your sweet friend."

"That's OK, Gabby." Colleen patted the shop owner's shoulder.

"Thank you, dear." Gabby smiled at her gratefully. "Fortunately, they did find a last-minute replacement for the butter sculpture artist on short notice."

"Athena?" I guessed.

Gabby put a finger to her lips. "Shh, don't tell anyone. It's not public information yet. But you're exactly right. She's the perfect person for the job, in my opinion. Between us, though, I'm not sure she was happy about stepping in for her father."

"Why not?" Colleen asked.

Gabby tapped her chin as she thought. "What was it she told me when she delivered the gnomes? Oh yes. The project 'wasn't suited to her current artistic and business goals,' or some such. But again—and I'm telling you girls this strictly in confidence—it sounded to me as if she didn't care for the way Mayor Flanagan approached her with the idea. He was rather pushy, apparently." The shop owner lowered her voice again. "To be honest, she used more colorful language."

So Athena and I had something in common other than our advanced ages. I wasn't a big fan of His Dishonor

Raymond F. Flanagan, either. While he could be outwardly charming, the mayor's ego—and appetite for cold, green cash—knew no bounds.

I was about to suggest to Colleen that we continue on our way when a series of loud thuds sounded at the front of the store.

"Oh, dear. That heavy wooden door," Gabby said. "It keeps expanding in this nasty heat. It's so hard to open."

All three of us hurried toward the entrance to assist the person on the other side. As Colleen and I pulled hard on the door, it suddenly flew open.

The customer stumbled into the shop, and Gabby caught her by the arm.

"Oh, hello." The newcomer, her dark hair pulled back in a neat French twist, smoothed her light blue linen suit and smiled as if she hadn't nearly fallen on her face. "Perhaps you could help me. I'm just off the plane from Shannon and in a terrible rush. I need to buy some Shamrock T-shirts for my daughter. She's fourteen years of age." Her eyes swept the store. "Nothing too tacky, please."

Gabby pursed her lips. "I'll see what we can find."

Chapter Six

Colleen and I quickly said good-bye to Gabby and exited Gifts of Gab. I can't say I was overly sad to leave behind those weapon-wielding gremlins in the window.

A loud rumble of thunder sounded the second we stepped onto the sidewalk. The sky had turned an odd grayish green. In the distance, I glimpsed a bright flash of heat lightning.

"We'd better decide on our next stop fast," Colleen said. "It's about to start lashing."

I gazed around the Square. For once it was nearly empty of foot traffic, other than people running to their cars or hailing green cabs. The Shamrock Trolley rumbled past, briefly blocking my view. I had no idea where we should go, other than somewhere Colleen and I could talk privately. There'd be zero chance of that back at the house until who knew when tonight.

The fake gaslights started to flicker in the growing darkness, and the Irish flags outside Molly's Fish and Ale House flapped wildly in the increasing wind. A Great Shamrock Fair banner hung precariously by one end over Main Street. A wayward trash bag was caught on the nearest fire hydrant.

"How about that new place, halfway down?" I said, as the first fat raindrop hit my nose. The sign outside showed a teapot with an adorable goat jumping over it. Tea would be perfect.

"The Jumping Goat?" Colleen shrugged. "OK. I haven't been in there yet."

"It's hard to mess up tea," I said. "Plus there have to be pastries, right?"

In no time we were settled comfortably at a table in the far corner of the shop. The only other customer was a woman in a booth with her back to us. All I really glimpsed of her as we sat down was a long, white chiffon scarf woven around her head and over one shoulder like Grace Kelly. And a pair of large, heavy black shoes.

There was no server at the counter, or anywhere in sight. Well, that was OK. We weren't in a rush, and rain pelted the front bay window. We'd made it inside just in time.

Those chocolate cupcakes with green sprinkled frosting in the display counter sure looked good. I was starving.

Colleen twirled her clean teaspoon. "So I guess we should talk about how we're going to handle everything with Bliz, right? Having Ian show up in town right now sort of complicates everything."

I sighed. "Yup." Complicated didn't begin to cover it.

Short version of a long story: Ian was Maeve's biological dad, but not Bliz's. Technically, the girls were cousins as well as sisters. I'd adopted Bliz not long after she was born, just after Ian and I officially divorced. He'd returned to Ireland to concentrate on his music, promising to visit and send money whenever he could.

Neither of those things ever really happened. Not too often, anyway. It broke my heart. And Maeve's especially, I was sure. She didn't talk about her dad a lot.

Anyway, when Colleen found out she was expecting Bliz before her senior year of high school, we'd come up with The Plan. It was actually my sister's idea, and we thankfully had our family's full support. Twelve years older than Colleen and already mom to a seven-year-old, I was thrilled to welcome my second daughter, even though I knew it wouldn't be easy. Everyone agreed Colleen wasn't ready to raise a child, and our mom had her hands full with the Chief still recovering from his injuries.

Other than my and Ian's divorce soon after—which might have happened anyway, to be honest—things had worked out smoothly so far. Colleen and I had intended to tell the girls the whole truth about our family situation and the choices we'd made when they were both old enough to understand.

But during our visit last March, Maeve overheard a conversation between me and Colleen about the timing. Total disaster. And of course it wasn't the way I'd wanted my older daughter to find out.

Waiting this long to tell the girls may not have been the best decision, I realized now. Maeve knew; Bliz didn't. But there was also the issue of Bliz's dad. Colleen had never revealed his identity, not even to me. And she hadn't told him about Bliz.

She'd promised she would. Soon. Since I worked with clients remotely during the tax off-season, we had agreed to spend the summer as a family and try to work things through.

And I would decide if the girls and I would stay in Shamrock for good. Even if it meant big changes to all of our lives.

"So do we wait to tell Bliz?" Colleen asked. "For now?"

"I think so," I said slowly. "At least until after Ian goes back to Ireland. The dad issue will just make things more confusing for her. She and I haven't really talked about the birds and the bees yet."

"Maybe you should," Colleen said.

I sighed. "I don't know if she's ready for that yet. As far as specific details are concerned, at least. I want her to enjoy being a kid for as long as possible. She still believes in Santa, for heaven's sake. Or she did last Christmas, anyway."

"Mm." I'm not sure my sister agreed with me. Maybe I was wrong. I'd been going back and forth on the timing for the last three months.

"I've always taught Bliz about different kinds of families," I said. "And plenty of her friends live in nontraditional households. Bliz won't think twice about that. I've gotten books out of the library about kids with two mommies, too, but that's not the same thing. I haven't found any yet that explain our particular situation."

"Does it matter that much, really?" Colleen said. "She knows she's safe and how much we all love her."

"Of course she does." I sighed. "But if I'd told her from the beginning, this would have been so much easier."

"So do we keep letting Bliz think Ian's her dad?"

"Well, he's been OK with it so far," I said. "But she's getting older, and she doesn't even know him, really. I don't know how she'll feel. But it's not fair to either of them. He's been playing daddy from afar, in some sense, but I guess having a second kid right then wasn't what he signed up for. Especially under the circumstances."

Colleen looked stricken, and I regretted that last line. "He didn't actually say that, but still." I paused. "And a lot of this depends on you, Colleen. What exactly do you want me to tell Bliz about her real dad? Because she deserves to know when we bring the subject up. Plus we need her full family health history. When are you going to tell Bliz's dad? And me, by the way? You can't put this off forever."

Colleen twisted her hair. "I'll tell him. Really soon. I promise. I just can't, not quite yet. For all kinds of reasons."

"I guess we're in the same boat, then. Me with telling Bliz, and you with telling her bio dad. We have to do it soon. As in, this summer."

"I know." She gazed down at the table. "Look, Kate, you're her mom. I'll follow your lead. And I'll talk to . . . her dad. Just give me a little more time. And a heads-up if you decide to say anything to Bliz before that, OK?"

"Agreed." I reached across the table and laid my hand over my sister's, Claddagh ring to Claddagh ring. "Don't worry, Colleen Queen. We'll figure this out."

We had to. And the sooner, the better. For Bliz, and everyone else involved.

Where was our server? I really wanted that cupcake and tea now. I looked around the shop again. Other than apparently having zero employees, The Jumping Goat seemed like a nice place. Cozy and chill with pictures everywhere of goats and the Irish countryside, displayed around shelves of teapots and related tea paraphernalia. Ireland was known more for its sheep than goats, but they were just as cute.

"Guess no one's going to serve us," I said. "Should we just leave?"

"Yeah, this is pretty ridiculous." Colleen leaned out of the booth and looked over her shoulder. "Did that other customer get her order?"

"Doubt it," I said. "I may help myself to one of those cupcakes and leave some cash on the counter. I'm that hungry."

"Wait." Colleen spun around again. "Is that person in the booth . . . Moira McShane?"

Oh no. How could I have missed that zebra-striped coat on the peg near the ladies' room when we walked in?

"Yup, that's her, all right." I lowered my voice. "Do you think she heard us talking just now?"

"One way to find out." Colleen was off toward the booth faster than a shot of Irish whiskey.

I hesitated, then followed. I had no idea how this convo would go, but I couldn't let my sister face Moira alone. Not after the standoff between them after Deirdre's murder.

Someone must have brought Moira that tea with the fancy plate of lemons, but they appeared untouched. And why was she wearing those huge, cat-eye sunglasses indoors on a dark and stormy afternoon?

Obviously she hadn't wanted to be seen—or disturbed—by anyone. Especially if they had the last name of Buckley.

"Moira?" Colleen said.

The young woman quickly adjusted her scarf to cover even more of her face. "Um, hi, Colleen. And . . . Kate."

Her voice was muffled, and not just by the crazy scarf. Had Moira been crying alone in a goat-themed tea shop?

Colleen frowned, and I could tell she was taking in Moira's outfit du jour. Usually her frenemy wore dramatic, attention-seeking outfits paired with randomly retro accessories from a closet that had to rival my sister's in volume. But aside from the distinctive scarf and glasses, today Moira wore a knee-length black skirt and stiff, white button-up shirt with those industrial black shoes I'd noticed earlier. Her bright, frizzy red hair looked duller today, pulled in a tight bun with a few stray wispies left around her face.

Other than the scarf and sunglasses, Moira was the perfect image of a Central Casting server at Bewley's Café, the famous coffeehouse on Grafton Street in Dublin.

"Do you *work* here?" Colleen sounded incredulous.

"No." Moira glanced furtively toward the door, as if she might make a break for it. "I mean, yes." She sniffled. "Sort of."

I couldn't help feeling sorry for her. Moira was a hot mess on a good day. Not to mention rude, overly driven, jealous, pushy, competitive and condescending. She always had an agenda of some sort, too—usually one that involved trying to best the Buckleys. But she'd been through a lot since last spring, too. Not more than my sister, who'd lost her best friend, but still.

"Moira," I said gently. "Are you all right? You seem upset."

She blew her nose on a paper napkin. "I am," she said in a wobbly voice. "My life is in the toilet."

Beside me, I sensed Colleen in instant empathy mode. "Scoot over, Moira," my sister said, and plopped down into the booth.

Moira seemed surprised, but she did as she was told. Unsure whether it was a good idea, I sat across from the two of them.

"You should be really happy right now," Colleen said. "I heard the Smiling Shamrock is doing great, with Aidan and all the Crossroads dancers staying there. That's a good thing, right?"

"No," Moira said. "Not for me, anyway. Auntie Una is delighted, and yeah, we've been super busy." She paused to let her next words sink in. "A lot busier than the Buckley House, I bet."

Now that sounded like the Moira McShane Kelly we knew. I gazed up at the Jumping Goat's green tin ceiling and mentally counted to ten.

Colleen ignored the dig. "If you're so busy over there, why are you working here instead of the Shamrock?"

Moira stared into her full cup of tea. It had to be ice cold by now. Plus she'd left in the tea bag, so the hue had turned from amber to practically black. Irish Breakfast Tea, according to the tag at the end of the string. Seemed to me that any tea place worth their cream and sugar would steep loose tea leaves. Anyone could pick up the bag kind at the Value Castle over on Kilkenny Parkway.

But then, this was a tea place named The Jumping Goat.

"Oh, I'm still working at the Shamrock, all right," Moira said. "But Auntie Una pays me practically nothing, and I need more money. I want to go back to New York."

I sometimes felt the same in this crazy town.

"So this is your side gig," Colleen asked. "Does your aunt know?"

"No." Moira tapped a long black fingernail on the table. "She's been distracted lately because my other auntie Zita is over from Ireland. You know, helping out with the B&B while Auntie Nuala is in the . . . medical place. I gave notice here this morning, because I can't make my hours work with the Shamrock's anymore. It's, like, twenty-four/seven there now."

"You must be exhausted," Colleen said.

Moira nodded. "I wanted to just quit the Goat, but I couldn't leave my boss in the lurch. Plus I didn't want her blabbing around that I was a bad employee. People hate me enough already."

"They don't hate you, Moira." That may not have been exactly true, but I wanted to make her feel better. Sad, mopey Moira was even worse than regular Moira.

"I'm such a failure." The floodgates were wide open now. "Do you know how hard it is to be around all those happy dancers at the Shamrock? They're so excited about the show and getting their big breaks. But I got fired from Irish Steps, and Aidan doesn't want me in Crossroad Dreams. I know he's your boyfriend and everything, Colleen, but it's so hard. Where's my big break? You don't even practice, and everyone thinks you're an amazing dancer."

I held my breath for a second, awaiting my sister's reaction.

But Colleen reached over and patted Moira's bony hand. "Now, now," she crooned, like Mom used to when we were little. "It's not that bad, Moira. Have some faith, and don't give up. Good things will happen. I promise."

"I'm not good at anything," Moira moaned on. "My dance school in the city never got off the ground, and I can't compete with you and Bernie at the Donnelly School. Especially now." Moira gestured toward her teacup. "I can't even make a decent cuppa." With that, she dropped her frizzy head on my sister's shoulder and started full-out bawling. Colleen looked at me in alarm.

"You know what you're really good at, Moira?" I tried, racking my brain. "PR. When you were thinking about launching your new Irish dance academy here in Shamrock last spring, you did an amazing job of getting the word out. And you're a whiz at social media."

Moira sniffed and sat up again. "I am, aren't I?"

"Oh, yes," Colleen said. "Maybe you can get a publicity job with Crossroad Dreams, and Aidan will let you be an understudy or something, too. You can work your way back on stage."

I raised an eyebrow. Colleen knew full well that Moira's dancing ability wasn't the issue. The problem was . . . well, her entire personality.

"Bernie and I do have things running pretty smoothly at the Donnelly School," Colleen said. "For now, anyway. But we could use help with social media. Let me check with Bernie. And here's another idea, too. What if I talked to the Miss Shamrock Committee about hiring you to do PR? Like, a last-minute media blitz."

"I never got to be a Miss Shamrock like you," Moira said. "Or even a Little Miss Shamrock. I was always a runner-up."

"That means you were a member of the Celtic Court," Colleen pointed out. "Twice. That's a big honor, too."

"Well, yeah." Moira was warming to the idea, I could tell. And my sister was on a roll.

"You could help with the talent segment as well," Colleen said. "There will be a ton of Irish dancers. Do you know anything about music or singing, too? No, wait. How about costumes? You're a whiz with design."

Moira perked right up. "Yes! I love fashion. Remember all my Irish dance solo dresses? They were one-of-a-kind."

Were they ever. I tried not to shudder.

"And I can do makeup, too. I'm amazing at that." Moira forgot herself in her eagerness and pushed up her sunglasses.

Eek. Even not counting the puffy, swollen eyes and nose and the mascara running down her cheeks, she looked a fright. Elizabeth Arden meets Beetlejuice level.

"Mmhm," Colleen said. "You're a perfect fit to join the Miss Shamrock team. I'll talk to the committee and let you know as soon as I hear anything."

"OK." Moira was positively beaming now, like a banshee who'd gotten an unexpected glow up. "I'll get started with a bunch of promo ideas in the meantime. Thanks, Colleen. You're a peach. I owe you one."

Colleen smiled and rose gracefully out of the booth. "You're welcome. Now go splash some nice cold water on your face and redo your makeup, and you'll be our Moira again. Kate and I have to scoot, but we'll see you soon. Bye now."

"Bye!" Moira waved happily. When I glanced over my shoulder on our way out the door, she was already pulling a giant train-style cosmetics case from her equally massive tote to put herself together.

I really wanted to believe that the completely out of character heart-to-heart on Moira's end was genuine. But had my sister just been cleverly manipulated by a pro? Impossible to tell.

Hopefully Colleen's off-the-cuff suggestions worked out for both of them. Maybe it was my negativity popping up again, but I felt a strange sense of uneasiness. Not just about the Moira situation. More like everything in general since the girls and I had arrived in Shamrock this afternoon.

I couldn't seem to shake that same creeping dread I'd experienced last March. As soon as I had some time to myself, I'd run into Our Lady of Angels and light a candle. Just in case.

It wasn't the first time I'd promised myself that. But this time I really meant it.

Chapter Seven

After our unexpected run-in with Moira McShane Kelly at the Jumping Goat, neither Colleen nor I felt much like hanging around in town much longer. We'd had our conversation, everything seemed fine with Moira now, and the storm had blown away, but I'd lost my appetite. I wasn't even sorry I missed out on that cupcake.

Mom called from the Irish dance practice in progress at Angels Hall to let us know everything was going well. She'd head home when Colleen arrived, but the girls wanted to stick around to watch the older kids. And the Chief was already off to Farrell's with the Limerick Lads.

I decided I'd drive my sister to the practice after she changed into her dance clothes at home. That way, I could hang out for a while with Maeve and Bliz. And to be honest, an hour or two of jigs and reels and overall chaos beat pacing around the Buckley House, fretting about Ian. Hopefully my ex—and his new beloved—wouldn't show up at the B&B tonight to greet the rest of the band. That might make things extra awkward.

* * *

"I ordered a bunch of pies from Erin Go Pizza," Colleen announced, bounding into the living room in a hot pink athletic top, black dance shorts, and an oversized Donnelly School tank. She expertly twisted her hair on top of her head in a messy bun, securing it with a metallic gold scrunchie as she glanced out the window at the driveway. "The delivery person should be here soon. I charged everything on the Buckley House credit card. And gave them a big tip. Hope that's OK."

I shrugged. "Sure. The new guests may be hungry tonight after such a long trip. I might even snag a slice or two to take to practice."

"Oh, the pizza's not for the guests. Unless there's any left over. It's for my friends."

"Your *friends*?"

"Yup. The ones moving all the stuff from the garage into the basement, remember?" She cocked her head and frowned slightly, as if considering something for the first time. "Hopefully everything will fit."

I leaned over from the armchair and pulled aside a floral drape. "Wow, they're here already." Six or seven fit-looking twenty-somethings, with a couple of pickups and a Toyota Corolla parked at the curb. "I can't believe they showed up so quick."

"Of course they did," Colleen said. "They said they'd be happy to help."

I sighed. "Guess I'd better stay home to pitch in, then. Especially since a lot of that junk belongs to me and the girls."

"Nah." Colleen shouldered her dance bag. "We'll just leave the side door unlocked in case anyone needs to use the bathroom. Mom will be back soon anyway."

"I doubt the Chief would be thrilled about us leaving the house open for even two minutes," I said. "He's on that big security system kick."

Colleen waved. "Dad will be fine with it. They're all Shamrock PD and Fire. Come on, we can say hi on our way out and wait until the pizza shows up."

I sighed. "Let me grab my purse."

"Pocketbook," Colleen reminded me. "You're back in Massachusetts now."

"Whatever."

We stepped out the side door to enthusiastic greetings. Unreal. How did my sister manage to get so many people—including me—to do things for her like this?

I had to admit, her persuasive abilities were far better than mine. And they definitely came in handy sometimes.

* * *

The parish hall at Our Lady of Angels was crowded, noisy, and hot, despite the recent heavy rain. The doors were propped open with folding chairs, and strategically placed fans whirred in a futile effort to move the stagnant air. Beside the stage at the far end of the huge space—which also served as the school gym and auditorium—flags drooped like multicolored shrouds. American and state on one side. Irish on the other, next to the old black piano.

My heart tightened as I scanned the hall for Mom and the girls. This was where Colleen and I had found poor Deirdre. Well, technically behind the stage, at the bottom of a flight of stairs. I'd never get over the shock and horror of that stormy night. Maeve probably wouldn't, either.

Colleen never mentioned it now.

"Sorry, Ms. B!" I was momentarily knocked off balance by a young dancer rushing past me, texting at the same time. Kids were in motion all through the hall, hurrying to their spots or the bathrooms or practicing steps with their friends as they waited for their turns on stage. Older kids amused themselves with electronic devices, books, and cards. Elementary school siblings ran screaming after each other in games of hide-and-seek or tag. Sneakers squeaked and hard dance shoes clicked across the shiny blond-wood floor. Parents chatted near the snack table—cookies and brownies twenty-five cents—or fanned themselves in sticky folding chairs brought out from beneath the stage.

From the middle of the bleachers across the room, Mom waved and started gathering Bliz and their bags.

I finally spotted Maeve, too. Cross-legged on the floor under a wall of Angels sports championship banners, drinking from a PJ Scoops water bottle. Zoe Koo—her best friend in Shamrock and an ace Irish dancer—was doubled over beside her in a warm-up stretch, face to right knee. Their mutual buddy Conor, Siobhan's eldest, leaned against the wall, scrolling his phone. He wasn't a dancer, but he often helped with the music or sound tech. No sign of his mom, so he was probably on babysitting duty for his little sisters. Sure enough, the Murphy triplets sorted M&Ms by color nearby.

The owner of the Donnelly School of Irish dance, Bernadette Donnelly—known to the adults in town as Bernie—stood in the middle of the stage, surrounded by preteens. Mostly girls, but not all. Wearing her usual tracksuit—a lilac-hued summer version—she looked hot and slightly exasperated, but her expression brightened as Colleen hopped lightly onto the stage.

"OK, dancers, listen up!" Bernie shouted to the room in general. "Miss Colleen is in charge now. I want you all to—" Her gravelly voice suddenly gave out, probably as much due to her multi-pack-a-day cigarette habit as the challenges of making herself heard over the noise. Colleen handed her a bottle of water and executed an ear-splitting whistle.

Silence.

"Hi, everyone!" Colleen called. "The sooner you all pay attention, the sooner we get out of here!"

Beside me, a profusely perspiring dad clapped silently.

Colleen looked at Bernie, who motioned for her to continue as she chugged the water. My sister turned back to the crowd. "OK, thanks, guys. Everybody who's dancing in the fair, go see Theresa Meaney over by the door to check your groups and times, if you haven't already. They may change before the fair opens"—adults groaned—"but hopefully not. Before anyone else leaves, I want to mention a couple of important things about the Miss Shamrock contests."

Now everyone was really paying attention. Other than Maeve, who got up and headed toward one of the bathrooms in the hall. Zoe stopped her stretching and frowned.

"If you are interested in entering one of the contests—remember, twelve and under for Little Miss Shamrock and thirteen and up for Miss Shamrock—today is last call. The first rounds start on Monday, with a rehearsal tomorrow night. Please sign up with your or your guardian's name and email on the clipboard at the snack table. Use your best handwriting, OK? If we can't read your email, we can't contact you with more info. We will need your parent or guardian's permission. But there's a new addition to the contest for the final rounds this year." She paused. "A short essay of 150 words or less for the younger girls, and up to 300 words for the teen group."

The room filled with chatter again. And a few more groans.

"The topic, chosen by the Miss Shamrock Committee and approved by Mayor Flanagan is, 'What My Heritage Means to Me.' Got it?"

A chorus of drawn-out yeses sounded around the hall, along with more than a few less enthusiastic reactions.

"And remember this, because it's really important," Colleen added. "You have to write your essays yourselves. No help from anyone. That means parents, guardians, relatives, teachers, siblings. Even your friends." She waited a beat. "And I know it's tempting, but please, no cheating by using any kind of AI, OK? The Miss Shamrock Committee wants to know what *you* think. From your heart. Not a computer program."

Some of the adults in the crowd clapped. Others looked worried.

I craned my neck, looking for Mom and Bliz. Someone must have stopped Mom to talk. Eileen Buckley knew even more people in town than Colleen.

I was startled when someone came up beside me. The rude woman with the French twist who'd come into Gifts of Gab looking for T-shirts. "Hello," she said, "I'm Lulu Cavanagh-Barry, from Dublin. I saw you and your—sister, is it?"—she cocked her head toward the stage—"in the shop today."

I nodded. "Yes, that's Colleen. Nice to meet you. I'm Kate Buckley. Hope you found what you needed for your daughter. Is she dancing at the fair?"

"She is." Lulu touched at her hair. "We were thrilled when we got the special invitation from Mayor Flanagan. Very kind of him, don't you think?" Before I could respond, she rushed on, "Cassandra was going to appear at a *feis* in County Clare this week, but we dropped everything to come to the Great Shamrock Fair. She qualifies for Worlds every year, so as you can imagine, our schedule is packed. It's so hard sometimes to fit everything in. There she is, on her own over there by the Irish flag. That's my Cassandra."

I turned toward the corner of the stage. Right away, I spotted Lulu's daughter. Long, wavy red hair in a side pony. Spray tan. A startling amount of makeup for a kid—not to mention a dance practice in 90-degree heat. She looked bored and attentive at the same time.

"I have a daughter her age," I said. "How nice you and Cassandra were able to come for the fair. I'm sure you'll enjoy it."

"She's performing several solos between the Donnelly School sets. And of course she's entering the Miss Shamrock contest, too. Why not? I heard your sister held the title years ago. Tell me, has a girl from over the pond ever won?"

I drew back slightly, unnerved by the woman's intensity. She didn't even try to hide it. "I'm not sure," I said. "But the contest has always been open to everyone."

"Has it?" Lulu gave a between-us wink. "Cassandra is used to being first, I'm afraid," she said, with a sorry-not-sorry sigh. "I hope she won't be disappointed. But for the talent portion she'll perform her last championship routine. And I imagine she'll be given extra points on the heritage essay. You know, since she's actually from Ireland."

I was literally speechless. This woman's attitude was unreal. Not in the least bit subtle and very . . . well, un-Irish, in my experience. Overly competitive mothers with attitudes like Lulu Cavanagh-Barry's were exactly the reason I was wary of Bliz entering competitions of any kind. Even Irish dance, which she loved.

"Well, I'm not on the committee," I said finally, "but I can assure you, girls from all backgrounds and ethnicities are eligible to be Miss Shamrock. There's no extra credit for being Irish or Irish American."

"Ah, of course." Lulu waggled her fingers. "I'm off to see if Cassandra needs me. And to watch the dancing. Bye now. It was lovely to meet you. I'm sure I'll see you again soon." She glided away in the direction of the stage.

My mouth was probably still hanging open as Mom and Bliz came up.

"Mommy, please please *please* can we stay the whole time?" Bliz, who'd started Irish dance in March and swiftly declared it her future profession, gazed up at me in her Donnelly School T-shirt, eyes shining. "Cassandra Cavanagh-Barry is here. She's an amazing dancer. And I don't want to go back to the Buckley House yet."

That made two of us. I wasn't looking forward to welcoming the guests from Peat—one of them in particular. "Sure, sweetie," I said. "We'll stay as long as you want."

* * *

It was late when Colleen and I got home with the girls. Mom was already in bed. Between the practice and the heat, no one had much energy left, even my sister. I offered to wait up for the arriving guests, after getting the girls settled in the Nest. I needed to make sure it wasn't too hot up there in the cozy attic space under the eaves. Maeve and Bliz both loved their shared room-away-from-home, but it could get stuffy in the summer. We'd already brought up extra fans and set up the portable AC tower.

Before I wished my daughters good night, I sat down at the end of the antique iron bed. "Guess who's coming to see you, girls?" I paused, smoothing the quilt my Irish grandmother had sewn. "Dad."

"Really?" Maeve's expression was unreadable. "We haven't seen him in forever. Why didn't he tell me?"

"I don't know," I said truthfully. "Maybe he wanted to surprise you. From what I heard, it was a last-minute plan."

"Right." Maeve looked out the round window.

"He and his band are playing the Great Shamrock Fair."

"So that's why Dad will be here, then." Maeve crossed her arms.

"It's not the only reason, honey."

Bliz sat up from under a pile of decorative pillows. "Will he take us for ice cream?"

I smiled. "I'm sure he will, if you ask nicely."

"Good," Bliz said, and disappeared under the pillows again. Maeve pulled out her phone.

End of conversation. I'd try again later. "Good night, sweethearts," I said, giving them each a kiss. "Sleep tight. Is it cool enough in here with the AC tower?"

"We're fine." Maeve sounded annoyed that I was still there.

I looked back as I was halfway down the folding stairs from the Nest's trap door. Phone still in hand, Maeve was staring out the window again into the darkness.

I sighed as I pulled up the stairs and double-checked the chain. Ian wasn't a bad person or entirely insensitive. He hadn't always been this self-absorbed or thoughtless. If he had been, I would never have married him.

But it was true he had changed somehow—into a person I hardly recognized. How had he become such an absent dad, even taking into consideration he lived an ocean away? I'd never seen that coming. In my heart, I was sure Ian had no idea how much he'd hurt our daughters, especially Maeve, with his silence. Maybe he thought it would be better for him to be less involved in their lives. That he'd be in the way, or that too much contact between him and Maeve would hurt her more. But neither of those excuses were true or justified his actions. Or nonactions. And whenever I'd brought up the subject—not often enough, I had to admit—he did the dodge, dip, dive.

It was hard for me to accept, but it seemed as if all Ian thought about now was his music. And Fallon, I supposed. They were getting married, for heaven's sake. Well, best of luck to them both.

For the zillionth time, I was thankful for my family. For better or for worse, we had each other's backs. Jokes and bickering and mini dramas aside, we could always count on each other. My parents and siblings had given me and the girls so much support when Ian and I went our separate ways.

The Chief and the Limerick Lads—including Noel, whom I learned had joined his dad's band last March when a founding member retired—were back from Farrell's when I returned downstairs. All of them except Noel went directly up to bed. No impromptu music in the living room. Not even tea and biscuit requests.

My dad would be awake soon anyway. Ever since the life-changing incident at the Shamrock PD when a perp he'd helped bring to justice escaped from jail and shot him behind his desk, he rarely slept for long stretches at a time.

"The lads are all completely knackered," Noel said with a chuckle as he joined me in the parlor. "Especially me."

"I bet none of them were too tired to argue with you about leaving the pub," I said.

"Exactly right."

"It's the jet lag," I said. "It looked like my dad was worn out, too, though. He hasn't been much of a party animal lately. Doctor's orders. And my mom's," I added half-jokingly.

These days, the Chief enjoyed an occasional nip at home or a beer or two with his buddies, unless he was driving. Farrell's was just down the street from the B&B, but he preferred to make the short trip in his own specially outfitted van. A point of pride, I suspected.

"Ah, well, they enjoyed the good time," Noel said. "The *craic*, as we say."

For some reason, things felt a little awkward between us, sitting in matching striped armchairs in the parlor. Maybe because this room was a bit more formal than the others. Or maybe because Noel had always been good friends with Ian.

A few years younger, he was handsome in a clean-cut, Irish soap ad way. Even though the two guys had practically opposite personalities, they'd always bonded over music.

"It's been such a long time since we've seen each other," I said.

He nodded. "It has."

"By the way," I said casually, "what was the deal there between your dad and Fallon O' Malley? He sure doesn't seem to like her much."

Noel looked uncomfortable but waved my question away. "Ah, it was nothing. Old business."

"Oh. Right," I said, disappointed. It didn't sound as if I would get much more out of Marty's son.

I offered to bring Noel a mug of tea or a Leprechaun Lager, but he declined. "I may call it an early night as well," he said.

But as Noel stood up to leave, his cell phone buzzed. Two more text alerts arrived as he pulled it from his pocket and checked the screen. "A friend," he said. "Looks like I'm heading back to the pub after all. Maybe one pint."

"Did your friend just arrive?" I asked politely.

He nodded. "I won't be out long," he said. "Some of us need to be at the fairgrounds at the crack of dawn. Stage setup. But that's hours off. And while in Shamrock . . ." He winked, then bounded toward the doorway with renewed energy.

"Have a good time," I called.

But he was already gone.

It was after ten. I was dying to go up to bed after such a long day, but I had to wait up for the new guests. Somehow I fell asleep reading there in the parlor. I must have been too comfortable—or too hot—curled up in the armchair nearest the doorway. Or maybe I was lulled by the loud ticking of the grandfather clock in the still B&B.

The book was a terrible choice anyway. *Notes from the Heart*, a sappy and depressing memoir by an American woman who'd spent a year in her twenties busking on the streets of Galway. She'd fallen in love with a local and almost stayed in Ireland with him but didn't. She'd long ago given up on music and romance and now she regretted her choices. But she'd learned a lot about life and longing and comforted herself by making costumes for her four pet ferrets.

Oh, please.

I don't know who the book belonged to, if anyone—I'd found it on an overstuffed bookshelf—but I tossed it directly in the trash. As I returned through the foyer, congratulating myself on a job well done, I heard a soft knock at the front door. Finally. Our guests were here.

Hopefully not with Ian.

I was surprised to find just one member of Peat on the Buckley House porch. After I welcomed him in, I soon learned that Liam played guitar, banjo, mandola, saxophone, bodhran, flute, and . . . hurdy-gurdy. OK, then. A pale, soft-spoken guy in a rumpled, button-up shirt, with hair so blond it was almost white, he offered to let his bandmates in for me when they arrived. Apparently the Peat contingent had gone directly from Logan to the pub. Now all of them except Liam had scattered in different directions to continue the party.

I almost turned down his offer. For the second time today, I risked my cop's daughter card by throwing caution to the wind. Especially in light of the Chief's latest security kick. But it was almost midnight. I could be up for another two hours, when Shamrock's pubs closed. And Liam seemed like a standup guy. "Thanks," I said. "Appreciate it."

I left Liam in the kitchen with everyone's room assignments and keys and the can of Leprechaun Lager Noel had refused. Rover snoozed happily at his feet.

Yup, it had been a long day. Tomorrow, I suspected, would be even longer.

Chapter Eight

I was showered, dressed, and down in the kitchen early the next morning. I hadn't gotten much sleep, but I felt extra virtuous and perky. A room to myself—even if it was the small spare room on the top floor, across from the Chief's office—made all the difference. No sharing with Colleen this time.

Mom, just back from 6 AM Mass, was tossing flour around and rolling dough. The Chief sat at the table in his plaid summer robe, engrossed in the *Shamrock Sentinel* with a mug of steaming coffee. I sniffed the air, recognizing the alluring aroma of freshly cooked Irish bacon, aka rashers. Even though the sun had barely been up for a couple of hours, everything seemed brighter today.

No sign of Bliz yet. And who knew if any of the musicians from either band had made it out to the fairgrounds. Maeve would lie in for as long as we'd let her.

"Morning." I opened the top oven door and extracted an extra crispy rasher from the broiler pan with an antique turning fork.

"You're out of bed with the chickens, Kathleen," the Chief said. "Will you be going to eight o'clock Mass?"

"I'll take the girls tonight," I said. "What can I do to help, Mom?"

We usually served a simple Continental buffet for our guests, but the Lads were friends of the family. And we couldn't exactly offer them full hot breakfast and not the other guests.

"Nothing, dear, thanks. I'm almost done." Mom swiped a spot of flour from her cheek with the side of her arm.

"Dad, want to take your coffee out on the patio with me?"

"Sure, you go on," he said. "I'll be there in a bit."

That meant no. "OK." I looked around the kitchen. "Where's Rover? I should probably take him out for a quick walk. Maeve can do the next one."

"Haven't seen him," Mom answered. "Still sleeping, I suppose."

I headed to the mudroom and stuck my head in the door. "Morning, boyo!" I called. "Rise and shine. Time for walkies."

No answer. Not even a rustle. Rover's towel bed was disheveled. And empty.

I checked the hall. The butler's pantry. The entire main floor of the house. I even went down to the stuffy, spidery basement. No elderly golden retrievers. I ran to the top of the front stairs and looked in every direction. No luck.

Don't panic. Maybe he'd gotten out into the yard somehow. Reversing course, I headed downstairs again, avoiding the kitchen-mudroom route this time. No sense in worrying Mom and the Chief.

I stepped out the main back door and made a quick tour of the yard, arms crossed against my old Notre Dame sweatshirt. "Rover!" I called, trying to keep my voice down. "Here, boy. Where are you, buddy?"

Not even a blade of grass moved. The only sound was a window being pushed up in the house next door. Mrs. Sheehan, her thin white hair rolled up in those old school pink plastic-and-foam curlers, stuck her head out. "Katie Buckley, is that you? Everything all right, dearie?"

"Just fine, Mrs. Sheehan. Trying to find our dog."

"You have a dog now, did you say? How nice." Mrs. Sheehan leaned further out the window, displaying the top of her pale green bathrobe. "When did you get him? How we do miss our Rusty."

"Yesterday." I lowered my voice even more, so I wouldn't wake up every other house on Galway Court. "He's a big, golden dog, very friendly. Have you seen him?"

"What's that?" Mrs. Sheehan cupped a hand to her ear.

I repeated myself, surreptitiously scanning the yard again. I didn't want to be rude, but if Rover was really missing, I needed to get moving.

"Oh yes." Mrs. Sheehan nodded vigorously. "The poor fella wanted to go out. He went that-a-way." She pointed toward the gate. "With the nice gentleman."

I squeezed my eyes shut for a second in frustration. The gate with the broken latch. But I'd already checked the gate, first thing. It was closed. No signs of tunneling underneath. The "nice gentleman," whoever he was, had let Rover out.

A voice called to Mrs. Sheehan from inside her house. "Bye now, dearie," she said to me, sounding a little frazzled. "Jimmy needs to get in the shower. Hope you find your friend." She struggled to shut the window, then disappeared.

Well, this wasn't good. Our newly adopted dog was out here somewhere, either with a stranger or on his own. What if he got lost or hit by a car?

I had to find him before he got hurt—or the girls woke up. Avoiding Mom and Dad once again in the kitchen, I grabbed Rover's beer mug leash from the hook in the mudroom, then my pocketbook and car keys from upstairs. I'd try to retrace his steps. He couldn't have gotten far with that arthritis. If he really had it. I found myself almost wishing he did, in just this one instance. A touch of hobble would make it easier to catch him.

I checked the gate more carefully, then searched for any canine clues in the damp grass and dirt around it. Negative. Who was that gentleman in our yard Mrs. Sheehan had mentioned? And what were they doing here at this hour of the morning?

Too bad we didn't have those security cameras my dad was itching to install.

I was wasting precious time here. I needed to start scouring the neighborhood. As I straightened from peering for pawprints, the sound of cheerful whistling drifted through the early morning air. And straight up our driveway.

"Good mornin'," Marty greeted me as he came up. "Out for a dander as well?"

Was this Mrs. Sheehan's alleged "gentleman"?

"Morning, Marty," I said. "You're up early."

"The jet lag," he said. "'Twas dark when I woke up in me bed."

"Oh no, Marty, did you hurt yourself?" I pointed toward his left hand. "You're bleeding."

He looked down, and I noticed a bright red splotch on the wrist of his light sweater as well. "So I am," he said. "I may have taken a wee tumble."

"That looks pretty deep. You need to go inside and have Mom fix you up," I said. "She's an expert in first aid."

"Ah, it's nothing." He kept walking toward the house.

"Well, let her take a look anyway."

"I will, yeah," he said. That meant no.

"Marty, wait," I called as he ambled to the door. "I'm looking for our dog. The one digging in the yard yesterday. Did he go out the gate with you?"

Marty considered. "He did. He stayed with me for a while. A fine companion. Then he went off somewhere on his own."

"Which direction?"

"That way." Marty pointed toward Farrell's and Our Lady of Angels. Then he frowned and pointed in the other direction, past the Sheehans'. "Or that way, maybe."

Not helpful. Poor Marty. But I was losing time here. "OK, thanks," I said, breaking into a jog down the driveway. "Take care of that hand," I added over my shoulder, waving the dog leash.

As I searched the neighborhood, starting with both sides of our block, I tried not to be furious that my dad's buddy had let Rover out of the yard. Not only that, but Marty seemed completely unconcerned our dog was wandering the streets of Shamrock on his own.

Marty was elderly, I reminded myself. He'd taken a fall. I was being too hard on the poor man. Maybe he'd hit his head.

If so, Mom would take him straight to urgent care. I needed to find Rover before he got hurt, too.

No sign of a wayward retriever anywhere on Galway Court or Windsor Terrace. I jumped in the Subaru and widened my search, eyes peeled for any sudden movements or flashes of gold.

My cell rang through the dashboard. Siobhan. What was I going to tell her? I'd lost her former foster fur baby in less than twenty-four hours. But I needed her help. I stabbed my finger on the screen to accept the call.

"Hey, Kate, heard Rover got out."

How had she gotten that news already? "Siobhan, I am really sorry," I said, fighting tears. "He followed one of our guests out of the yard this morning and—"

"No worries," Siobhan said. "He sneaks out all the time. My neighbors all know him. He may be trying to find his way back to our house."

That did not make me feel much better. The Murphys didn't live that close to us. Rover would have to cross several streets, if he even knew the way. Hopefully there wouldn't be much traffic this early.

"He's microchipped," Siobhan said. "And he has an ID tag on his collar. Still has my name and number on it. We'll have to get him a new one. But anyway, this guy I know, Fergal, saw him and picked him up in his truck."

Thank heavens. Why hadn't she led with that info? I stopped at a red light and collapsed over the steering wheel in relief.

"I didn't want to bother you this early. But Fergal was on his way out to the fairgrounds to deliver some equipment, and he called me again. Rover jumped out while he was unloading the truck. I'm getting the girls up so we can help look for him, but Garrett said he'll try to—"

The light turned green, and I floored the gas. "Thanks, I'm on it," I said. "I'll keep you posted."

I had my Shamrock PD courtesy card in my wallet. I could make it to the fairgrounds in seven minutes.

Or less.

No sooner had I disconnected Siobhan than a text alert flashed on the car screen. The ID said, "Ian."

Nope nope nope. I hit "Ignore" and kept my attention on the road. I'd deal with my ex later.

* * *

I pulled into a space at the far edge of the fairgrounds parking lot and jumped out of the car, leash in hand. If only I'd thought to grab some dog treats from those bags Siobhan had given us.

First I had to find Rover. Then I'd worry about persuading him to come home with me.

Where should I look first? Somewhere near food. The fair didn't officially begin for a few more days, and I wasn't sure the food trucks had started arriving yet. So far the first parking lot was filling up with campers and trucks hauling equipment for the carnival strip, aka the Emerald Way.

Beyond the midway were the animal and farm equipment barns, plus several livestock and horse show rings, a roped-off area for the antique car show, and even a tractor pull. But on the two main fairground fields, striped green and white tents had been set up, with performance stages already in place. I purposely didn't focus on any of the people working around the stages, in case Ian was among them.

Instead I turned my attention to the out-of-town vendors staking out their camping areas. Some might have started cooking on camp stoves or using the microwaves in their RVs. That meant food scraps and wrapping. Trash bins and dumpsters had already been placed in the grassy parking lot.

The Kerrygold butter sculpture building, mostly brick with a huge glass enclosure at one end, was set not far from the main music stage, the Castle Pavilion. An unmarked, refrigerated truck was parked outside with workers moving around it. Beyond the Kerrygold building was an enticing stand of shady maples, and beyond them, a dog-friendly mini-wood of pine trees.

I headed toward the truck first. Maybe the workers had seen my family's darned dog.

They hadn't. "Look, lady," one guy said, tossing a huge carton marked *Fragile* on the ground. I glared at him for the "lady," but his back was already turned as he reached into the truck for another box. "We got stuff to do here, OK? We can't be payin' attention to no stray animals."

"Talk to the boss lady," another man wearing a lifting belt said.

"The boss, you mean?" I said.

He shrugged. "Whatever. That's her." He jerked his thumb toward a very tall woman visible inside the glass structure.

That had to be Athena Sweeney. I took in her close-cropped black hair and long black cape tied at the neck. In the summer.

But hey, who was I to judge her choice of outfit? I'd lost the sweatshirt, but my white T-shirt, navy shorts, and tennis shoes made me look like a camp counselor. All that was missing was the whistle.

And my mission right now wasn't to corral a bunch of rowdy kids into supervised activities. Just one tricky golden retriever. I smoothed my hair and let myself into the ice sculpture building.

"Close that door!" the woman greeted me. "You're letting all the heat in."

"Oh. Sorry." I pushed on the heavy steel door behind me as hard as I could, then leaned against it until I heard a click. Up close, the artist looked even taller. And a whole lot angrier than the situation called for, in my opinion. "You must be Athena Sweeney." I smiled hesitantly. "I'm Kate Buckley. Big fan."

I'd never even heard of her before yesterday. But Gabby had spoken glowingly of her talent. And maybe I could butter her up, so to speak.

Athena gave a sharp nod of her pointy chin. "No one is supposed to be in here. The space needs to reach optimum temperature as soon as possible."

I rubbed my bare arms. It was definitely cool inside the glass area. No wonder the sculptor was wearing an extra layer. But still. A cape? Guess she wanted to make some kind of artistic statement.

"I'm looking for a dog. About this big." I approximated Rover's height with the flat of my hand. "Golden retriever. Friendly. Have you seen him?"

Her dark eyes narrowed. "Yes. He was hanging around my studio a couple of hours ago."

"Studio?" I couldn't recall any other structures at the fairgrounds, other than a few barns for the horses, sheep, and other livestock the local farmers and 4H kids showed.

"The caretaker's cottage." Athena's cape swirled as she turned to point through the glass, in the direction of the trees. "My family has a special lease from the town."

"Ah," I said. "So the dog is still around there, do you think?" My teeth were beginning to chatter now.

Athena turned just her head. "He was a pest. Kept nosing around. I got rid of him."

I must have looked alarmed, because she added with a frown, "Oh, please. Not literally. But he was quite persistent, so I locked him up very securely in the old chicken coop. Then I left a voice mail for the dogcatcher."

"Shamrock doesn't have a dogcatcher," I said. "Animal control is handled by the police department. And Rover has a tag on his collar with a phone number."

Athena sniffed. "I didn't see one. In any case, my works in progress are top secret. The studio is a restricted area. No people. No animals. I've already had more than one unwanted intruder this morning."

"Got it." I'd hardly call Rover an intruder. He was a harmless senior dog, for heaven's sake. And who hated golden retrievers? "I'll just go grab him, OK?"

The sculptor gathered her cape. "Fine. Make it quick."

"Do I need a key?" I asked.

Athena looked disgusted. "Are you always so literal, or just dense? No, there is no key for the chicken coop." She pointed toward the exit with a jagged fingernail.

"Right." I was already pulling on the heavy door.

"And be quick about it, like I said!" she called after me. "No peeking."

Oh, I'd be quick, all right. The sooner I removed myself—and poor Rover—from anywhere near Athena Sweeney, the better.

Chapter Nine

I headed straight for the trees and the former caretaker's cottage to retrieve our new retriever.

The Seven Dwarfs-style dwelling looked rundown in what might be considered an arty way. Or a needed-to-be-condemned way. But right now I had zero interest in anything but getting Rover back into the Subaru and home.

The chicken coop area was located on the side of Athena's ramshackle studio, surrounded by a rusty, chain-link fence. And it was empty, with a good-sized pile of fresh dirt next to the open door. My heart sank. Hairy Houdini had escaped again.

"Rover! Here boy!" I ran through the pine trees behind the house, swatting early morning mosquitoes and the branches grazing my arms. He had to be here somewhere.

The pines ended sooner than I'd expected, the property line marked with flagged sticks. I found myself at the edge of another field, much smaller than the fairgrounds area. This expanse was more brown than green, other than occasional patches of clover with buzzing furry bumblebees. Giant rocks provided added potential cover for a largish dog.

I shaded my eyes with my hand. Why hadn't I brought my sunglasses from the car? The morning was already getting brighter and warmer. A nice change from the chill of the butter sculpture building.

A main road ran alongside one end of the field, behind a stone wall with a rustic log gate in the middle. Closed, thank heavens, so at least Rover wasn't running in the street. Stone walls bordered the far end and parallel side of the field as well.

Still no Rover. Now what? Maybe someone from the PD had taken him out of Athena's improvised dog run and returned him to Siobhan's house. Or maybe Garrett had beaten me here and found him. He could even have brought him back to the Buckley House. I hoped so.

My phone buzzed in my shorts pocket. That could be one of them with an answer right now. I anxiously checked my cell screen.

Ian. Texting me on the international app we used for rare communications. He always called the girls at Christmas and on their birthdays.

In Shamrock. Know you're here as well.

Text me back. Or call.

Have been trying to reach you. In bits.

In bits? What was Mr. Trad-Punk Rock Star so upset about? Maeve was the one in bits, with him jumping in and out of our lives when it was convenient. Well, he could cool his heels. Or lean on his snobby fiancée.

Finding Rover was more important than my ex suddenly feeling nostalgic or whatever. It wasn't my business to care about his feelings anymore, unless they concerned Maeve or Bliz.

I stuffed my cell back in my pocket, feeling a little guilty anyway. Ian wasn't an emotional guy. More the quiet type, in an intriguing way. Which made him extra dangerous. To me, anyway.

At almost the exact moment I turned my attention back to the field in front of me, the barking began. If sounded as if it were coming from everywhere.

I'd never heard Rover bark much, if at all, so I couldn't tell for sure if it was him. But this dog was frantic. It had to be him.

I entered the field at a run, calling his name. A flock of startled birds took to the air from the trees behind me, flapping above me as I ran faster and faster. Rover needed me. The barking was everywhere now, in surround sound.

Just as I started to lose my breath, a flash of gold shot out from behind one of the largest rocks. Still barking furiously, Rover circled my feet, nearly knocking me off of them.

"Buddy, stop!" I jumped aside. "Everything's OK. I'm here. We're going home."

Rover was really freaking me out now. He wouldn't stop barking. What was the matter with him? Physically he seemed unhurt, but he was acting like a crazy puppy.

I reached for his collar—still there. How could Athena not have seen it? I tried to snap him onto the leash, but he deftly avoided my grasp. He kept running a short distance ahead of me and doubling back, as if to make sure I was still following him.

Something was seriously wrong. I stopped and looked around the field again, frowning. This time Rover came up and leaned in against my legs, gazing up at me with intense dog eyes. I gently hooked the leash and gave him calming pets. "It's OK," I said. "Good boy."

While my words sounded soothing and steady to my ears—and hopefully Rover's—my heart was beating double time. I couldn't shake the growing feeling that we were not alone, and the wide-open space made me extra nervous. Rover stood at full attention now, sniffing the air, his eyes zeroed in on the log gate. But there was no one in sight.

Finally he gave a soft growl deep in his throat and crept slowly forward in the direction of the gate. I tentatively followed, taking baby steps. The two of us stopped and started as if we were playing a twisted game of Mother May I?

Then I spotted a flash of movement between the rocks in the stone wall. It disappeared in a blink, but I heard the distinct crunch of gravel. Rover lunged on the leash, but I held tight. “Easy, boy,” I said. “Just someone walking by. Stay.”

Rover obeyed, standing motionless again, tail feathers up, until the person was gone. Well, hopefully gone. What were they doing, scuttling along behind a stone wall? A kid, maybe, playing spy.

When Rover relaxed and looked back at me, as if to say the coast was clear, I breathed a huge sigh of relief.

It lasted until the end of the exhale. Rover gave another bark and banged a U-ie, zooming back toward that rock. I held onto the leash for my life, tennis shoes barely skimming the grass. I couldn’t lose him again. No matter what.

When we reached the boulder, the dog skidded to a halt and sat beside it. He looked straight at me. Back at the rock. Then back to me. Another bark.

Rover might not be a K-9 officer with the Shamrock PD, but the message was clear.

I peered around the rock.

A woman lay in the damp green clover, face down. Young. Fit. Blond ponytail pulled through the back of a crisp white tennis visor. Trendy running shoes, pastel pink and gray. Black sports bra and athletic short-shorts like Colleen’s with a swirly-patterned, maroon-and-mauve tank over them.

It took a moment or two for my brain to correct itself. The woman's tank top was solid mauve. The paisley-style pattern had been created by . . . blood. The early summer grass beside the body—she could not possibly be alive—was soaked in red. Here and there, dark red drops had hit the creamy white clover blossoms.

No no no. Not again.

I peered closer, still holding on to Rover, who leaned even harder against my legs. The logo on the running shoes: Gucci.

The dead woman at my feet was Fallon O'Malley.

Terrified screams sounded through the sunny field, followed by caws and flapping wings. The birds had been startled into flight again. Even the brazen crows.

I didn't realize right away that the screams came from me.

Chapter Ten

After a few moments of alternating fear and horror, I tried to pull myself together. This wasn't the first time I'd encountered a dead body.

I just never thought it would happen again.

And especially not so soon.

Three months ago I had helped solved a murder. I was a police chief's daughter, with a sibling and not-boyfriend in law enforcement. I knew the drill.

I forced myself to focus. Deep breath.

Fallon O'Malley was dead.

In the very brief time I'd spent with the woman, I hadn't liked her, to be honest. And I'd liked even less the idea she was my ex's new fiancée. But Fallon hadn't deserved to die. Especially not like this.

She couldn't have been a terrible person. Not if Ian was in love with her.

I slowly approached the body, careful not to disturb the crime scene. I needed to check for a pulse, even though I knew there was no use. Rover whined and shrank low to the ground, reluctantly following on the leash. I didn't want to let go in case he made a bolt for it—or worse, got too close to Fallon.

There was so much blood. I didn't see a weapon, just a gaping wound in her back where one had been. Likely some kind of knife. Nausea swirled in my gut, and I tried not to gag.

I reached down carefully, lightly touching Fallon's left wrist. Cold and slightly blue, like the rest of the arm stretched above her head. I tried to avoid looking at her face, but I couldn't miss a glimpse of one dull eye. Wide open, staring lifelessly at the ground.

I quickly jumped back, barely missing stepping on Rover's paws as he cowered behind me. "Sorry, fella," I said, as we both backed away.

I had zero training as a medical professional or first responder, but it was clear there was no hope. Like Deirdre, Fallon was gone.

"Rest in peace," I whispered, making a quick sign of the cross. "I'm so sorry. We'll find whoever did this to you. I promise."

Running footsteps thudded the ground behind me as I slipped my phone from my pocket to dial 911. I whirled, instinctively shielding Rover. But he pushed past me, jerking the leash from my hand as he shot forward.

Wagging his tail.

"Easy, fella." Garrett disengaged Rover's front paws from his chest, grabbed the leash, and took me in his arms. "You OK, Kate?"

For the shortest of seconds I rested my face on the soft cotton of his USMC tee, feeling his fast heartbeat. He was still breathing hard from his run.

I raised my head and stepped back, extricating myself from the leash Rover had wound around our legs, rom-com style. "I'm fine." I gestured toward the patch of grass and clover hiding Fallon's still body. "But someone's . . ."

I couldn't bring myself to say the word "dead" out loud.

Garrett gave a short nod and moved toward the deceased, swiftly taking in the crime scene.

"Looks like she was stabbed," I said. "But there's no knife anywhere. Not that I saw, anyway. I didn't call 911 yet."

"Uh-huh." Garrett turned back to me. He looked tired. "Give me a minute."

He walked away and made a few calls on his phone. I strained to catch his words, but the birds were making a racket again. I knelt, and this time I was the one who leaned against Rover. "It's OK," I assured the dog as he gave a sad whine, staring after Garrett. "He's coming back."

When he did, Garrett's expression was grim. "Medics and PD are on the way. So is your dad. It'll take a while to process the scene, but in the meantime, no details of anything you saw to anyone. No speculation about cause of death, no—"

Seriously? The last thing I wanted to do was talk to anyone about this right now. Especially Mitzi Dolan-Yung, the relentless reporter at WSCK-TV. And I definitely didn't want to share any specifics concerning Fallon's death with my daughters.

Plus, I'd grown up Buckley. I knew the rules.

"Garrett, I got it. This isn't my first murder, remember?"

"True." He smiled ruefully.

"You don't really expect me not to discuss this with my dad, right?" It wasn't a question.

Garrett didn't answer. He was checking out the scene again, peering more closely at the blood in the grass. I noticed now there were more spots and patches behind me, leading slightly to the left—in the direction of the trees and the caretaker's cottage. Had Fallon first been attacked somewhere other than the spot where her body lay? Had she struggled to get away from her killer—or had her body been dragged here into the clover?

"How'd you find me so fast?" I asked.

Garrett took a couple of photos on his phone. "I was at the fairgrounds already, looking for you and Rover. And then I, uh, heard you."

Oh. The screaming. "Guess I lost it for a bit."

"Hey, who wouldn't?" He rose from his squat, and his tone softened. "You sure you're all right, Kate? Your dad's going to take you home."

After he got a firsthand investigation of the scene himself, no doubt. But even with the Chief's boundless determination, I doubted my dad could navigate this field in his wheelchair. The ground was uneven, with long stretches of mud from the heavy rains last night. And there were rocks everywhere. It would take more than the Chief's dogged efforts to get through this obstacle course.

The emergency vehicles might have trouble getting here, too, through the stone wall's narrow gate. But they obviously couldn't come through the trees from the fairgrounds.

That would really send Athena Sweeney into a tizzy.

I shaded my eyes again to view the gate and remembered the flash of tan I'd noticed through the stones. I quickly filled Garrett in. "Whoever it was, they probably had nothing to do with what happened to Fallon."

Garrett raised an eyebrow. "Fallon? Wait, you knew the vic? Thought maybe she was a tourist, by her clothes."

"I didn't know her, exactly. She came by the Buckley House yesterday, to book rooms for three other people. She said she was from Dublin, and her name was Fallon O'Malley."

"What else?" Garrett was making notes on his phone.

"Colleen talked to her a lot more than I did." I took a deep breath. "But bottom line, she's the publicist and manager for Peat."

"Ian's band?"

"Yup. And she's also—well, she was—his fiancée."

Garrett's only visible reaction was a blink. Just one. Then he was back to detective mode. He glanced back at the body. "No ring."

"Well, she was wearing one at the house yesterday," I said. "I remember that distinctly. She could have taken it off before she went on her run."

"Maybe. If not, there's a good chance this was a robbery."

That was an even more awful thought: Fallon killed for a ring? A beautiful and very valuable one, I reminded myself.

And I had begrudged her that ring.

"Anything else you saw, besides a movement behind the wall?" Garrett asked.

"No. And like I said, I didn't really see a person, to be honest," I said. "It was more like a movement. A flash of tan. Rover noticed it, too."

"Could have been an animal," Garrett said. "But we'll check it out."

Emergency vehicles began arriving at the gate and parking along the road. Lights, no sirens. A medic jumped out of the first van, joined by two cops from the patrol car behind it. A Shamrock FD truck took up most of the narrow street.

As a line of other responding vehicles began squeezing through the now-open gate and fanned onto the field, my brother jogged up behind me. "Hey, sis, are you all right?"

"I'm fine." I nodded toward Fallon's body, the view blocked by a half-circle of first responders. "Other than the circumstances."

"Good," Frank said. "Let's go, then. Dad's waiting in the parking lot."

"I'm staying here."

"For what?" My brother sounded extra grumpy. It looked as if he'd just woken up. His Shamrock PD sweatshirt was inside out. And for once his hair spiked in every direction.

"I found the body," I said. "And I knew the vic. Sort of."

"Yeah?" Frank looked puzzled, then craned his neck past me toward Garrett, which made me even madder. "McGavin, you got her statement?"

Garrett held up his phone. "A start. We'll have more questions, though."

"Time for that later. Walker's on her way."

Uh-oh. That would be the newly-promoted Detective Captain Shirley Walker, aka Surly Shirley. As the Statie detective assigned to the Cloverhill County DA's office, she was the lead homicide investigator for Shamrock, working in conjunction with the PD.

Maybe it *was* time for me to go. Shirley and I had shared a few flashes of understanding, though, during the investigation into Deirdre's murder. I think.

"What about Dad?" I asked my brother. "He must be chomping at the bit to get out here."

"You could put it that way," Frank said. "But this field is a hazard for him in that chair. I almost broke my ankle jogging through it. Let him feel useful, getting you home in the van. We'll fill you both in as soon as we're done here, OK? I'll drive the Subaru back."

I looked over my shoulder at Garrett. He held up his hands. "Hey, I'm Switzerland here."

"Fine." I glared at them both, letting them know it wasn't. But there was another thing to consider. I needed to get home to the girls before they heard about any of this.

I dropped my car keys into Frank's open palm and gathered Rover just as Surly Shirley's state police vehicle pulled onto the scene.

"I'll see you through the woods," Garrett said.

* * *

Garrett and I didn't talk much on our walk through the trees. Rover trotted happily along beside us. I was glad to have our new Buckley family member safely in hand, but it was hard to put the image of Fallon O'Malley's body lying in the clover out of my mind.

I guess Garrett was trying to give me some space after the trauma of stumbling upon a crime scene. Again. Or else he was mentally cataloging the initial details of the investigation for his report.

Then it dawned on me. There might be a completely different reason for his unusual silence.

And it wasn't good.

"Garrett, hold up a sec," I said as the caretaker's cottage came into view. Rover instantly sat beside me, like a blue-ribbon obedience dog. He probably needed the rest. "No one's going to think *I* killed Fallon, right? I mean, that's ridiculous."

Garrett stopped, but didn't look at me right away. Instead he stuffed his hands in the pockets of his sweats and rocked in his sneakers.

High-school Garrett. The one who hadn't finished his history paper due the next day because he'd spent too much time at the gym. The Garrett who had TPed the Buckley House on Mischief Night, which had infuriated my dad. Also the Garrett who'd asked me to junior prom outside my locker in the middle of the hall during class changing.

"Right?" I repeated. "I won't be a suspect?"

This time he gazed straight at me. "I know you didn't kill her, Katie."

"Yeah, but will everyone else believe that, too? Like Detective Walker?" I gestured in the direction of the salt-and-pepper-haired detective in the khaki blazer emerging from the passenger side of the Cloverhill County vehicle. I could barely see her through the trees from this distance, but I felt her scowling.

Garrett probably did, too.

"I mean, just because Fallon was Ian's fiancée, and she showed up at the Buckley House, and then I found her body," I rushed on. "And her ring that looked a lot like the one I wore when I was engaged to Ian is missing." I paused for breath. "All a bunch of ridiculous coincidences."

I didn't mention running into Fallon outside Gifts of Gab. That didn't count. She'd had no interaction with me and Colleen whatsoever. I was sure she hadn't even seen us. And of course I hadn't been stalking her.

Garrett stayed silent. A smart move on his part.

Tears pricked my eyes. This was all Ian's fault. He should never have agreed to come to Shamrock and play the fair with his stupid band. He should never have brought his snobby fiancée here.

And he should never have left me and the girls.

"Aw, Katie." Garrett stepped forward and wrapped his arms tightly around my slumped shoulders. "Don't cry. Everything will turn out fine. You know how these investigations go. You've got to trust the process. Trust the PD. And me."

I nodded, and an escaped tear or two made a damp spot on his T-shirt. How embarrassing. "I do trust you," I said. My cell buzzed in my pocket with another incoming text, but I ignored it.

"You again?" The sharp woman's voice made me pull away from Garrett sooner than I'd wanted to. I felt his body tense as we both turned to see Athena Sweeney standing a couple of yards away on the overgrown path. "This is private property."

"Town property, ma'am," Garrett said, but I could tell he was embarrassed, too. Nothing like a detective caught in an embrace with the person who'd just discovered the body in his latest case.

The detective who was supposed to be escorting said person to the former police chief's van, chip-chop.

Chapter Eleven

Athena Sweeney didn't step off the path. Instead she stood there with her arms crossed, glaring at me and Garrett. "I don't appreciate trespassers snooping around my studio," she said. "Which also happens to be my home. Particularly when the projects I've been commissioned to create are highly confidential."

The nepo-daughter sculptor sure had a high opinion of herself. And her "art." Wasn't she working on a butter sculpture? And her other body of work included a bunch of very ugly garden gnomes.

Garrett stepped forward, that all-business look on his face again. "Detective Captain Garrett McGavin, Shamrock PD." He took out his wallet and displayed his flat badge. "You've seen people trespassing around here recently?"

"Absolutely." Athena pointed toward me. "Your girlfriend there was one of them."

"What?" I said. "I was looking for my dog, for heaven's sake." Rover wagged his tail beside me. "You had him locked up."

"I did not," Athena said, with a sniff. "I told you, the chicken coop area has no lock. Did you find him in there?"

"Well, no," I admitted. "But—"

"Ma'am, can I get your name, please?" Garrett had his phone in hand. "This is your permanent address?"

Athena sighed and gave him her information.

"So did you see anyone else come through here this morning?" Garrett pressed. "Or notice anything unusual?"

"No."

I frowned. Athena's answer was short, but I got the distinct feeling she was lying.

"Look, I have serious work to do," the grand artiste said. "And I'm sweltering out here." She fiddled with the tie of her cape and pulled it from her shoulders, looking highly annoyed.

Her simple black tank was nothing special, but the large pendant she wore on a black leather cord caught my attention.

Amber. That was sort of tan, wasn't it? Maybe if it caught the light the right way.

"So no other, uh, trespassers?" Garrett asked. If he'd noticed the color of the gemstone, he didn't let on.

"People have definitely been around my studio. Since you're a detective, maybe you can find out who stole my sculpting tools."

"What are you missing, exactly?" Garrett asked.

Athena threw up her hands, and the edge of the cape she held brushed the dirt path. "An entire set of hand tools," she said. "I had them on my tool roll to sharpen and stepped out for half an hour to supervise things at the butter sculpture building. Left them right on my table under the window. Next thing I know, they're gone. They didn't just walk away on their own."

"What kind of tools, exactly?" Garrett's tone was casual.

The sculptor shrugged. "Potter's knife, chisels, fettling knife. Maybe a couple of others. Whoever it was must have grabbed through the window, rolled them up, and taken off.

If you want to look for them, knock yourself out. I can work with some of my dad's tools in the meantime. But right now, if you don't mind, I've got half a ton of butter about to melt."

"Right." Garrett stuck his cell phone, which he'd been using to make notes, back in his pocket. "We'll see what we can do. We'll be back if we have more questions."

Athena shrugged. "Sure. But make an appointment with my assistant, Bronya, at the gallery. And don't bring that dog back with you."

Before Garrett and I could say good-bye, she stomped back to her dwarf cottage.

"So what did you think?" I asked Garrett as we started walking again. The main fairgrounds area was visible now at the edge of the trees. "She said she's missing a bunch of sharp tools. And did you see her necklace? The stone was tan. Sort of."

Garrett nodded. "I'll talk to her again. We need more info first."

"She was lying about not seeing anyone today," I said. "I could tell. Shouldn't we at least try to—"

"Look, Kate," Garrett said. "I really appreciate you trying to help. But hey, you just found a body. You should take it easy, give this a rest for a while. The team has everything under control now. Let us handle it. And look, your dad's here," he added in an upbeat tone as we stepped out onto the large field.

The sunshine was nearly blinding. But I could see the Chief's white van parked almost straight in front of us. Past the butter sculpture building, as close to the woods as possible.

In another second, my dad would be out of his vehicle.

"Thanks, Garrett," I said, pulling Rover along. The traitor clearly wanted to stay with Garrett. "Really glad you showed up back there. Talk to you later, OK?"

"You bet," he said, as I started toward the van with Rover. "Take care of yourself," he called.

I nodded and waved, but didn't turn around. Again, I didn't glance in the direction of the music stages. At this point I was glad to be getting out of here.

I was in the passenger seat of the van, with Rover in the back, before my dad had a chance to hit the ground in his chair.

"Hi Dad," I said. "Thanks for picking us up. Frank's got the Subaru."

"Katie Margaret," he said as I buckled my seat belt. "Are you sure you're all right?"

I wished everyone would stop asking me if I was OK. But they meant well. "I'm fine, Dad. I sort of lost it for a minute or two, maybe, but things are fine now."

He nodded and hit the gas using the van's left hand control. "Tell me all the details. Don't leave anything out."

I gave him the full debrief, including my encounters with Athena Sweeney and the flash of tan behind the stone wall. Hopefully I remembered everything correctly. My brain was already trying to erase the image of Fallon lying dead in the grass. But I recalled the red blood drops on the white clover blossoms with chilling clarity.

The Chief didn't pepper me with questions the way I'd expected. He was actually quieter than usual, his lips set in a thin line. He didn't even drive like a crazy maniac, as he was fond of doing whenever there was an investigation in progress.

I also noticed that he took the long way back to town, out by Emerald Lake. Probably so I would have more time to keep talking. I had no idea what he was thinking.

"A bad business, Kathleen," he said finally. No Katie Margaret this time. "I'm sorry you had to see that."

"Me too," I said. "And I know the news will be everywhere soon, but I'd like to keep as much of this as possible from the girls. Especially anything about the way Fallon was killed. It was truly disturbing, with the blood. And Maeve was there when Colleen and I found Deirdre, so another murder . . . well, that could be even more traumatic for her."

The Chief nodded. "Understood. She seemed to handle everything well the last time. I was very proud of her."

"Well, yes, we all were. But still. It's too much. She's a kid." A kid who claimed she wanted to be a forensic investigator someday, thanks to all those true crime shows she watched. And some Buckley family gene. As her mom, I wasn't sure how I felt about that career path. But it would be her decision. Someday.

"So is there anything else?" the Chief asked.

I suddenly realized I'd left the part about Fallon being Ian's fiancée out of my debrief. I should have mentioned that up front. All I'd said was that she had shown up at the Buckley House yesterday and booked rooms for three other guests. I didn't know whether the Chief had met the new members of Peat yet, unless he'd seen them at Farrell's last night.

But he had to have noticed the garage was cleared out.

I took a deep breath. "Dad, there's something else."

"Hold on, Kathleen." The Chief swerved into Patsy's Petrol Pump. "We're running on fumes."

"I've got it." Clutching the credit card my dad handed over, I jumped down from the van to fill the tank. A temporary reprieve from thinking about Fallon. Or Ian.

For about two seconds. My phone buzzed with an incoming text just after I got the gas cap off and placed the nozzle in the tank. When I saw Ian's name, I was tempted to ignore the message again.

But everything had changed now. Did he know Fallon was dead? What should I say?

Better to call him than text.

I flipped the lever at the pump to start the flow of gas and squeezed the trigger on the nozzle extra hard. Then I dialed. "Hi, Ian," I said. "What's up?"

"Hey." His voice sounded muffled and shaky. "Kate, I really need to talk to you. Alone. Can you come over here? I don't want to run into anyone who knows me. I'm at an Airbnb."

What was going on with my ex? I stood frozen beside the van, watching the digital green numbers run faster and faster on the pump. None of them registered in my brain. The Chief had told me to put in half a tank. I had no clue when to stop.

"What's the address?" I forgot to even ask Ian if he was all right.

He gave it to me, and I told him I was on my way. The pump stopped with a jolt the instant we hung up.

"Dad, I need a favor," I said as I clambered back into the van.

Chapter Twelve

Ian opened the door to the huge stone building a second before I reached the top of the wide concrete steps.

"That was quick," I said as I stepped across the white marble threshold. He must have been looking out the window.

"Camera." Ian turned his phone toward me to display the mini split-screens. Yup, there I was, standing next to him in the foyer. Looking as stupid as I felt.

"Oh. Right." I'd been back at the Buckley House less than a day, and modern technology was already a dim memory. I was worse than the Chief.

Or maybe I was just nervous. I wasn't looking forward to this conversation.

"Good to see you, Kate." Ian gave me a feather-light hug, leaving plenty of space between us. "You're looking well."

"You too," I said, but that was a flat-out lie. I'd never seen him so tired-looking and pale. His wavy brown hair might have been whipped up by one of Mom's vintage crank eggbeaters.

My ex led me down the short hall, then through an arched doorway and into an enormous open space. The cathedral-style ceiling soared to the top of the building. Sunlight filtered through a spectacular stained-glass window at the far end.

The design showed a giant image of St. Patrick against a bright blue background, holding a sprig of shamrock in one hand. In the other the saint carried a book and a golden staff. The glass art was framed in a golden braid with green shamrocks, entwined with dark serpents.

Huh. A deconsecrated church. Maybe not my personal choice for a hotel, but OK.

Other than the stained-glass window, the whole place was a blinding vision in white. Painted white brick, exposed white beams and pipes, white couch, spare white chairs, throws and pillows. One wall held white cabinets with no visible hardware. The kitchen was set off by a white-marble counter with bar stools and a built-in sink. The appliances had to be hidden somewhere. Assuming anyone cooked or cleaned or ate anything.

"Nice place," I said.

"It is, yeah." Ian dropped down at the far end of the couch, ruining the monochrome effect in his brown Peat T-shirt and black skinny jeans. I perched on one of the midcentury chairs. I doubted anyone lived here more than one short stay at a time.

The Airbnb host was brave to rent this place out. I could only imagine the red wine stains.

Without warning, my mind flashed an image of a clover field with white blossoms spattered in red. I blinked hard to reset.

"I almost expected your dad to show up," Ian said.

"Believe me, he wanted to come," I said. No need to mention the Chief was waiting for me in the parking lot of a nearby outlet store. I'd offered to catch the trolley back into town and walk the rest of the way home, but he'd assured me he needed to do an errand in the vicinity. At the Twelve Months of Irish Christmas Shoppe. The flagship store had a location on the Square downtown.

Sure, Dad.

Ian leaned back against the couch, looking exhausted again. Or maybe hungover. He didn't look much different than the last time I'd seen him—Maeve's Confirmation in the city, maybe?—but I hardly recognized the guy I'd been married to for years.

How would I break the news that his fiancée was dead? Whatever the reason he'd summoned me here, it couldn't be anything more devastating than that.

I cleared my throat. "I'm glad you called, Ian. We need to talk."

He picked up a white bouclé pillow and crossed his arms over it against his chest. "You didn't answer my texts earlier. I saw that you read them, you know."

"Sorry." I took a deep but silent breath. If I let him talk first, it might help break the ice between us. And also delay my having to deliver the horrible news. I needed more time to find the right words. "Why are you in bits?"

"Fallon—my fiancée. She's dead."

Oh. My pulse pounded in my head. He already knew. The police must have beaten me to it. But hadn't Ian started texting me before I'd found Fallon's body?

He tossed the pillow back onto the cushion beside him. His tone sounded emotionless, but he had to be devastated. And probably still stunned. "She managed our band." He glanced at me, then quickly away. "She mentioned she met you and Colleen at the Buckley House yesterday. Not my idea, the drop-in, by the way."

I nodded. "Go on."

He took a deep breath. "I left early for the stage set-up this morning. And I found her in the field next to the fairgrounds. She was . . . gone."

It took a few seconds for his words to register in my brain. What? I hadn't been the first person to find Fallon's body? He'd somehow stumbled upon that awful crime scene nowhere near the performance stage and done *nothing*? I tried not to let the shock show on my face.

"I am truly sorry for your loss," I said.

Elbows on knees, he covered his face. "I know that was a lot of news in one go," he said. "And the engagement thing was out of the blue. It just happened. Like, a couple of weeks ago. I planned to tell you and the girls while I was here. Not that it matters anymore."

I held up one hand. "Ian, please. Don't even think about that right now." I hesitated. How could I ask this?

"Go on," he said, with a sigh.

"You did call for help, right?'

"I, em, didn't," he said. "It was too late. And I . . . I dunno, I freaked out or something. I left."

I rubbed my temples. "So you found your fiancée stabbed and somehow didn't even call for help? You left her there in the field and came back here? To a fake church hotel?"

I could hear the shaking in my voice. Disbelief, anger, fear—my emotions ran up and down like notes on a creepy musical scale.

Ian drew back. "How did you know Fallon was stabbed?"

"Because I found her, too, when I was looking for my dog. I was the one who called 911. Well, Garrett did."

"Garrett McGavin?" Ian frowned. "He's still around?" My ex had to be the only person in Shamrock who didn't like Garrett. Why he wasn't a fan, I had no idea.

I'd never cheated on Ian. With anyone.

"He's a detective now with the Shamrock PD," I said. "He was off-duty and responded to the scene. But back to Fallon. You found her and didn't make an emergency call? Why not?"

"I know that sounds bad," Ian said. "And it is. I was in shock. Still am, I think. But I promise, there was no way anyone could have saved her. I could tell for sure she was . . . not there anymore. I called you instead of the gardaí. The police, I mean. But I knew you'd tell your dad."

This was hardly the time or reason to feel flattered that my ex had put his trust in me. "You're still not giving me a straight answer. Why did you run away like some kind of coward?"

He sighed. "A lot of reasons, I guess. I was scared." His voice dropped to a mumble. "And I knew you'd believe me when I said I had nothing to do with what happened to Fallon."

"Ian, why wouldn't the cops believe you?"

He shrugged. "Dunno. Different reasons, maybe."

I leaned forward in my uncomfortable chair. "There's no way around this, Ian. You need to talk to the detectives. Like, right now. They have to gather all the information they can about Fallon as soon as possible, to catch whoever did it. There's a killer on the loose out there. That means anyone in Shamrock could be in danger."

Silence. I felt St. Patrick staring down at my neck from the window.

"Do you even realize how much trouble you could be in now?" I said softly. "Even if you didn't kill Fallon? Or . . . good Lord. Was it some kind of accident?"

It sure hadn't looked like an accident to me. But I had to ask.

"Jayzus, Kate." Ian looked away.

"Tell me the truth, or I can't help you."

More color drained from his face, if that were possible. "You must be joking," he said. "You know I'm not a murderer. And there was no accident. I've made a few bad moves in my life, yeah, but nothing like that. I'm not some kind of monster." He stared down at the white coffee table between us. "Even if Maeve thinks I am."

"That's ridiculous. You're her dad, Ian. She loves you. You know that."

He held out his phone, screen turned in my direction. "As of last night, she never wants to talk to me again."

"Well, of course Maeve didn't mean that literally," I said. "I know that for a fact. She tells me the same thing all the time. But let's deal with one issue at a time here. Do you want me to call the police for you right now? You can get on the phone and talk with them. They'll probably want you to come down to the station in person, though."

Ian nervously drummed his knees. "Actually, I was hoping maybe I could talk to your dad first."

Aha. There it was. The real reason he'd called me. But the Chief wasn't a huge admirer of my ex-husband's, to put it mildly. "I'm not sure if that's such a good idea," I said slowly.

"I know he and I don't see eye to eye much," Ian said. "Mostly on his part. But I trust him. He's a man of his word."

"Dad wouldn't help anyone get away with a crime," I pointed out. "And he won't be impressed that you fled the scene. Especially a murder scene."

Your fiancée's murder, I wanted to add. But no need to drive that point home again. My ex really was in bits.

"I just want to talk to him first." Ian's voice was pleading. "Before I go to the police."

I sighed. "OK, but don't say I didn't warn you." I glanced around the massive apartment again. Nothing much of a personal sense anywhere, as far as I could tell. A guitar propped in a corner. Beat-up leather jacket and olive-hued duffel tossed beside it on the floor. "Where's all your stuff? Yours and Fallon's?"

"Didn't bring much," he said. "We shipped things ahead, and we're renting most of the equipment for the band. Fallon had a couple of suitcases and—what do you call that yoke?—a bag to hang fancy clothes. They're in the bedroom."

"Well, the cops will be here in no time," I said. "I'm surprised they haven't shown up yet, to inform you about Fallon and interview you. They'll look for evidence, too. If you want to talk to the Chief before anyone else, get whatever stuff you need for now, and let's go."

I was dying to snoop around the bedroom and en suite bathroom myself, for anything that might give me more insights into Fallon herself. But I'd been specifically directed not to interfere. And we had to get a move on if Ian wanted a chance to talk to the Chief before the investigators.

He left me in the sitting area with St. Patrick and disappeared through a well-concealed pocket door. Hopefully it led to the bedroom suite, and not outside somehow.

The minutes ticked by slowly. I tapped my phone impatiently. What was taking my ex so long? And what should I tell the Chief to start things off?

A slight rattling sound came from somewhere in the direction of St. Patrick. A branch from an extremely tall tree, maybe, brushing against the glass. But as I turned to check, I spotted a crumpled piece of paper near the baseboard molding. Not far from Ian's leather jacket, but not next to it either.

Probably a receipt, or some such. Ian wasn't the neatest guy I knew. But it stood out in this super clean place, and that bugged me. I walked over to pick it up and throw it in a trash basket. If I could find one.

As I bent down, I hesitated. There were ink letters on the outside part of the paper ball. Some kind of note. Or reminder, maybe. Should I just point it out to Ian? Leave it for the detectives?

That last option was the clear and correct answer. But my curiosity got the best of me. Using my fingernails like a pair of forceps, I snagged the ball of paper. Then I returned to the sitting area, stuffed it in my shorts pocket, and returned to the sitting area. This time I sat on the couch.

"Would you ever hurry up in there?" I called to Ian.

No response. Maybe he was in the bathroom. Hopefully he hadn't snuck out of the suite somehow.

My ex wasn't that stupid. The Chief was probably right outside waiting for him.

Of course I had to take a tiny peek at that little ball of trash in my pocket. I couldn't help it. Uncrumpling what appeared to be a hastily torn piece of printer paper, I carefully flattened it out on the coffee table, securing one corner with a Connemara marble coaster.

Yup, a note. Careful block letters, penned in black ink with a felt-tip marker. The message was short and to the point:

I know the truth.

Field next to fairgrounds. Tomorrow am.

half-6

Just you.

A chill shot through me as I stared at the wavy scrap of paper.

The truth? What did that mean? Had this note been intended for Ian or Fallon? And either way, who had sent such an ominous-sounding demand?

My ex was still out of sight, but I heard the definitive zip of a suitcase from the bedroom.

I jammed the note back in my pocket for safekeeping.

Chapter Thirteen

I hadn't bothered texting my dad to let him know Ian and I were headed his way. Just as I had expected, the Chiefmobile was parked directly across the street from the church Airbnb.

My dad seemed equally unsurprised to see his former son-in-law trailing behind me, carrying a duffel and his guitar case. I pulled Ian's carry-on roller bag. Apparently he wasn't planning to go back to the trendy church hotel. He said the place gave him the willies now.

"Mind the dog in the back there, and sit well away from my chair," the Chief directed Ian. "And hold onto those bags."

That was it. The entire greeting.

"Yes, sir." Ian scrambled in through the sliding door and folded his lanky self as much as possible on the side bench.

Rover warmly greeted my ex—a complete stranger, I noted without a shred of bitterness—by slobbering all over him and licking his face. What a traitor. Ian put his hands up to shield himself, but it was no use. His cool black leather rocker jacket—like Athena's cape, so handy in July—definitely needed to be dry cleaned.

Luckily, Ian didn't seem to mind Rover's enthusiasm. He still seemed a little out of it, as far as I could tell. Functioning. But distracted.

"Hi, Dad," I said, twisting toward him from the passenger seat. The blasting AC felt great. "How was that early holiday shopping? Any doorbuster specials?"

"Don't be smart, missy." He started the car with a grunt.

"Just kidding," I said lightly. "Thanks for picking us up, Dad. I'll text the girls and give Mom a heads-up we're on our way."

"Not quite yet," the Chief said. "We're making a stop. Just tell your mother and Maeve everything's fine."

"OK," I said, puzzled. I would have thought he'd be eager to get home and start pummeling Ian with questions for the new investigation. I had a bunch of them myself.

Of course, Dad didn't know the half of it yet. And Ian had no clue, either, that I had a piece of possible evidence in my pocket.

It might help him.

Or hurt him.

Had he ever even seen this scary note? Someone had balled it up and discarded it. But Ian wasn't the kind of guy who paid a lot of attention to everyday details or garden-variety rubbish. When we were together, he'd rarely glanced at the mail. I paid all the bills.

The note could have been intended for either Ian or Fallon. Neither was likely to have written it because it was already balled up, as if it had been read. And one of them hadn't written it to the other. They shared an Airbnb, so why bother meeting in a field?

Unless, of course, the note writer had wanted to avoid close monitoring by St. Patrick.

The Chief glanced toward the back seat and cleared his throat. "I'm sorry for your loss, son. May she rest in peace, your . . . fiancée, wasn't it?"

"Thank you." Ian's words were muffled by emotion. Or maybe the dog.

That was it on the conversation front. No pointless chit-chat. No interrogation. Not yet.

It was a loud, bumpy ride anyway as we rode back through the still-awakening town. The floor of the van, specially out-fitted to transport the Chief's chair, was low to the ground, with less room for shock absorption.

We also hit a few impressive potholes. Shamrock's sea-sonal freezing winters, crazy rains, and extreme humidity had created some doozies. My dad blamed the town—and especially the mayor—for negligence and rerouting of road funds. Mayor Flanagan blamed the State of Massachusetts.

At least the Chief wasn't tuned to his twenty-four/seven police scanner. Out of respect for Ian, I guessed. But I was dying to know what might be going down at the fairgrounds. I'm sure my dad was, too.

I snuck a look over my shoulder at my ex. He had to be grieving his new fiancée, but his expression gave away noth-ing. Ian had never been much of a crier. He was a pro at keep-ing his inner feelings in check. They went straight into his music—and toward a select few people.

In my heart I knew the girls and I were still included in that group. He just didn't show it much.

Getting back together was out of the question. We'd been split up since Bliz was a baby. But now I'd suddenly found myself involved in his personal affairs as well as a murder investigation. I even felt responsible for his safety, at least while he was here in Shamrock.

When he was in trouble, I was the one he'd called first.

I put that thought straight out of my mind. It didn't matter why he'd immediately turned to me for help. That kind of thinking wasn't healthy for either of us.

I checked my phone again. Mom had reported that both girls were up and weeding the patio before it got too hot. Colleen was holding down the fort inside, serving a late breakfast to the musicians who had just returned from the fairgrounds. And after his dad's wee jaunt this morning with Rover, Noel was securing the gate to hold us—and any wayward dogs—over until the hardware supplies were delivered.

Well, that was nice of Marty's son. One thing checked off the Buckley House to-do list. No one else would have gotten to it today.

The Chief pulled into the small lot behind Farrell's and parked the van in what he considered his private space. A small, rusty sign above the accessibility designation said, "Reserved for Shamrock PD."

"This is our stop?" I asked.

"It's a good place to talk at this hour," my dad said.

"Dogs aren't allowed inside, though," I said. "And we can't leave Rover in the van. It's already too hot."

The Chief pushed the button to lift the back door, swiveled the driver's seat to slide into his wheelchair, then unhooked the restraints holding it in place. "Bring the meat hound," he said. "We'll sit in the far room."

Rover didn't exactly qualify as a working support dog. But he'd already filled in as a K-9 officer this morning. No one at Farrell's was likely to say no to the Chief, anyway.

Ian was already outside the van, seeming more alert now. And nervous. His eyes darted around, as if someone might recognize him, as we took the ramp and walked through the pub's back entrance. If I were Ian, I'd be more worried about sitting down with my dad for a chat.

As any of the Chief's former suspects—and us Buckley kids—had learned fast, innocent until proven guilty didn't mean he wouldn't be tough. Sometimes he directly grilled the questionee so they'd feel the heat. Other times he'd lob softball questions so the person would let their guard down. And then, wham! The hotseater and their bogus story were Irish toast.

No one ever used the back room of Farrell's unless there was a private party or a major overflow situation. A Limerick Lads ballad played through speakers set up on corner shelves among sports trophies, ancient whiskey bottles, tin whistles, and decorative beer mugs.

I shuddered to think of how long it had been since any of those items were dusted. Judging by the cobwebs, I'd estimate that job was last done in the 1950s. And that was being generous.

I slid into the accessible snug, divided off from the booths by a wooden panel with frosted glass at the top. Ian squeezed in beside me, and the Chief rolled his chair up to the other side of the table. Rover settled at our feet.

I felt a little strange sitting so close to my ex. It had been such a long time. On one hand, I knew Ian really well. And on the other, I didn't know him at all. Not anymore.

"I'll let them know we're here," I said, popping up from my seat again. "No one saw us come in."

"They're aware." My dad waved me back down. "Damien's on the bar."

Sure enough, practically the second he finished his sentence, my favorite server popped her head around the panel. "Good mornin' to you, Chief. And your other daughter, is it? Not Colleen."

I sighed. "Kate."

At least she didn't comment on Rover. Maybe she hadn't seen him yet. He was playing the senior dog card at my feet.

"And is that Ian Forde there? From Peat?" The young woman's dark monobrow quivered with excitement. She'd reacted the same way to Aidan O'Hearne when she'd waited on us last March.

"Right you are." Ian pointed at her and smiled.

"I'm Carmel," she gushed. "From Donegal. I heard you were here last night. My friends and I saw Peat live ages ago. You opened for the Limerick Lads. Will you be playing your new music here at the festival?"

"We will, yeah," Ian said.

Hopefully. Who knew what might happen before the fair kicked off in a few short days? And what if the town's biggest tourist event of the summer had to be canceled to ensure the safety of all? Those were two whole other issues.

The Chief leaned toward our enthusiastic server and said in a low voice, "Carmel, we wouldn't want everyone knowing Ian was here now, would we? All the fuss and people following him about. The poor lad just arrived. It'll be our little secret, right?" He gave her a conspiratorial wink.

"Oh. Sure." Carmel's big smile dropped. "Not even a selfie, then?"

"How about if I sign this just to you?" A switch seemed to turn on in Ian. He smoothly reached across me and extracted a bar napkin from the stack in the iron holder. "Do you have a pen?"

"I do." Carmel removed the black and gold Farrell's pen from behind her ear. Ugh.

My ex scribbled something on the napkin and handed it over with a smile. "There you go."

"Ah, thanks loads. I'm over the moon." Carmel stuffed the napkin into the low scoop neck of her black tank, which partially covered her trinity knot tattoo. "What'll you have?"

"Coffee," the Chief said. "Black."

"The shepherd's pie, if it's still on the menu," Ian said. "And Guinness."

"The pies aren't finished baking yet, but I'll see if we can speed them up for you." Carmel gave him a reassuring pat on the shoulder.

Barf. "I'd like a nonfat cappuccino, please," I spoke up.

"Machine's banjaxed."

"Tea, then, please. And an English muffin with the scallion cream cheese."

"That's the *Irish* muffin," Carmel corrected.

"She hates me, I swear," I said when the server was gone.

"Nonsense, Kathleen," my dad said, with a chuckle. "You need to grow a thicker skin. You've lived in New York too long." His sharp blue eyes bored into Ian's. "Now let's get down to business."

Before my ex could reply, Carmel returned with his pint and the Chief's coffee. No tea, no muffin of any kind. She nodded when I asked if she could bring them soon, but she kept hovering by our snug for some reason. What was she waiting for?

Oh. I tried not to cringe at the heart design swirled in Ian's Guinness foam. Instead I concentrated my gaze on the collection of colorful rugby scarves hanging along the far wall.

"Made it meself," she said proudly.

"Thanks very much." My ex stared into the foam. Maybe a heart wasn't what he needed to see right now, with his fiancée barely cold. After Carmel flounced off again toward the main room, he gave the foam a quick stir with his finger. The heart disappeared.

The Chief noticed as well. He cleared his throat. "Go ahead and tell us what happened, son."

"Do I need a lawyer?" Ian looked from me to my dad.

"Depends." The Chief shrugged. "Are you guilty?"

"Dad!" I protested. "He's been through enough this morning." I turned to Ian. "It's up to you about the legal representation. But you did say you wanted to talk to him."

Ian nodded. "I do."

"Understand, son, I'm not acting in any official capacity here," the Chief said. "I'm retired, as you know. But I do keep my hand in the game regarding matters of local law enforcement. From time to time. An unofficial consultant, you might say."

Yup, you could call it that. As opposed to official meddler. Full-time.

"I don't know if I can help you," the Chief went on. "But you're still a member of our family."

My ex gazed down at his pint again. He might not have noticed my dad's slight hesitation before the word "family," but I did. "Thanks," Ian said finally. "Appreciate that."

"All right, then." My dad sat back in his chair. "Start from before you left home. Any unusual activities or communications you were aware of concerning your fiancée?"

"Everything's a muddle in my head at the moment. But nothing I noticed recently." Ian paused, considering. "Fallon came to America a few days early—she flew from London into New York for a meeting or two. Then she took the Acela train into South Station in Boston and an Uber to Shamrock on Thursday. I think."

"You're not sure which day?" The Chief raised a brow.

"Em, no," Ian said. "We weren't in touch last week, until I got here yesterday. I traveled with the band from Dublin. And there was the time difference and all. Fallon met us here at the pub last night."

The Chief nodded. "I saw your group, briefly."

"Then we went some other places." Ian pressed his eyes, as if he had a headache. He probably did, after the late night and the events of the morning. "Not sure where, precisely. The others could tell you, maybe. We went our own ways after a while."

"So Fallon was with you all night?" I asked.

"She was, yeah. Well, for the first part. She left early from here. Think she took one of those green cabs back to our B&B."

That sounded a bit off to me. The two of them had just reunited, after being apart for days. With minimal communication. "Why did Fallon leave so soon?" I asked.

My ex shrugged. "She told me she wanted to go for a run in the morning. Really early."

"Which she did, I take it," the Chief said. "Judging by what she was wearing when she was attacked."

"How do you know those details already?" I asked my dad.

He shrugged. "I made a few calls. After I finished my shop."

"Did you buy anything for Christmas?" I asked sweetly. "A nice ornament for Mom, perhaps? Snow globe for your office? No, wait. A tin of last year's fruitcake on overstock?"

He swirled his black coffee with a green plastic stirrer and scowled. "Nah. The stuff was all rubbish."

Beside me, Ian fidgeted with his drink coaster. He'd left something out, I was sure. Should I bring out the note in my pocket?

Not yet, I decided. "Did Fallon give any other reason for leaving here early last night?" I asked, trying to sound casual.

Unfortunately, Carmel chose that moment to show up and present Ian with his shepherd's pie. Just out of the oven.

"Grand," Ian said. "It smells lovely. Thanks."

She was so happy, she actually remembered to go back for my tea. Then she grudgingly slapped a cracked plate with my Irish muffin in front of me. "Will there be anything else, then?" she asked us hopefully.

"We're good, thanks, Carmel," my dad said. "We'll settle up at the bar on our way out. No need to bother yourself coming back."

She looked disappointed, but she got the hint. "Right, then. Bye now," she told Ian, with a waggle of her fingers. "See you again. Very soon, I hope."

"Go on with your story, lad," the Chief said, the second she disappeared from view.

Ian turned to me. "What was it you asked? My brain is losing track again."

I didn't want to doubt that, but I knew when my ex was being evasive. The same way I could tell when my sister or Maeve tried to avoid giving a direct answer. I'd had plenty of practice with all three of them.

I was more straightforward this time. "Ian, what was the real reason Fallon left?"

He tapped the coaster on its edge against the worn table. "The band didn't agree with her on a few things. And I didn't exactly support her, I guess. She was upset at that, maybe. I went to the jacks, and when I got back she was gone. Never said anything to anyone. Just slipped out."

The old "Irish good-bye"—the art of slipping away from a gathering without a farewell to anyone.

Except Fallon's Irish good-bye was permanent.

The Chief leaned back in his chair and crossed his arms. Was it my imagination, or did his eyes narrow a teensy bit? So he didn't believe Ian was telling the whole story, either. No matter what my dad always said about going on facts, his strong intuition had served him well over his long career in law enforcement.

I'd gone with my intuition, too, to help find Deirde Donnelly's killer last spring. But that had gotten me into trouble a few times. The dangerous kind.

The Chief changed course. "The vic—" He cleared his throat. "The *deceased* was known to wear jewelry of some value. That's what Kate told investigators at the scene. A ring. Is that correct?"

Ian nodded. "An engagement ring. She had it made here in America. Picked it up in New York a few days ago. She designed it herself." He glanced my way. "Based on my old family ring. I, uh, didn't know that until I got here. I swear, I had no idea."

I nodded, but didn't reply. It made me feel a little better that Ian hadn't known. But it made no sense. Fallon had wanted a ring a lot like the one his ex-wife had worn. But better. What kind of bride thought like that?

I stirred my stone-cold tea, watching the sad lemon deteriorate into spidery wisps. I'd been so thrilled with that faux-gem ring when Ian proposed at Emerald Lake.

He didn't look at me now. Probably embarrassed.

"Did Fallon wear the ring on her running expedition?" the Chief pressed.

"I didn't notice when I found her. But it was brand new, like I said. She had it on at the pub the night before." He started tapping the coaster again. "I don't know whether she would have worn it to go running or not. She was used to running in Dublin and London, though. She knew how to take care of herself, pretty much."

"Wait. Let's back up, son. What did you mean, when you found her?" The Chief reached across the table and placed his hand firmly over Ian's. The coaster tapping ceased. "You were there at the scene? Before my daughter?" He looked at me and frowned, as if waiting for me to correct him. I gave a tiny nod of my head.

The Chief whirled back to Ian. "I want to make sure I understand this. You found the poor girl and left her dead in the middle of the bloody field? And didn't call 911?"

And there it was. The hammer.

"Em, yes." Ian's voice was almost inaudible. "And no."

The Chief, for once, was momentarily speechless. "What were you doing in that field? What time did you find Fallon?"

Ian hesitated. "I was going out to the fairgrounds anyway. I just got there a little early. She told me she was going for a run, and I knew she'd be at the stage setup after. I thought I'd, uh, surprise her."

My dad was still staring at him. "What time?" he pressed. "Be precise, lad. It's important for the investigation."

"Seven?" Ian said, then reconsidered when he saw my dad's glare. "Around then. Seven-twenty, maybe."

The Chief's body language was totally different now. Stiffer. Sharper. "We'll discuss this back at the house," he said, glancing toward the doorway to the front room. No lurking Carmen, thankfully. "I'll arrange for a meeting with the detectives as soon as possible."

"Yes sir." Ian sounded even more miserable, if that were possible.

To be honest, though, the one I felt sorry for right now wasn't him. It was Fallon. The rude, snobby ring-one-upper. I just didn't get it. The Ian I'd known would never have deserted someone he loved like that.

I glanced at my own ringless finger. *Or maybe he would have.*

"You understand that being on the scene near the time of death—and failing to render assistance and report a crime—changes the equation here?" the Chief said.

"I do." Ian stared at the table, jonesing for his coaster.

"And not in your favor."

"I wasn't myself," Ian said. "That's not an excuse, I know, but . . ." He mumbled something else I didn't catch.

"Hmph." Now it was the Chief's turn to drum the table. My ex had to know that significant others, especially ones without an alibi, always topped the suspect list in a murder case. Ian had served himself up on a shining silver tea tray.

Finally my dad held up one hand. "Let's stop right here for now. I saw that you brought your bags. I strongly suggest that you stay with us at the Buckley House, son. That way I can keep an eye on you. You don't need to be running about town. And your hotel will be a secondary crime scene."

Ian nodded. At this point, he seemed past caring.

I hardly cared, either. My insides churned with more than tea and Irish muffin. Should I confess and produce the note right now? Put everything out on the table, so to speak? Or could it somehow make things worse for my ex?

Huge mistake. If only I'd told Ian about the note on our way out of the Airbnb. Or even better, left it on the floor for the CSI team to find.

Not as bad as leaving Fallon dead in a field, maybe. But close.

My dad wanted to carry on this convo more privately back at the Buckley House. It would be better for me to reveal the note's existence then. Hopefully I could speak to Ian first, in private, so I wouldn't blindside him in front of the Chief.

That way, maybe Ian could give my dad the note himself, as a sign of good faith. And his innocence.

In the meantime, though, I could be in hot water as well. For withholding information related to a crime.

"Kate, can you settle up for us at the bar?" my dad asked. "Make it quick, please."

A temporary reprieve, even if it meant dealing with Carmel again. But I'd made my decision. Either Ian or I would hand over the note to my dad. Right after my ex and I had talked. No ifs, ands, or buts.

"Sure, Dad," I said, as Ian stepped out of the snug to let me past. "I'll meet you guys at the van." I was already mentally calculating how low a tip I could ethically leave for Carmen.

"Yer man here will pay the charges later," the Chief called after me.

Yup. I had a feeling my ex would pay, all right. One way or the other.

Chapter Fourteen

The WSCK-TV news van was parked at the curb outside the Buckley House as the Chief, Ian, and I pulled into the driveway.

Great. Investigative reporter Mitzi Dolan-Yung had wasted zero time in sniffing out the latest Shamrock crime news. And she'd headed straight to the B&B to try to grill my dad. She must have already struck out with Chief Ryan. Or bypassed him altogether, more likely.

As if either of them would cough up any additional information on an hours-old case.

But there was another possibility. Had Mitzi somehow learned Ian was connected to the murder—and our family—and headed straight here? In no time we'd have Peat fans like Carmen showing up in our front yard. Guaranteed.

"What do we do now?" I said. "Mitzi is relentless."

"You get out with the dog, Kathleen," my dad said. "Duck down, Ian. You and I will keep driving."

"Where are we going?" My ex sounded nervous.

"Christmas shopping," I told him over my shoulder as I hustled Rover out of the van.

It helped that the Chiefmobile's windows were tinted. Another one of my dad's security extras.

The Chief backed up the van and roared off with Ian, leaving Mitzi standing in Mom's petunias.

I didn't know if I was sorry or not that I'd miss out on hearing any continued discussions between my dad and my ex. Maybe they'd even drop by the PD to talk to the detectives.

But I had to get back to the girls. And pull myself together.

Heading quickly up the stairs toward the porch with Rover, I noticed someone had straightened and reinforced the vacancy sign on the lawn. Nice.

Even better, the sign now read: *No Vacancy.* Miracle of miracles.

Of course Mitzi followed me up the steps with her microphone and tablet, trailed by her camera person. The local news anchor wasn't wearing her Serious Journalist trench coat today. I hoped she was sweating in her green knit dress and blazer with the gold scarf.

"Kate Buckley, what can you tell us about the current death investigation at the fairgrounds?" Mitzi asked breathlessly.

I suppressed my sigh, so it wouldn't be caught by the hot mic. "No comment." Why in the name of everything holy hadn't I used the garage entrance into the house? Mitzi couldn't follow me through there.

"Is it true Fallon O'Malley was the fiancée of Ian Forde from the band Peat? And he is your former husband?"

"No comment." How had Mitzi learned the dead woman's identity so fast? I hoped Carmel hadn't overheard us talking at Farrell's and flapped her jaws.

"Is your father consulting in the investigation with Shamrock PD? Where is Ian Forde right now? Have you spoken with him?"

I shook my head as I reached for the front doorknob, Rover dancing around my feet. Mom appeared and held the door open for us without a word. She was an old hand with the Shamrock media.

"Kate, this is the second murder you've discovered in just over three months," Mitzi called after me. "What do you have to say about that?"

Nothing, nada, zilch. As Rover and I stepped past Mom, she frowned and shook her head at Mitzi, then firmly shut the door. "That one's a perfect pest."

"Couldn't agree more." I unsnapped Rover's leash, and he made a beeline for the kitchen. Multiple conversations drifted toward us down the hall from the living room. "What's going on?" I asked Mom.

She sighed. "The guests have all heard the terrible news about Fallon O'Malley. Some of them were at the fairgrounds this morning and heard the commotion." She shook her head. "Such a sad business. I'm giving them their privacy now. And a fair amount of brandy."

"Good idea," I said.

"They'll be answering questions for the police soon enough, since they knew the poor girl. And there are details some will need to attend to, of course."

"How are Bliz and Maeve doing?" I asked. "Did they hear the news yet?"

"Yes, from Maeve's phone, I'm afraid," Mom said. "And the TV. But not many details are being given out to the public yet, thank goodness. The girls took things well enough, I think, but they were worried about you. They're in the kitchen."

"And Colleen?" I hoped my sister wasn't having flashbacks from Deirdre's murder after hearing the news.

"She stayed with the girls for a while. But she's upstairs right now, preparing the Connemara Suite for two new guests." Mom hesitated. "And if Ian joins us as well, we'll be up to full capacity."

So the Chief had called her about the updated accommodations plan. Hopefully Mitzi wouldn't find out anytime soon.

"No problem, Mom," I said. "I'll move in with Colleen. I'll pack up my stuff right after I've I talked to the girls."

"No need. Colleen already handled moving your things." Mom peeked out the window beside the front door. "Where did your father and Ian go off to?"

"Dad didn't say. To talk somewhere private, I guess. Or maybe the PD."

My mom sighed. "It does make sense for Ian to stay with us, I suppose, under the circumstances. He shouldn't be on his own at a time like this."

And she didn't even know the whole story. Actually, none of us did.

"I'm sorry, Kate," she added. "About all of it. I know it won't be easy."

"Thanks, Mom." I hadn't had much time to really consider the logistics of having Ian here at the B&B. Or the awkwardness. It wasn't the most important thing I needed to worry about at the moment, but the reality of the housing situation was beginning to hit. "You didn't mention anything to Maeve yet about Ian staying here, did you, Mom?"

"No," she said. "I thought that might be best left to you."

I nodded, trying not to panic. How would I explain this temporary arrangement to my older daughter? I'd tell her the truth: It would be the best thing for all of us.

Depending on how the investigation went.

"Honey, I never even asked yet how you were doing." Mom folded me into a hug. "I should have done that straight away."

"I'm fine," I said, my voice muffled. I felt like I was ten again. Maybe that wasn't such a bad thing.

"It's madness for lightning to strike again so soon." Mom shook her head.

"Not lightning," I said. "A killer." *Another one.*

"Well, you don't need to get involved this time, Kate." Mom stepped away and gave me an encouraging smile. "Let your father and the PD handle it."

"Mm."

My mom knew as well as I did that my response was technically not an agreement. But she didn't push the point. Instead she headed upstairs to join Colleen. I hurried straight to the kitchen.

Maeve sat at the table in an old Holy Innocents T-shirt of Colleen's, huddled over her phone. "Hi, Mom," she greeted me. Bliz was cross-legged on the floor near the stove, petting an appreciative Rover. The second she spotted me, she scrambled up from the linoleum and tore in my direction. "Mommy!" she said, throwing her arms around my waist. "We were so worried about you and Rover."

"No need to worry anymore, sweetie." I smiled as I knelt and smoothed my younger daughter's French braid. "See? Rover and I are both just fine."

Bliz didn't loosen her grip. "There's another bad person out there, Mommy. They hurt a friend of Dad's and now she's in heaven with Miss Deirdre."

"Dad's *fiancée*," Maeve said. "No one told me he was getting married again."

"I just found out myself," I said, trying not to notice her steady glare. "We can talk about that later, honey." Then I turned back to Bliz. "Sweetie, it's true Dad's friend got hurt, but like I said, there's no need to worry about anything," I said. "We're safe here at Gram and the Chief's house." I pointed to the now-snoring dog. "And Rover is such a good protector. No one is in danger."

My words sounded lame, even to me, but my youngest nodded trustingly.

"It was breaking news." Maeve jerked her chin toward Mom's small countertop TV. "I changed the channel to cartoons, but I couldn't find the remote right away." She got up from the table and came over to give me a hug as well. "Glad you're home, Mom."

"Thanks, me too." I hoped neither of my daughters had heard yet that I was the person who'd officially found Fallon.

"Hey Blizzie B, guess what?"

We all turned as Colleen whirled into the kitchen in a cute lime green skort with a tie at the hip and a green-and-white polka dot halter top. She plopped herself onto a stool in the corner and triumphantly held up her phone, her charm bracelet jangling. "You're in!"

"In what?" I said. Maeve gave a little leave-me-out-of-this shrug.

"Yay!" Bliz jumped up and down, her blue eyes shining. "I'm going to be Little Miss Shamrock!"

"You get to be in the contest, Blizzie," Maeve corrected. "That doesn't necessarily mean you'll win."

"Yes, I will." Bliz's Buckley dimple deepened. "I'll ask St. Jude." Maeve groaned in mock despair.

"Wait just a minute here," I broke in. "Bliz, we didn't talk about you entering the Little Miss Shamrock contest. You need a parent or guardian's permission. And Colleen, didn't you announce at the dance practice that last night was the deadline?"

"Moira's on the Committee now," my sister said. "She got Bliz's name on the list. I would have asked them myself, but I didn't want to seem like I was asking for an exception for a family member or anything."

"Which you were, basically."

Colleen's dimple matched Bliz's. "I told Moira you'd sign the form later, and she said fine."

I hesitated for half a second, and Bliz's little face dropped. "Mommy, I want to be like Aunt Colleen and Maeve. They were Little Miss Shamrocks, and Aunt Colleen was the big-girl one too."

"It isn't all fun, Blizzie," Maeve warned. "There's a lot of hard work when you're in the contest. And even more if you win. You'll have to write an essay, remember? And wear a fancy dress and pose for a lot of dumb pictures."

"That's OK." Bliz was undeterred. "I want to do all that."

Colleen looked from Maeve to me and threw up her hands. "For heaven's sake, you two. It's not like she wants to be queen of the world. It's supposed to be *fun*. And the contest entries and tickets raise money for Shamrock House. You know, the nursing home."

"Please, Mommy?" Bliz gave me the same beseeching look as Colleen did when she wanted something.

Begging in stereo from my sister and my youngest. I tried to resist. But to be honest, the Little Miss Shamrock contest prep and festivities might be the perfect distraction for Bliz from any murder news. "All right, sweetie," I said. "But I don't want you to be too upset if you don't win."

Or if the contest gets canceled, I almost added, before I caught myself.

"I won't be upset," Bliz promised. "I need to tell Gram I'm going to be Little Miss Shamrock," she called over her shoulder as she tore out of the kitchen.

"Well, that's settled, then," Colleen said. "Don't worry, she'll be amazing. It'll be a great learning experience for her."

"Right," I said. No sense in bringing up the possibility that the contest—and even the entire Great Shamrock Fair itself—might be in jeopardy due to the murder investigation. "I still wish you'd asked me first."

"I get it, Katie," my sister said. "It was a timing issue, I swear. They were finalizing everything this morning, and if we waited any longer it would have been too late. I mean, you were busy with the cops and the Chief out at the fairgrounds. That must have been so awful for you."

No. I squeezed my eyes shut, but not before I saw Maeve bolt up in her chair. "What? Mom, you were at the crime scene?"

I gathered myself together and headed over to the table to sit beside her. "Yes," I said. "Just for a little while."

For a second Maeve was speechless. Then, her voice barely a whisper, she said, "You found the body, didn't you?"

"I can't believe it happened to you again, Kate." Colleen shook her head. "I mean, what were the chances? And Fallon was just here at the house, talking with us. It's all so sad and horrible."

"So what happened, Mom? How did that woman get murdered?"

"Honey, it's all confidential police info right now. I can't go into any kind of details."

"Are you going to investigate this murder, too? Why don't you just join the Shamrock PD?"

"She's too old," Colleen said.

I frowned at my sister. "For your information, there is no age limit to become a police officer in Shamrock."

She raised one, perfectly shaped eyebrow. "And you know that how?"

"It doesn't matter," I said. "And the answer to both of your questions, Maeve, is absolutely not." I turned back to my sister. "Colleen, you spoke with Fallon the most. Did she seem stressed about anything to you? Say or do anything that seemed out of the ordinary?"

"You *are* going to investigate," Maeve said. "I can help you again, you know."

"Nope. Sorry, honey. This time the cops are handling everything, as they should. I'm just . . . asking a few questions."

And as soon as I had a spare moment, I would change all the passwords on our family streaming accounts and podcasts. Maeve didn't need to see or listen to any more crime shows. She already had a front row seat here in Shamrock.

My sister tapped a finger on her cheek, still considering my Fallon question. "The girl was definitely nosy," Colleen said. "And kind of snobby, to be honest. Maybe a little high-strung. But what she really seemed super worried about was having things set up perfectly for the band to rehearse. I got the idea they were working on something they wanted to keep under wraps. She seemed pretty focused on it."

"If you ask me, the stressed one was the Chief's friend, Marty," Maeve said. "Remember how he freaked out when he saw Fallon yesterday? He called her the devil. And now she's dead. Maybe we should talk to him first."

"There is no 'we,'" I corrected. "Honey, I know how interested you are in all of this, and you were a big help on Deirdre's investigation. But this time your job is to stay safe and try to enjoy your summer. You know, be a kid."

Uh-oh. I immediately realized the "kid" had been a mistake. I braced for my daughter's response. But she *was* a kid, right? And I was the parent here.

Whose own mother had just told her not to get involved in a second murder case.

"Sure, Mom." Maeve's voice was a smidge saccharine.

Colleen glanced at the rooster clock and jumped off her kitchen stool. "Oops, it's later than I thought. I've got a ton of stuff to get at the store now that we have actual guests. Counting your friends, Kate, and now Ian, the B&B is officially full. Isn't that awesome? Don't worry, I moved all your stuff into my room already."

"Mom mentioned that," I said. "Thanks. Who are these alleged friends of mine, by the way?"

"Wait a minute, back up. *Dad's* staying here?" Maeve's mouth dropped open as far as the tiny elastic bands of her pricey orthodontia would allow. "You didn't bother to tell me that, either?"

"I'm sorry, honey, I really didn't have a chance," I said. "It was just decided. The Chief thought it would be a good idea for your dad to be at the B&B with us, under the circumstances. And so do I. Your father is very upset about Fallon. It was a horrible shock to him."

Maeve sighed. "Yeah, I guess that makes sense."

I didn't add that her dad might end up as a murder suspect in his fiancée's murder. No need to borrow trouble and make the situation any worse.

"Hey, want to come with me to the store, Maeve?" Colleen broke in. "I could use an extra set of hands with all the bags. And we can grab a late lunch at the Piggety Diner. You love that place."

"Sure, I'll go," Maeve said, getting up from the table. "No sense hanging around here. This place is like a morgue." She caught herself and covered her mouth. "Oops. I didn't mean *morgue*, exactly."

"That's OK. Bring a cinnamon bun for me," I called after her and Colleen.

They had been out of the kitchen for less than a second before Colleen skittered back in her daisy heels and stuck her head through the doorway. "Hey Kate, can you check in your friends when they get here? They should show up any minute. Thanks a mil."

She was gone before I could ask her again about the identity of my so-called "friends." Well, I'd find out soon enough.

I had more important things to think about right now. Like who—other than my ex—might have killed Fallon O'Malley. And why.

True, everyone kept telling me not to get involved. They were probably right. But I had to. For Ian, the guy I'd once thought was the love of my life. And for Maeve, because he was her dad. But also for the young woman left lying in a field in a foreign country, stabbed in the back.

True, the two of us had never set eyes on each other until yesterday. We were strangers, really, connected solely through a man one of us hardly knew anymore.

But that didn't matter.

Fallon didn't deserve to die, no matter what she might have done. Or what the mysterious note writer thought she'd done.

Someone out there needed to face the music.

Chapter Fifteen

I stood outside the living room, my back against the gold and green striped wallpaper in the hallway, preparing to face the guests mourning Fallon O'Malley.

Or maybe *not* mourning.

At least one of the gathered Irish musicians was not a huge fan of the deceased. Marty had made that pretty clear with the drama he'd thrown in the backyard yesterday. Hopefully poor Fallon—I made a quick sign of the cross—never heard him call her out as the devil.

Would she have cared? I had no idea.

But why had Marty insisted Ian's fiancée was evil? Someone far more nefarious than Fallon might have agreed with him—and removed her from this earth.

Unless Marty himself was Fallon's killer.

Jayzus, Mary, and Joseph. Could that be possible? I had a hard time even considering the idea. I'd known Marty since I was a kid. A sometimes-stormy, sometimes-twinkly little man fond of jokes, sweets, and longwinded stories, he liked nothing better than to entertain a crowd. Especially with his fiddle. Not to mention, he was also my dad's longtime pal. I wasn't sure why, exactly, because in a lot of ways they had opposite personalities. But Marty was an amiable enough companion. In small doses.

I wasn't sure about his general health and physical strength, but the leader of the Limerick Lads had enjoyed a long life in pubs and on the road. I bet Fallon would have squished Marty like a New England black fly if he'd attempted to attack her. Weapon or no weapon.

But what about the blood I'd seen on his hands this morning when he returned from his walk? Could it have been not his, but Fallon's? What if Marty hadn't taken a tumble, as he'd claimed?

No, that was ridiculous. I was stalling now, dreading my duty to face the assembled guests. I wasn't always the best at cheering people up. Colleen and Mom were the pros in the social outreach department.

But our visitors from Ireland deserved consolation and assistance. Also, I needed to start somewhere if I was going to find Fallon's killer. I'd take any crumbs of information I could get.

I drew a deep breath, wiped my nervous-sweaty palms on my jeans, and stepped into the living room with a respectful smile.

The musicians were conveniently grouped with Limerick Lads on one side of the coffee table and Peat members on the other. Except for Liam, who sat over by himself on the piano bench. Neither contingent seemed thrilled to be together.

Or more likely they were just upset.

"Hello, everyone," I said, trying my best not to sound fake-perky. "I'm Kate, for those of you who haven't met me yet. My parents are the owners of the Buckley House, and my daughters and I live here, too." *For now.* "We're all so very sorry for your loss."

The guests returned mumbled greetings. Or at least nodded. Even Marty looked somber. No one seemed to be full-out crying, but the one young woman from Peat had red eyes and a puffy face.

"Can I get anyone anything?" I said. "Tea? Another round of brandy? More biscuits?"

I don't know why I bothered asking about the cookies. The plate on the coffee table was untouched. For once.

"I'll take a beer, thanks."

The young woman who'd spoken up was in her late twenties, I guessed. Petite, with a sharp, pale face, her arms were covered in elaborate Celtic tattoos. "I'm Macker, by the way," she added.

"Nice to meet you," I said.

"Tell us now, Macker, is that the name your mammy gave you?" one of the twins from the Limerick Lads asked. Timmy, I guessed. I could never tell him and Jimmy apart. It was extra confusing because all of the Lads' names ended in "y."

Well, they used to, until Christy—short for Christopher—retired and Marty's son Noel joined the group. Noel was missing from the room, I noticed now.

"My legal name is Beatrice McWilliams." The girl glared at Timmy. "If you really must know."

"Ah, I'm only codding you," he said. "Macker is a lovely name." Beside him, his twin stifled an amused snort.

I frowned at him. So did Liam, the guy across the room who had let his Peat bandmates into the B&B for me last night. Neither of us said anything, though.

Marty was quiet too. The old man sat with his arms crossed, chin on his chest. Oh. Had he nodded off, or . . . ?

One of the twins tapped him on the knee, and Marty snapped to attention. Phew. For a moment there, I'd worried we might have lost him. The way the day had been going so far, it was possible.

I perched on the arm of an empty overstuffed chair. "Fallon's passing must have come as a terrible shock," I said. "What can any of us here at the Buckley House do to make things easier for you?"

"We're good, thanks." Liam rose from the bench and held up his phone. "Just got a text from Ian. He's on his way."

Macker twisted in his direction, her pale face pinched in concern. "How did he sound? Is he OK?"

Liam shrugged. "Hard to tell. He didn't say much. But he wants to have a band meeting as soon as he gets back. We have some special business to take care of."

"Tell him the rest of our rental gear arrived this morning," said the guy sitting next to Macker. His skin was as dark as hers was pale. If I remembered correctly, he was Noel's recent replacement in Peat, after Noel left to join the Limerick Lads. "It's out in the studio," he added.

The studio? Ah. Our repurposed garage.

"So were any of you over at the fairgrounds this morning?" I asked, looking around the group. "Before Fallon was, um, found?"

By me. After Ian.

"I went over there early, yeah," Liam said. "To meet with one of the sound guys." He nodded toward the newest member of Peat on the other sofa. "Jaymes was having a lie-in with a sore head. Ian never made it over, either. I couldn't tell you about Macker here."

"I was in my bed as well," she said. "And I'm still tired." She sniffed. "Allergies."

"Noel represented for the Lads." Timmy shrugged. "We're old hands at this. Didn't need more than one person to check on things. Just give us a stage or a tent or a room, and we're off to the races. Marty's boy is a stickler for every detail, though. Haven't seen him since. Marty, where's Noel?"

"Noel?" Marty started awake, and I glimpsed the neatly wrapped white gauze bandage on his hand.

Mom's signature handiwork. All of us Buckleys had been on the receiving end.

Timmy leaned closer to Marty. "Your son," he said, louder. "Where is the lad?"

"Noel? Ah, he's off somewhere. Who knows?" Marty said. "I'll have a beer as well, Kate, since you're bringin' one to the young lady here."

This time he was the one who got the evil eye from Macker. Apparently she didn't like the term "young lady." Marty didn't seem to notice.

But he hadn't been dozing this whole time. He had full awareness of Macker's drink order.

Selective hearing, maybe. Just like the Chief.

"I'll get those beers right now," I said, jumping off the armchair. "Be right back." I doubted I'd get much more from this group about the morning's events anyway. Not as a group, anyway.

Divide and conquer. Another of the Chief's specialties.

"Did you find your dog, now?" Marty called, as I reached the doorway.

"Yes, Rover's safely home, thanks." *After you let him out of the gate, I wanted to add.*

"He's a sly one, that pup," Marty said.

"Sure is," I agreed. But Marty was the real sly dog, in my book. And on my list for a private chat.

After my ex.

* * *

When I returned to the living room less than five minutes later, Leprechaun Lagers in hand for the guests who'd requested them, I was surprised to find only Macker left. She was still in her place on the couch, frowning at her ragged nails. They were bitten down to the quick.

"Where did everyone go?" I handed Macker one of the lagers.

"Just leave Marty's there on the coffee table." She pointed in front of her. "He went off with the others. If he doesn't come back, I'll drink it. Or you can."

"Thanks, I'm good." I set down the beer and dropped into the armchair across from her. Macker would be my first guest interrogee. "Again, I am so sorry about Fallon. Were the two of you close?"

Macker drew back. "Not so much," she said. "We had a business relationship. We weren't exactly BFFs."

"Oh, right." I shouldn't have assumed two women involved in a band would be friends. "Did you know anything at all about Fallon on a personal level, though?"

"Not really." Macker shrugged. "She was a decent manager. A real pro at PR. Got us some brilliant gigs, too. She had a knack for getting people to do things. Especially if they didn't want to do them."

"Like what?" The way Macker had thrown that last line out, it didn't sound like much of a compliment.

Macker took a swig of her beer. "Well, for one thing, she had all the guys wrapped around her finger," she said. "Like your sister."

I immediately bristled. How did this young woman from an ocean away know anything about Colleen?

"I didn't mean that in a bad way," Macker said. "More like, knowing how to get whatever they want."

"That's not true," I defended my sister. "Have you ever even talked to Colleen?"

"She's just the type. I can tell." Macker flopped back against the couch. The cushions almost swallowed her up, making her look even smaller. "There was some talk about her in the pub last night. Nothing bad," she added quickly, before I opened my mouth. "People were just saying she'd been the perfect Miss Shamrock. And that she was a brilliant dancer and Aidan O'Hearne is over the moon for her and she was best friends with his Irish Steps partner. The one who got murdered, so people felt really sorry for her. They did back home, too. It was big news in Ireland, the whole thing."

"I can imagine," I murmured. Macker was on a roll now. I reached for Marty's abandoned beer and cracked it open to keep her company.

"I'll give you an example of how Fallon always got her way," Macker said. "She flew into New York last week before she came here and got a meeting with the top exec at Emerald Records. Johnny Myer. Just like that."

"Wow." I'd never heard of the guy.

"She walked right in off the street to his fancy office in Manhattan. Got past the lobby reception desk and through security and everything. She told his admin she wasn't leaving until she spoke with him."

"She told you all of this?" I asked.

Macker nodded. "Last night at the pub. "Bragged about it, even. But not everyone in the band was thrilled she went to see Johnny Myer."

"Why did she want to talk to him, exactly?"

Macker bounced back from the cushions and leaned in my direction. "I probably shouldn't tell you this, but the word will be out soon enough. Fallon wanted Peat to do the music and official soundtrack for Crossroad Dreams."

I frowned in confusion. "I thought the Limerick Lads were already signed on for that."

"They are." Macker regarded her raggedy nails again with a smug little smile. "For now."

"Huh," I said. "Let me get this straight. Fallon walks into the offices of a big New York record label without an appointment. And the top exec meets with her, just like that. Then she convinces this Johnny Myer guy to sign Peat to do the music and soundtrack for Aidan O'Hearne's new show. Which would mean Emerald Records dumping the Limerick Lads, who they have a contract with. All of that solely on her recommendation?"

"Pretty much, yeah," Macker said. "The way Fallon told it, anyway. Contracts get broken all the time in the music biz. There are always loopholes and escape clauses built in on both sides. Like, say, if the artists aren't performing up to par. Anyway, Johnny Myer was probably already on board with the idea. Everyone knows the Limerick Lads are going downhill. They need to retire already."

Ouch. Macker's tone was matter-of-fact. Maybe what she'd said was true. Marty was definitely a lot slower than he used to be. Hadn't he just dozed off a few minutes ago? But I had to feel bad for him and the Lads. They were practically icons in Irish music. Their CDs and vinyl records were sold in half the stores in town.

"Fallon said she invited Johnny out to Shamrock this week," Macker continued. "To hear us play live, since Peat has top billing at the fair now. The Limerick Lads are opening for *us*."

That was news to me. On the other hand, a couple of days ago I'd had no idea Peat was even playing the fair.

"So no one in the band knew anything about Fallon's whole Crossroad Dreams takeover plan before she flew to New York?" I asked.

"Well . . ." Macker didn't seem quite as eager to continue the story now. "I wouldn't exactly say that. We had a few discussions. In theory."

"But nothing's final yet?" I pressed.

Macker shrugged. "It's no secret Aidan's not happy with the Lads' work so far. The music is wrecking the whole show. He'll be on board with changing artists."

I wasn't so sure about that. But I waited, letting the sudden silence between us grow. Another handy strategy of the Chief's. Lulls in conversation made most people uncomfortable, and chances were one person would jump in to fill the void. And the longer they talked to empty air, the more likely they were to spill information they hadn't intended. *Three, two, one, and . . .*

"Fallon had been talking about us doing Crossroad Dreams for ages," Macker went on. "Right after Deirdre Donnelly quit Irish Steps, and Aidan announced his own show. He asked the Limerick Lads to do the music right away, the eejit. They're still popular with what Fallon called 'the mature demographic.' Geezers, mostly."

Peat's fans were younger, true. But Ian was the oldest member of the band. And as Colleen had pointed out, thirty-six was ancient. Especially in the music biz.

"Isn't the mature demographic the target audience for Crossroad Dreams?" I asked.

"Well, yeah," Macker said. "But we incorporate trad elements into our work too. Peat just has a cooler style. You know. Celtic punk, like."

"I'm familiar." This young woman probably had no idea I'd been in Ian's first band. Long ago and far away. Our music wasn't punk, but it wasn't just traditional Irish folk music, either. Did Macker have any clue I used to be married to Ian? It didn't sound like it. She'd find out eventually, but I wasn't about to mention it right now. "What instruments do you play, Macker?"

"Drums, mostly. And keyboards." She grinned. "I play a mad triangle as well."

"Nice." Time to get this convo back on track. "So you said when Fallon told the band she'd met with Johnny Myer in New York, not everyone was happy about that?"

Macker fussed with a small knot in one of her thread bracelets. "Jaymes was OK with it, but he hasn't been with the band that long. And Liam doesn't care much one way or the other. He plays a ton of instruments. He's down for any kind of music."

"And Ian?" I already knew the answer.

"He's a musical genius. Don't you agree?"

"Um, sure," I said.

"Well, in my opinion, he hasn't been the same since Noel quit the band after Paddy's Day. The two of them hardly even speak now. But they were amazing together. Musicwise, I mean. Noel did the writing, and Ian focused on the music. They worked on covers, too."

"Those two have been working together forever," I said. As long as I'd known them, anyway. Ian and Noel never used to fight, so if they were at odds now over Noel leaving Peat, it was a big deal.

"They were both dead picky about the kind of stuff they wanted to play." Macker stopped to take another sip of her lager.

"So maybe doing the music for an Irish dance show, even a potential blockbuster with Aidan O'Hearne, felt like going backward for them," I said slowly. "Artistically." That sounded like Ian, all right.

"Ian said we'd be selling out," Macker went on. "Going too commercial."

I tried not to imagine Maeve's school tuition and future university fees being magically disappeared by all that commercialism.

Focus, I reminded myself.

"But Noel left to join the Limerick Lads," I pointed out. "They're about as traditional as Irish music gets." I paused. "They also happen to be the band with the actual Crossroad Dreams contract at the moment."

Macker sighed. "True. I don't think Noel had much choice about leaving Peat, though. Christy left the Lads in a bind. Fallon tried really hard to talk Noel out of it. Like I said, she's usually good at convincing people. But the Lads needed another member right away who knew all the music and could easily step in."

"And Noel didn't want to let his dad down," I said.

"Yeah. Everyone knows Marty's been slipping for years. Nothing serious as far as I know. But the Lads are still popular enough, and the old timer refuses to retire."

Like the Chief. Technically, my dad was retired, but in his mind—and almost everyone else's—Dermot Buckley was still the face of the Shamrock PD.

"Noel made a huge mistake, though. He sacrificed his own music career to look after Marty," Macker said. "He grew up in the traditional Irish music scene—learning the songs from his dad and playing in pubs for tourists. Now he's stuck. He ruined Peat and his whole life. I heard his girlfriend—none of us ever even met her—dumped him like a hot spud."

"Wow," I said. "That's rough."

Macker polished off her lager. "He's a sound fella, Noel. But he tries too hard to make everyone happy. He can't ever say no."

"Noel did quit Peat," I pointed out. "That was a no."

"I guess."

Poor Noel. The whole situation was so sad. I felt bad for both him and his dad.

I also felt sorry for my own dad. I hadn't broached the idea of Marty as a possible suspect yet to the Chief. He'd probably be in denial about that, as well as his old friend's decline. But there was no denying the strikes against Marty.

His obvious dislike for Fallon. The blood on his hands around the time of her death. Right outside our gate the morning I'd looked for Rover.

What if Marty hated the woman so much he'd somehow snapped and managed to stab her after all? He might have had no clue what he was doing. Maybe he had some kind of dementia.

Or maybe he was sharp as a tack.

Marty could easily have gotten himself to the fairgrounds. He had definitely been up and out of the B&B early. He could have confronted Fallon in the field.

Would he have written that creepy note, though? It didn't seem like Marty's style.

Across from me, Macker was staring out the window now. I'd almost forgotten she was there. A strange young woman, in my book. But much more talkative than I'd expected.

"What about you, Macker?" I asked. "Did you think Fallon's Crossroad Dreams plan was right for the band?"

She blinked, seeming startled. "I guess so," she said. "The money would have been grand, that's for sure. But Ian is always right about music."

I knew I might be pushing it, but I had a few more things to ask. This might be my only chance.

"Do you think the Limerick Lads knew Fallon was angling to have their contract for Crossroad Dreams canceled?" I asked. "So Peat could replace them? Is that even possible?"

If so, anyone in Marty's band could have had a motive to nip the situation—and Fallon—in the bud. And it might explain why Marty had been so furious with her.

Macker fiddled with her bracelet again. "Maybe for breach of contract, like. Dodgy work. Like I said, there's a rumor going around that Aidan O'Hearne isn't pleased with the Lads' work so far. They might have heard it. I dunno."

"And when you said that Peat has top billing at the fair now," I said. "Do the Limerick Lads know that?"

"Well, maybe the top-billing thing was a wee exaggeration on my part," Macker said. "I didn't mean top billing, like, literally. But your Mayor Flanagan flew us out to America for free—first class, can you believe it?"

Nope. And yes.

"We weren't going to play the Great Shamrock Fair this year, because we've been in the studio in Dublin. But he was very persuasive."

Just like the mayor's other VIP invitation I'd heard about from that overzealous Irish dance mom. Lolo or LeeLee or whatever her name was. My brain was overloaded at this point.

Macker leaned forward again. "Between you, me, and the kettle, Ian didn't seem thrilled about doing this Shamrock gig. I tried to talk to him about it to find out why. But like I said, when Fallon wanted something . . ." Her voice trailed away.

"Got it," I said.

Ian had never been a total pushover like that. Not with me, or anyone else, as far as I knew. When my ex really cared about something—like his music—he poured his heart and soul and all of his focus into it. He wouldn't have folded like a parish hall chair.

Macker rose from the couch and held up her empty beer can. "Where do I bin this?"

I got to my feet as well. "Give it to me, and I'll recycle it. Oh, and one more thing before you go, if you don't mind."

This time, the petite musician seemed wary. "You do ask a lot of questions," she said. "So American of you."

I ignored that. "Guilty," I said lightly. "As your B&B host, I just thought I should get a bit of background on things. I'd hate to say the wrong thing to anyone somehow. You know, under the circumstances."

Macker cocked her head. Uh-oh. She wasn't buying that explanation. It was pretty lame, I had to admit. "What is it you want to ask?" she said finally.

"What exactly happened last night at Farrell's when Fallon told the band about the Crossroad Dreams meeting?"

Macker shrugged. "At first it was like a normal conversation. We don't always agree on stuff. But then it turned into a huge row. Ian was raging. I guess Fallon thought we'd be delighted she went behind our backs. I tried to calm Ian down. Jaymes was useless—he stayed neutral. Liam got Misty-eyed."

"Misty-eyed?"

"Irish Mist. The whiskey, like," Macker said. "Anyway, Ian told Fallon she'd sold us out. That she hadn't even talked to him about it, and he was her fiancé. And she said none of us knew our arses from our elbows about branding and career building." She paused. "That's kinda true, actually. Fallon's the one who got us all our gigs."

No doubt about it, the woman had been good at her job. "And she left Farrell's on her own?'

"She did, yeah," Macker said. "But not before she called us all ungrateful eejits. Well, worse, actually. Last words I ever heard her say."

"Gosh, that's terrible. I'm really sorry," I said.

I was even sorrier that Fallon had been unpleasant to so many people in her life. It made it a lot tougher to figure out who'd wanted her dead.

"There was one other thing, though," Macker said.

"What's that?" I said, happy she was volunteering info on her own.

"Fallon was showing off her fancy new engagement ring at the pub. Ian wasn't thrilled about that, I could tell. His eyes were out on stalks when she started flashing it around." She lowered her voice conspiratorially. "He looked a little sick to his stomach, if you ask me."

Macker started out of the living room but stopped and turned. "I have a question for *you,* Kate."

I smiled. "Fire away."

"Are you the one who was married to Ian and has a kid?"

My chest felt like it had been hit by a soccer ball. "Two kids."

"Huh. Hard to imagine you two together."

"Thanks," I said, before I realized that was the wrong response. It didn't matter. She was already gone.

Chapter Sixteen

I waited a good minute or two before I followed Macker out of the living room. I wanted to put as much distance between me and Little Mary Sunshine as possible.

I was halfway across the hall toward the kitchen when a two-toned, retro chime sounded in the foyer. We actually had a working front doorbell now. A miracle.

Frank was still on shift, as far as I knew. That left Saint Noel, who'd been AWOL since late morning.

Why was the guy being so nice? Maybe he was trying to make up for his dad and the rest of the band. If he ever wanted to dump the Limerick Lads gig and stay on at the Buckley House as our resident jack-of-all-trades, I would personally sign off on his free room and board. I'd even throw in the garage/music studio and cookies in perpetuity to sweeten the deal.

The Chief wasn't back yet with Ian. They'd been gone so long, my ex was probably being questioned down at the Shamrock PD right now. And no one involved would have any idea about the note in my pocketbook.

Shifting Macker's empty Leprechaun Lager can to the crook of my elbow as I clutched my own almost-full beer in my left hand, I opened the door. I tried to retain my automatic smile when I saw who stood on our porch. The pushy woman from the dance practice. Beside her was her teen daughter, an extra-large dance duffel slung over her shoulder.

"Hello," the woman said, waggling her French manicure. "Lulu Cavanagh-Barry here. And you remember my Cassandra."

I hadn't actually met her daughter yet. The redhead wore a cropped dance top, light purple terry shorts, and a completely neutral expression.

"Of course." I smiled. "What can I do for you ladies?"

"Oh, we're here to check in," Lulu said breezily. "I'm sure Colleen mentioned we'd be arriving this afternoon. She told us she would."

"Ah, right. She did." My stomach made a surface dive. So these were my "friends" who needed a room. Wonderful. The Cavanagh-Barrys would be the perfect guests to bring our three-shamrock B&B to full-misery occupancy.

Immediately, I felt ashamed—and sorry for Cassandra. She was just a kid. It was unfair of me to lump her in with her annoying mom.

And hadn't I been overly eager to fill every room for fair week? Now I'd pay the price for it: a Lulu of a week with nonstop bragging.

The girl in the doorway seemed less confident than the cool-cucumber dance champion I'd seen in Angels Hall. This kid, her face still bearing traces of heavy stage makeup, seemed slightly embarrassed as she gave me a tentative one-sided smile. She reminded me a bit of Maeve, actually. Without the eyeroll.

Her mother nudged her slightly. As if a light had switched on, the girl's expression changed to one of perfect composure.

Her smile broadened, her teeth startlingly white against the residual self-tanner streaking her cheeks. “Hello,” she said, gracefully stepping forward and extending her hand. “I’m Cassandra. Mum and I are delighted to be here at the Buckley House. Looking forward to our stay.”

Clearly Cassandra’s mother had trained her to interact politely with the public. The girl sounded even more adult than Maeve’s friend Zoe, and a lot more formal. Almost like a robot, to be honest. I shook her hand. “Thanks, Cassandra, we’re so happy to have you. My daughters will love the company.”

As I finished speaking, sounding equally stiff, I felt rather than saw Bliz watching from halfway up the stairs. Her sparkly gold Crocs with the shamrock shoe charms skimmed the carpet the rest of the way down before she jumped from the last step.

“Hi Cassandra!” my youngest said, her eyes shining with joy. “I’m Bliz, remember? You gave me your autograph at dance practice. On my arm.” She held it out as evidence, and I tried not to shudder at the laundry marker ink. “Want to come play with me and my Irish dance doll? She has lots of dresses, just like you.”

“Oh, Cassandra won’t have much time to socialize while she’s here,” Lulu said. “She’ll be so busy with practices and the fair events. You’ll hardly see her.”

Bliz’s face instantly fell.

Was it my imagination, or did Cassandra look a little sad at her mother’s words, too? “Maybe later,” she told Bliz. “We have to unpack first.”

“That’s OK,” Bliz said. “I understand.”

“So may we come in, then?” Lulu asked me. She sounded a little impatient now.

I suddenly realized I'd been standing there with the front door half closed and two beer cans in tow. "Heavens, my brain must be half-baked in this heat," I said. "Welcome to the Buckley House." I threw the door open all the way, then reached behind it to surreptitiously put the beer cans down on the small side table set against the wall. When I turned back to our new guests, Lulu was frowning slightly. Not due to the beer cans, it dawned on me. "Don't worry," I added quickly, "we'll get some awesome AC cranked up in your room."

Hopefully.

As Cassandra stepped further into the foyer, Lulu motioned to the green cab waiting at the curb. The driver jumped out and began unloading their bags from the trunk.

There were quite a few of them, so the driver made three trips. Bliz's eyes widened as the pile grew. "That's a lot of stuff."

"We sent some of it ahead," Lulu said.

"Is that box for wigs?" Bliz pointed.

"It is," Cassandra said. "And that one has extra shoes. You need a lot of solo dresses when you're competing at the Worlds level, too."

"Wow." Bliz was in complete awe. "I didn't know you had *this* many. Even more than Ciara. Will you show them all to me?"

Cassandra shrugged. "If you want. Who's Ciara?"

"Oh, you'll get to meet her soon," Bliz said. "She's coming to every Miss Shamrock rehearsal."

I tried not to smile at Lulu Cavanagh-Barry's reaction. Was she looking high-level annoyed because the driver was dumping the bags and boxes in the doorway willy-nilly? Or at the possibility of unexpected competition for her daughter in the contest?

Either way, Lulu gave the driver a hefty tip, and I led her and her daughter to the front desk. Bliz trailed behind us, practically at Cassandra's heels. The self-tanner either hadn't reached them or had been worn away by her shoes.

"Let me get your room keys and information," I said. "Then I'll show you right up." I consulted the computer, even though I knew full well which rooms they'd been assigned. "The Connemara Suite, how nice."

"Only the best for my princess." Lulu smoothed Cassandra's hair. The poor kid looked as if she wanted to go through the worn, green-carpeted floor. Lulu leaned toward me over the desk. "I really do appreciate your making room for us at the last minute," she said, in a confidential whisper. "I just happened to talk to your sister after the dance practice and learned you only had one suite left. Thank goodness Colleen said you could accommodate us. Since you and I know each other, of course."

"Yes, things have certainly been busy here," I said. That was no lie. "If you don't mind my asking, Lulu, how did you hear about the Buckley House?" I crossed my fingers she would mention amazing reviews. The ones Colleen and I hadn't seen yet.

"To be honest, we had other lodgings booked," the woman said. "But I decided to make this alternate arrangement for . . . other reasons."

"Oh?" I waited.

Lulu lowered her voice again. "We can have a chat later. Not in front of the children." She glanced over her shoulder at the girls. Bliz was talking Ciara's ears off about her new dog as the teen listened politely.

My interest level in whatever the woman from Dublin wanted to say had just taken a one-eighty. "Right. Well then, why don't we all head upstairs?" I said brightly. "May I help you with your bags?"

Lulu gave another teensy frown, but it disappeared in an instant. "Oh, no bell person? I suppose not. Some help would be grand, thanks."

"We have a cart." I hurried down the hall to retrieve it from the large hidden storage closet, half tempted to ride it back like a scooter to save time.

All those bags were heavier than I'd expected. Lulu watched me load every one of them, except for the wig box, which Bliz set carefully on top. Cassandra moved to help with some of the dress bags, but her mother placed a firm hand on her shoulder. "No, lovey, let Ms. Buckley do it. We don't need any shoulder strains before the festival."

I gritted my teeth as I loaded the last garment bag onto the cart's hanging rack.

The three of us headed toward the guest elevator, the last door before the Chief's private lift. The guest elevator had once been a dumbwaiter, so it was a tight squeeze.

"Quaint," Lulu said, with a brave smile, as we pressed against the walls. Bliz stood on the cart.

We made it safely to the Connemara Suite without incident. I fumbled for the light switch on the wall after I finally got the door open with its fancy, old-fashioned key. The summer heat was causing every piece of wood in the house to expand, and the AC hadn't been on for a while in here. No one had booked these connecting rooms lately. Hopefully Colleen had done a good job of dusting.

I pulled the chain on the charming blade fan, and the glass bead on the end came off in my hand. "We'll just leave this on for now, while the AC is cranking up," I said, closing my fist on the bead. Casually I stuck my hand in my back jeans pocket, depositing the fake crystal teardrop so the guests wouldn't notice.

"This is lovely, Kate," Lulu said, looking around. She sounded sincere.

The sitting room area did look nice. Welcoming, for sure. Framed prints in varying sizes of charming Irish castles, coasts, and farmlands, filmy Irish lace curtains, floral chintz couch, early-model flatscreen TV with an iffy remote, my great-grandma's writing desk with a hobnail lamp. Light green display candles in Belleek China holders set in the windows, a pair of midcentury recliners—from that actual century—a fringed floor lamp, an ornate Irish Georgian tea table.

"What charming antiques," Lulu said. "Is it all right for people to sit in that desk chair? We wouldn't want to break it or anything."

"It's much sturdier than it looks," I assured her. "All the furniture here at the B&B has stood the test of time." Including a couple of generations of Buckley kid shenanigans. I suppressed a shudder when I remembered Frank and me creating a climbing tower with the rest of that matched chair set. The remnants were probably in the garage/music studio somewhere to be "fixed." Someday.

She stepped into the next room, taking in the queen-sized bed with the European-down duvet and gold-tasseled drapes. Her gaze lingered on the small tray-top nightstand, my personal favorite. Then she moved on to the smaller adjoining room with the twin iron beds and pink mini-polka-dot curtains and bedding. Not very Irish-looking, but Colleen's personal touch, along with the braided wool rug dyed pink. The sheep woven into the center wore an old-fashioned sleep cap.

"Oh, this room is so cute," Cassandra said from behind us. "Look at that sheep."

"His name is Aran," Bliz offered. "I had a quilt with him on it back in the city."

I made a mental note to rescue Aran from the basement boxes as soon as possible and add him to the eclectic Nest décor.

"The suite is perfect," Lulu said, after a cursory check of the old-fashioned bathroom, complete with claw tub. The plumbing wasn't always the best, but it was clean. "Cassandra and I will be settled in no time."

My secret sigh of relief was interrupted when Rover bounded into the suite like a huge puppy, a blur of gold and floating fur.

"See, that's Rover!" Bliz said to Cassandra, as our rescue retriever dashed straight toward them. Cassandra took a step back, looking slightly alarmed, but Bliz dropped to her knees and wrapped him in a giant hug.

Tentatively, the older girl reached out to pat his furry head. "He's really soft." Rover looked up and gave her his best doggy smile.

"Rover, no!" I said, rushing forward when I saw Lulu frozen in horror from the corner of my eye. Her face was flipping shades from indigo to violet.

I gently but firmly reached for Rover's collar. "Bliz, we talked about this. It's not your fault, honey, but the dog is not allowed upstairs."

Rover passively resisted, making himself into a deadweight, as I tried to drag him toward the door. His tail waved enthusiastically as he enjoyed the game.

"I'll take him, Mommy," Bliz said. "Come on," she added to Cassandra. "I'll show you his room."

"Cassandra, your asthma!" Lulu called frantically, but the girls were already gone.

"Your daughter has asthma?" I asked.

"Exercise-induced," Lulu says. "But who knows how she'll do if she comes in contact with dog hair? Don't worry, Cassandra has an inhaler. She brings it everywhere she goes. She just needs to be careful."

I nodded. "I understand. If you need to cancel—"

Lulu waved. "It's quite all right. Cassandra and I will work around the dog. Though it would have been helpful to have the info on your website."

"Rover joined the family yesterday," I said. "We haven't updated things yet, I'm afraid. Um, will there be a problem with our cat, do you think?"

Where was Banshee, anyway? I hadn't seen him much since Rover's arrival. Maybe on my daughters' bed in the Nest once or twice. But judging by his food dish and litter box, he was very much around.

Lulu hadn't heard my question. Or maybe she'd ignored it. She was already busy transferring Cassandra's voluminous dress bags to the largest closet. "I'll need to get the wrinkles out of these right away," she said. "The Miss Shamrock prelims start tomorrow. Do you have a steamer?"

"Colleen might have one," I said. "To be honest, we usually settle for the poor man's dry clean."

Lulu looked horrified again. "The shower," I clarified quickly. "Let me go check for that steamer." I paused with my hand on the doorknob. Maybe not the best time to ask, but . . .

"Lulu, since it's just the two of us now," I said. "What was it you wanted to tell me about why you decided to move to the Buckley House?"

Cassandra's mother stepped out of the closet with three neatly folded empty garment bags held against her chest. "Sorry," she said. "I have so many things on my mind at the moment. Mainly, due to recent events, I felt Cassandra and I would be much safer staying in the home of Shamrock's former police chief. A highly regarded man in this town, I've heard."

"He is," I agreed. "The Chief is one of a kind."

"With zero tolerance for crime, I'd imagine."

"Absolutely." No need to mention we had potential murder suspects staying here at the B&B, right under the Chief's nose.

"I only hope that the fair and the Miss Shamrock contests won't be canceled due to that awful murder," the woman said. "That would be a shame. I've already given the mayor my input on the matter."

I had zero doubt about that. All this woman wanted was more attention for her daughter. With another sparkly crown, trophy, and winner's sash.

Lulu smoothed and stacked the garment bags on the floor of a vintage Irish oak wardrobe. A faded *Time* magazine cover featuring a long-ago pope had been taped to the inside door, but she didn't seem to notice. She had a lot more garment bags to empty.

"We had to forfeit our deposit at our previous lodgings, of course—the new Shamrock Grand Hibernian off the Square—but my husband agreed Cassandra's safety was much more important than hotel quality when I told him."

Ouch. Was that a compliment?

Her voice was muffled by the closet as she added, "And also, Colleen is on the Miss Shamrock committee. I'm sure she could be helpful to my daughter, since Cassandra doesn't know anyone here. People know *of* her, of course, but that isn't the same. These contests are so political these days."

I cleared my throat. "Lulu, I'm not sure you understand. Colleen isn't one of the judges. She has no part in any decisions regarding the Miss Shamrock contests. Zero."

Lulu stuck her head out of the closet. She didn't even seem embarrassed. "Oh, I know that, Kate. I meant in case Cassandra has any questions or needs assistance. Colleen has proven quite helpful to us so far." She smiled and swept her arm to indicate the Connemara Suite. "Like our room."

Trying to get through to this woman was a waste of time. "Right, then," I said, as Lulu returned to her task. "Let me go grab that steamer."

Chapter Seventeen

"Kate, did you say you were taking the girls to Mass tonight? They haven't been yet."

I paused with my hand on the doorknob to the room I was now sharing with my sister. Mom bustled toward me down the hall with her hands full of clean towels.

"Oh, um, gosh," I said. "It's been such a day, I forgot about church." The truth was, I'd just woken up from a much-needed nap, and I wasn't used to going to Mass on a late Sunday afternoon. Here in Shamrock, Our Lady of Angels offered services practically around the clock from Saturday afternoon until Sunday night. Even though only about a third of the town's residents were Catholic, and even fewer of them were regular churchgoers, the constant influx of tourists and special events kept the pews full. "What time is it now? Maeve is still out with Colleen, I think."

"It's three-thirty or so." Mom handed me a few sets of towels from her stack. "These are for you and the girls. Fresh out of the dryer."

"Thanks, I can tell," I said. The towels felt extra-warm against my skin, adding to the sticky heat in the hall. "Is the AC working, Mom?"

"Who knows?" she said with a sigh. "Off and on, I guess. Some of the rooms are cooler than others." She handed me even more towels. "Can you please take these up to Ian's room before he and your father get here? They should be back any minute."

"Sure, I'll go right now." The sooner the better. I wanted to talk to my ex privately about the note. But nowhere near his room, for heaven's sake. That would make things even more awkward between us.

"Remember, there's the Little Miss Shamrock practice starting at seven," Mom said. "I thought maybe you and the girls might want to grab a bite at the Blarney Bowl after Mass. It's new, a few blocks from the church. Very popular with the young people, I've heard. Colleen can help me prep dinner for the guests and meet up with you at the practice."

"OK," I said. Another practice? Oops. Lulu had mentioned the Miss Shamrock prelims started tomorrow. And I hadn't even checked my email yet for the contest info. I needed to get my act together for Bliz ASAP. "Sounds like a plan, Mom," I said. "If you're sure you don't need our help."

She smiled. "Oh, there will be plenty of opportunities to help later, dear. Believe me. I'm off to hunt down some extension cords. But another thing. The Limerick Lads are playing down at the Barleycorn tonight. It might be nice if you and Colleen went with your father."

Good thing I'd taken a nap. "That sounds fun." And even more worthwhile if my dad and I could pursue more info on the case while we enjoyed a night of Irish entertainment. You never knew when something might come up in this town. With the Chief in attendance, it was pretty much a given.

Or lately, whenever I stepped out of the house.

"He'd love to have your company, I know. The girls and I can have a nice quiet night at home. I have a few pies to make for the fair, and Bliz will probably be given her contestant banner to decorate at the practice."

"Thanks," I said. "She'll be excited about both of those projects. But I thought you weren't doing anything for the fair this year, Mom."

"I know." Mom sighed. "Ellen Lynch from the auction committee practically begged me, and I couldn't turn her down." She leaned forward and lowered her voice, even though there were no guests in sight. "If you ask me, your father is the one who could use a quiet night at home. But of course his friends from Ireland are here, and he's having such a good time." She rubbed her forehead, looking tired. "With the new investigation, I'm afraid he'll be burning the candle at both ends again. He gets so . . . involved."

Balancing the heavy stack of towels on my hip, I gave her shoulder a pat. "It'll be OK, Mom," I said. "Dad loves the thrill of the case. Much better for his health than all that tech stuff."

She gave me a small laugh. "I should be used to the constant worry after all these years. It never ends, I suppose."

No, it doesn't. I was an even bigger worrier than Mom. It had to be genetic. My concern for Frank and the Chief was always a given, especially after our dad was shot on duty. What if I'd been married to a cop instead of a musician? I'd be a total wreck.

For some reason, though, I didn't worry about Garrett's safety. Maybe because he was always so calm. Was there a difference in anxiety levels if you were only sort-of dating?

No, that made zero sense. Right now I was worrying about a musician I had almost zero relationship with at all.

Mom was halfway to the stairs. "Remember, five o'clock for Mass," she called over her shoulder. "Not five-thirty. We're on summer schedule now."

"Got it," I said. At least I'd get my chance to light that candle for Fallon.

* * *

No sooner had I arrived downstairs, quick-showered and ready for the first part of the summer evening marathon in a black cotton T-shirt dress and my all-purpose black sandals, when I was literally greeted on all sides by my family. Maeve and Colleen heading into the kitchen with bags full of groceries, the Chief trying to navigate a path to his private elevator, Bliz bouncing up from the bottom of the stairs, where she'd been waiting with Rover.

No sign of Ian. Maybe that was for the best. I couldn't talk to him now.

"Oh, hey, Kate." Colleen stopped short, peering at Bliz above the serious number of sour-cream-and-onion Tayto bags topping her haul. "Blizzie, who did your hair? And you're not wearing those striped shorts to the Little Miss Shamrock practice, are you? People will *see* you there, sweetie. You want to look extra-nice."

Bliz cocked her head. "Mommy said I looked fine."

"Maybe for a contest run-through, but not for Mass. Even on Sunday night. Really, Kate." Mom, just up from the basement, rushed to rescue the umbrella stand as it fell victim to Rover's sweeping tail.

"We'll be late," I protested.

Bliz hesitated in confusion.

"Kate and Maeve, you go ahead," Colleen said, adding Maeve's bags to her own. "There's plenty of time. I'll get Bliz changed real quick and drive her to church. That way I'll have time to do her hair, too."

"Fine," I muttered. I wanted to tell my sister that I'd decide for Bliz, thanks very much. But seeing Bliz's bewildered look—and my sister bite her lip at the sudden realization she might have overstepped—I changed my mind.

I grabbed my pocketbook from the bench near the stairs, and Maeve and I hit the Galway Court sidewalk on our own.

I was still silently fuming when I spotted Ian, a baseball cap pulled low over his face. Probably Frank's. My ex was just emerging from the garage, looking both ways first like a thief in the night. Or a murder suspect. He must have checked in with his fellow band members as soon as he got out of the Chief's van.

"Hey." He jogged down the driveway toward us. "Wait up."

Beside me, Maeve froze. "Do I have to do this?" she whispered, without moving her lips.

"It's OK, honey," I said. "Your dad is so excited to see you."

Ian stopped straight in front of us, an uncertain smile on his face. I gave him an encouraging nod as our daughter stared at the ground. "Hiya, Maeve. You're looking well. And shooting up, so you are. As tall as your mom." He leaned forward very slightly to give her a hug.

I gave Mave a tiny nudge, and she stepped toward her dad. He held her for the briefest minute, but I could tell it meant the world to him. And Maeve, too. Even if she refused to show it.

"I'm still mad at you," Maeve said.

"I know. I don't blame you," he said. "I'm sorry. I've had a lot going on, and I guess—"

She held up her hand. "I don't want to talk about it, OK? Maybe later."

"Where are you girls headed?" Ian raised an eyebrow at me.

"Mass," I said. "And so are you. Come on." I took him by the elbow and started walking. I caught Maeve's frown from the corner of my eye, but she followed, doubling her steps to catch up after a momentary pause.

"Kate, this is not a good idea," Ian said. "What if someone sees me?"

"Pull the ball cap lower," I said. He must have left his rocker jacket back in the garage.

"I haven't stepped in a church in ages."

Neither had I, to be honest. Back in the city, the girls usually went to a children's Mass on Saturday, and I said my silent prayers over coffee at a nearby bistro.

"Maybe you should," I told him lightly. Then I added in a low voice, "You don't have to go in. Just walk with us, for the love of Mike."

"Uh, sure." Ian glanced over his shoulder at our daughter and smiled. She returned a half-grimace.

"How did things go when you were out with my dad?" I asked.

Ian shrugged. "About as well as you'd expect, I guess. But like I said, he's a fair man. That head detective from the DA's office came to talk to me at the PD, though. I don't think she believed anything I told her."

"Detective Walker?" I asked. "Don't worry, she's like that with everyone." *Especially me.* "It's just her way. She's a good detective. So what did she say?"

"Nothing too good." Ian's lips set in a thin line as he ran his hand through his hair.

I knew better than to press right now. I'd find out more later, either from him or my dad.

The conversation died after that. Maybe asking Ian to join me and Maeve on the walk to church was a mistake. Another unfortunate impulse on my part.

Not exactly the first since I'd arrived in Shamrock.

But it wasn't like I could bring the note from my pocketbook to show him in front of Maeve. And we weren't getting any closer to a daughter-daddy reconciliation.

To make things worse, I could have sworn someone was following us as we walked. It had to be my imagination, but the feeling was so strong I glanced around us a couple of times. Nothing. I was just being paranoid.

Probably a Peat fan getting up the courage to ask for a selfie or Ian's autograph.

As we passed Farrell's at the corner, I could tell Ian was dying to take an Irish shortcut, as the locals called it. Even if the detour meant risking another fake-flirty encounter with Carmen. But he didn't.

"I wanted to tell you, we really need to talk later," I said when Maeve stopped for a moment to check something on her phone. "In private. It's important."

"About Fallon, right?" Ian squinted at me from under his visor.

"Sort of. It's a long story," I said. "And I don't have time to tell it right now."

Completely true, because we'd already arrived at Our Lady of Angels.

"OK," Ian said. "Back at the house, then."

I nodded. "It may not be til late, because tonight is pretty packed."

"Fair enough," he said.

"Well, we'll see you later, then," I said awkwardly as the three of us entered through the open gates of the parking lot and started across the blacktop toward the church's side door. Most people used the front steps to the main entrance, but I didn't want to run into anyone we knew. Or didn't know.

That went double for Ian, I was sure. Not because he was the lead guitarist and singer for an up-and-coming Irish rock band trying to stay under the radar. By now all of Shamrock probably knew his fiancée from Ireland had been murdered at the fairgrounds.

To my surprise, Ian accompanied us all the way to the door. He held it open for me and Maeve. "You're coming in?" I asked.

He nodded. "I am, yeah."

Maeve raised an eyebrow, but she seemed a tiny bit pleased.

Inside, the church seemed darker than usual, in contrast to the late afternoon sunshine. After I blinked once or twice I saw the pews were nearly empty. A thin turnout even for the last Mass of the weekend.

As we started down the pews toward the back of the church, I noticed the little red lights above the confessional doors. Oh. Mom was wrong. Mass was at five-thirty after all. We were half an hour early.

In the deep silence of the nave, a handful of souls waited for their turns to talk to the priest. In the shadows of the confessional box, identities hidden behind a screen, they'd declare their misdeeds. Then they'd be offered forgiveness by Father Declan and learn how many Our Fathers and Hail Marys they'd be required to say for their penance.

My hands felt sweaty, and not from the heat. I hadn't been to Confession in forever, but I had plenty of material for

Father Declan. Most recently, the sin of omission for not revealing the mysterious note currently burning up my pocketbook.

For the splittest of seconds, I glanced back at the neat little row of ornately carved confession boxes. The tiny shamrocks embedded in the mahogany jumped out at me accusingly, an unwelcome reminder of the bloodstained clover blossoms I'd seen this morning.

It had only been a matter of hours since then, but it already felt like an eternity.

What if Fallon's killer was kneeling before the screen right now behind one of those highly polished doors, confessing to their brutal crime? By the seal of the confessional and the State of Massachusetts, the priest could not divulge any confidential information he heard to authorities. Even for a murder investigation. He could only try to guide the guilty party toward giving themselves up.

That sounded like a plotline straight from one of Maeve's TV crime shows. But unfortunately for our local law enforcement, it worked that way in real life, too.

Maeve had already taken a seat in one of the back pews. After what must have been the briefest possible required prayer on the kneeler, she stared at the pale blue ceiling. Impassive painted angels floating among the fluffy white clouds stared back.

The service would start soon. All that gazing from the angels reminded me of the stained-glass St. Patrick from that church Airbnb. Where I'd found the creepy note.

It was now or never.

I stopped at the recessed area that held row upon row of flickering green votive candles.

"Kate?" Ian's voice was low.

"I need to show you something," I said.

As we left the semidarkness and stepped into the glowing recess, I felt rather than saw Ian's concerned gaze. "Kate, stop messing," he said. "Is it what you were talking about earlier?"

"Part of it," I said.

"All right, then." Ian looked over his shoulder. The church was getting more crowded now.

"Let's light some candles first," I said. Not to stall or anything. I needed to figure out what to say first. And I could use the strength from the rows of glowing votives.

Ian looked at me quizzically but nodded.

Our Lady of Angels was strictly old-school. No push-button candles here. My hand shook as I reached for a long matchstick from the little glass container beside the display. Ian did the same, and our hands briefly touched.

"Sorry." He fumbled in his front pocket for change and came up with nothing but two old Irish pennies. He shrugged and dropped them in the donation box. "My wallet is in my guitar case. Back in the garage."

"I've got cash." I reached into my pocketbook. "Go ahead and light a couple candles. For Fallon. One for me, one for you."

"Thanks." Ian carefully caught a flame from a nearby votive.

My hand closed on my wallet in its usual place, the inside pocket of my pocketbook. I'd carefully folded the note from Ian and Fallon's Airbnb right beside it when I got home from Farrell's. Much safer than my back pocket.

Except now the note was gone.

I felt a sudden rush of heat on my face, and not from the candles Ian had finished lighting. Had I misplaced the note somehow? How was that possible? I peered closer into my purse in the candle glow, rummaging all the way through it. Wallet, keys, mini brush, hand sanitizer. Travel-sized coconut sunblock, cinnamon TicTacs. A hair barrette of Bliz's. And a scrap of a torn Dunkin napkin.

No note.

"Kate, come on. What is it you're needing to tell me?" Ian whispered.

I snapped my pocketbook shut and slung the strap back on my shoulder. "This is the wrong place. We'll talk about it tonight, like we said. Light one more candle, OK?" I stuffed a fiver and two one-dollar bills in the donation box. "For the souls of all the deceased."

And the living, I added silently. In particular, him and me.

For once Ian's silence was a blessing. He knew I'd tell him when I was ready.

As soon as I found that note.

Maybe it had fallen out somewhere at the Buckley House. And hopefully no one would find it before I did. But I had Mass, dinner, and dance practice to get through first.

As Ian lit the candle, I offered one more prayer.

Chapter Eighteen

Mrs. Gogarty started revving up the opening hymn medley on the organ as Ian and I entered the pew our daughter had chosen. Maeve slid over, hastily returning her cell phone to the pocket of her denim skirt.

Ian skipped the kneeler and slouched beside her, removing his ball cap. He'd forgotten to do so when we'd first walked into the church. Like Maeve a few minutes earlier, he focused on the angelic ceiling mural. Appealing for an intercession with the Almighty, maybe.

Or, more likely, thinking of his fiancée and where she might be right now.

I couldn't help wondering that, too.

I knelt and quickly crossed myself. But instead of looking straight ahead at the altar my attention was caught by the round woman in the summer shawl exiting one of the confessionals.

Gabby, stopping in for Mass after work. And an anonymous conversation with Father Declan.

She entered a pew close to the confessionals and knelt to do her assigned penance.

The image I'd had earlier of Fallon's killer asking for forgiveness jumped back into my mind. I quickly batted it down.

Gabby was a talker, maybe, but such a sweet woman. My old boss, for heaven's sake. I hadn't really had a conversation with her in years, but she would never hurt anyone. Plus, she couldn't be in much better physical shape than Marty.

I did want to talk to Gabby more about Fallon and Athena, though. She had spoken with both women recently. And what was the connection between them and those ugly carved gnomes?

I wasn't sure where to put Athena on the suspect scale for Fallon's murder. What would be her motive? Fallon had wanted to buy her hideous art. That was a good thing, right? Athena should have been delighted.

I frowned to myself. What Athena didn't like—other than Mayor Flanagan, apparently—were trespassers near her studio. She'd made that perfectly clear to me and Garrett.

What was that top-secret project of hers, and how important could it be? Like me, Fallon must have cut through the woods between the fairgrounds and the field. That meant she would have passed the caretaker's cottage.

Was Athena's privacy worth her killing for? Had she picked up one of those sculptor's tools—that she'd later reported allegedly missing—and followed Fallon to the field in an angry rage?

That scenario seemed pretty farfetched to me. Bordering on ridiculous. But she'd had access to a possible weapon and proximity to the victim around the time of the murder.

Had she written that note, though? The last thing Athena would want was to meet anyone near her house. Hadn't she told Garrett and me to book an appointment with her assistant at the gallery?

Too bad I'd lost a major piece of evidence. I'd held it right in my hands and let it slip straight through my fingers, so to speak. Unless the note had fallen out of my pocketbook—highly unlikely with that inside pocket—someone had pinched it straight from my bag. But who?

As far as I knew, no one had any clue I had that note in my possession. The thief must have found it while snooping through my purse for something else. Money, I supposed. Or maybe they'd wanted some kind of info about me.

Well, good luck to anyone on that. Other than my New York State driver's license, the contents of my pocketbook pointed straight to Stressed-Out Mom.

I'd last seen the note in my purse when I paid the bill at Farrell's. I'd briefly left my pocketbook on the bench in the downstairs hallway at the Buckley House. And in the laundry room at some point, maybe. I could have left it locked in my room upstairs or, better yet, in the safe in my dad's office. I was a total idiot.

The Chief had been right about wanting to put in a security system. Mom, Colleen, and I hadn't taken it seriously enough.

As far as I knew, the only people in the B&B this afternoon—other than Buckleys—were the members of Peat and the Limerick Lads. Minus Noel. And Ian, of course.

I had to make things right, and fast. Or at least stop the situation from getting worse, if possible. But how?

I had jeopardized the entire investigation. Also my dad's sterling reputation among the Shamrock PD and the Staties alike.

I hadn't done Ian any favors, either. And I'd broken my promise to Fallon to help find her killer. What if I'd inadvertently let her murderer off scot-free?

I sat back from the kneeler just as the first altar girl, wearing jeans and sneakers under her robe and bearing a gold cross half as tall as she was, started up the center aisle of the church toward the altar. Everyone rose to greet the priest as Mrs. Gogarty frantically switched to the processional hymn.

I needed to check my purse for that note one more time. Maybe the lining of my pocketbook had ripped. I'd pretend I was looking for a tissue.

As I turned to scoop up my purse, I spotted a lone parishioner in the very last pew, staring straight at me as I stood next to Ian.

Garrett.

I threw him a quick church smile and left my pocketbook on the seat as I snapped back to face the altar beside my ex. The possible murder suspect.

Garrett had nodded, but there was no return smile. Not even a church one.

I sat when the rest of the sparse congregation sat, paying zero attention to the words of the Mass. I knew them all by heart anyway. Ian restlessly tapped his knees, as if playing that imaginary keyboard again. At one point he leaned toward Maeve and said something I didn't catch. I saw her mouth twitch very slightly, as if she were trying hard not to giggle.

Well, that was encouraging, at least.

To anyone around us, I'm sure I seemed entirely focused on the altar. But my mind kept recycling a seemingly endless loop of bad options. How would I tell Ian—and my dad—that I had somehow snagged and then *lost* a likely piece of evidence in Fallon's murder?

In a sudden rush of Innis-scented breeze, just as Father Declan launched into his homily, Colleen appeared at the end of our pew. My sister wore a swingy jersey dance dress with diagonal pink-and-white stripes. Her hair was pulled into a perfect bun with a matching pink-and-white ribbon tied around it. She had Bliz in tow—in the identical outfit and hairdo. One of those Mommy-and-me combo deals I always saw ads for while scrolling social media but never ordered.

Maybe I should have. Bliz was beaming. My heart gave a little squeeze.

"Sorry we're late," my sister whispered. She waved to an older woman with her grandchildren who had turned around disapprovingly—before realizing the Mass crasher was Colleen. The woman smiled and waved back. Bliz wiggled into the pew next to me.

"We were all ready to leave and then my same-day package arrived, so I thought Bliz and I should wear these dresses tonight." Colleen continued to whisper. "Cute, huh? Gotta go, so I can meet Bernie and get stuff set up for practice. See you there. I went to Mass with Mom this morning."

No chance to respond. My sister had already zipped back down the aisle and out through the propped-open front doors of Our Lady of Angels.

Bliz smoothed her new dress over her knees, still seeming pleased as punch. "Isn't my dress pretty?" she said to me. Then she leaned from her seat for Ian and Maeve for their approval.

My ex nodded, looking amused. And almost, for the briefest of moments, like the old Ian. Maeve smiled at her sister and placed a finger to her lips.

"You look very nice, sweetie." I took a tattered children's hymnal from the pew book holder and handed it to my younger daughter. "Now let's pay attention, OK? We're in church."

I guess the reminder wasn't just for Bliz. I didn't look upward, but I could feel those judgy angels smirking from the ceiling.

Chapter Nineteen

"I'm starving," Maeve said, as the girls and I stood outside the entrance of the Blarney Bowl. "What kind of bowls do they have? Like, Vietnamese? Poke? Ramen? Sushi?"

"Gram didn't say. But it's supposed to be good." I squinted at the trendy, retro-style sign above us. It looked vaguely familiar. "I can't believe you're hungry again, honey, after that late lunch at the Piggety Diner." I didn't have much appetite myself, even though I'd hardly eaten all day. My stomach was twisted in one big Celtic knot.

I had to admit I was relieved Ian had declined to join us for dinner. He'd headed back to the Buckley House to meet up with the band. And when I'd looked for Garrett after Mass let out, he'd disappeared. Didn't even say hello.

Bliz shaded her eyes as she peered into the window poster-painted with shamrocks. "Ooo! We can go bowling while we eat dinner."

Ohh. Actual *bowling* lanes. Now I knew where I'd seen that sign. It might be trendy now, but I remembered the original Blarney Bowl from when I was a kid, long before Shamrock turned green. My parents probably went on dates there in high school.

"We don't really have time to bowl tonight, sweetie," I said. "Mass started at five thirty, and we need to be at the Miss Shamrock practice soon. But we'll do it another day. You can ask the Murphy girls to go with us."

"OK," Bliz said as the three of us headed into the Blarney Bowl. "How about tomorrow?"

"Tomorrow is when the Miss Shamrock contest starts," Maeve said.

"We could go in the morning." Bliz pointed to the photo menu above the counter. "They have breakfast bowls, see?"

Maeve frowned. "A lot of oatmeal, with different add-ins. And . . . egg bowls."

"Look, there's one called Green Eggs and Ham. I'm never trying that, ever ever ever." Bliz collapsed in happy giggles.

"Katie Buckley!" the short, older man taking orders said. He wore a green Irish cap and bowling shirt under his striped apron. "You remember me, don't you?"

I did a double take. "Mr. Duffy!" I hadn't seen him for years, back when he worked at the Blarney Bowl in its original location off the Square. "How are you?"

"Wally, please," he said, holding up a hand. "And I'm keeping well. Just opened this place last month. Business is going gangbusters."

"Glad to hear that," I said. "Looks like a fun place." I introduced Maeve and Bliz to my old friend. "We're home for the summer." *Maybe longer,* I didn't add.

Wally beamed. "Nice to meet you, girls. What will you have?"

"I'll take the chicken and potato waffles with gravy bowl, please," Maeve said. "With the cheese add-in."

"Mommy, can I have the hot fudge and mint brownie bowl?" Bliz asked.

"How about a nice dinner instead?" I countered. "You need your strength for the Miss Shamrock practice."

"You're going to be in the contest this year, young lady?" Wally asked. "Another Buckley. Isn't that somethin'."

Bliz flashed her dimple. Not on purpose. It just came out whenever she smiled. "I'd like the barbecued hot dog bowl, then, please," she said. "With the brown sugar ketchup."

These were definitely not the kind of bowls we were used to in the city. I tried not to shudder at the nutritional content, but I didn't want to be a food snob. Or hurt Wally's feelings. "I'll have the bangers and broccoli bowl," I said. "And an extra-large Celtic coffee, please." I'd need it to get through what promised to be a very long evening.

"Excellent choice," Wally said, as a teenaged girl came up to the counter to take the next customer's order. Michi from Hogan's Hoagies, I realized. Maeve and I had met the blasé employee at the sandwich shop when we were in town last spring. She'd probably been fired for being on her phone all the time. This time I noticed that her cell was stuffed way down in the pocket of her khakis. Wally always kept a sharp eye on his employees.

When Wally returned with our bowls, Bliz put her hands on the counter and rested her chin. "Mr. Wally, do you have glow bowling here like in Brooklyn?"

"Just on weekends. Every color of the rainbow. We have a Win a Pot o' Gold contest on Friday nights."

Bliz's eyes widened. "Gold? Really?"

Wally chuckled. "Well, you can win gold token coins for a free game."

"Oh." My youngest looked disappointed. "And why is all the bowling stuff so little?"

I checked behind me to make sure we weren't holding up the line. Michi miraculously had things covered. "It's candlepin bowling," Wally explained. "But don't let the sizes fool you. It's just as hard as the tenpin. Ask your mom. She and that boy Garrett McGavin were pretty competitive back in their day."

I inwardly twinged at the mention of Garrett, who was probably not very happy with me right now.

"Who won?" Maeve asked.

"I did," I said quickly. "Well, most of the time."

"OK, Mom." Maeve rolled her eyes and walked away with her and Bliz's bowls to find us a table near the lanes. Bliz skipped along at her heels, then stopped to stare into a crane machine game with enticing green stuffie toys.

Wally winked. "Remember that time I caught you two trying to mess with the ball return?"

"It was stuck," I said. "We were, you know, helping."

"Pretty dangerous, back there behind the lanes." Wally shook his head. "Wonder what ever happened to that Garrett kid."

"He's a cop," I said, as I picked up my bowl to follow my daughters. "Right here in Shamrock."

Wally full-out laughed. "Yeah? Tell him to stop by, anytime. I'll give him bottomless coffee on the house. A cop, by golly. Who woulda thunk it?"

The girls polished off their salt-fat-and-sugar bowls before I did. As I picked at my broccoli, they threw a few free rounds of candlepin donated by a family that had to leave early. Bliz squealed in delight as her ball rolled down the lane, then gave a pouty twirl in frustration as it fell into the gutter.

"Like this, Blizzie." Maeve toed up like a pro, but she, too, threw a gutter ball. "Maybe we need the bumpers," she told her little sister with a sigh.

I set an alarm on my cell phone so we wouldn't be late for the practice. Then I sipped my thin coffee as I watched the local evening news. The clunky old TV above me on a rusty swing-arm mount had to be older than I was. Wally probably moved it from the original Blarney Bowl.

On the screen, Mitzi Dolan-Yung was her usual driven self. But she wasn't covering Fallon's murder right now.

Tonight Mitzi was conducting a bedside interview from Shamrock Hospital with the acclaimed sculptor Nick Sweeney. She perched on the seat of a black Colonial chair as she asked probing questions about his long career. Including the high honor of carving the famous annual butter sculpture for the Great Shamrock Fair.

Poor Nick, sporting extra stubble on his chin, was in some kind of brace from head to toe. He smiled for the camera, but it was obvious he couldn't move much. Eventually, Mitzi told us viewers, Nick would undergo a rigorous program of physical therapy. But fortunately, his daughter, Athena, would carry on the butter sculpture tradition for fair week.

I hadn't noticed Athena in the picture at first. She stood on the other side of the bed, arms crossed, near the drab, beige drapes.

"Athena, you must be thrilled to step in for your father on Shamrock's beloved butter sculpture," Mitzi said.

The sculptor stared back at her for a full second. "Yeah, it's a huge honor," she said. "Happy to do this for my dad." She reached toward the bed and patted his hand, giving him the first genuine smile I'd seen from her so far.

Once again, Athena wore a striking outfit. Not an off-season cape this time, but some kind of long black blouse with chiffon butterfly sleeves. Or maybe more like wasp sleeves. She'd also donned a 1930s-movie-usher cap that made her look like one of the Flying Monkeys in Oz.

Again I had to remind myself that I was the last person in Shamrock—maybe anywhere—qualified to critique anyone else's fashion choices.

"Athena, you're a rising star in your own right on the art scene," Mitzi said. "Would you like to tell our viewers a bit about your work?" Before Athena could open her mouth, the reporter motioned to the invisible control team back at the WSCK building. "Sam, can you give us some shots of Athena's most recent work?"

A photo featuring a group shot of the giant garden gnomes from Gifts of Gab's window display flashed on the screen. Just as hideous as in real life.

"So Athena, tell us about these unique sculptures. We understand they'll be auctioned off for charity on opening night at the Great Shamrock Fair."

"That's right," Athena said. "I—"

"And we've heard from Gabrielle Carroll, the owner of Gifts of Gab on Main Street, that there's a fabulous secret prize hidden inside one of these adorable Celtic gremlins. That will really up the ante for bidders, won't it?"

"Well, yes, and—" Athena tried.

"But there's one special thing our viewers are dying to know, Athena." Mitzi gave her television audience a dazzling smile. "Can you give us any hints about the top-secret theme of this year's butter sculpture?"

This time Athena was ready. "No."

"Oh, what a shame," Mitzi said, before smoothly finishing with, "Thank you, Athena Sweeney. And good luck with the butter sculpture to the daughter of Shamrock's very own, internationally acclaimed artist Nicholas Sweeney."

Yikes. Athena seemed even less pleased by the way she'd been abruptly signed off. The reporter was treating her like the opposite of a nepo baby.

The camera suddenly zoomed in on Mitzi. "So folks," the reporter said brightly, "remember to stop by Gifts of Gab to get an up close and personal look at just a few of this year's amazing auction items before the fair officially begins." In dizzying fashion, the camera panned back out to show the gnome photo as a full backdrop for an extra-tiny Mitzi. "Good luck to all you bidders out there. We can't wait to find out the secret surprise inside one of these whimsical pieces of art at the Great Shamrock Fair!"

Well, that was a mouthful. Luckily, Mitzi was a fast talker. "And now to our WSCK correspondent Imani Coby out at the fairgrounds," she said breathlessly. "Imani, what's the latest on the fair?"

Caught unaware by the camera, the on-scene reporter slipped the lipstick she'd been applying into her pocket and smiled. "Thank you, Mitzi. There's—"

"Any word on whether this year's Great Shamrock Fair might be canceled due to the suspicious death of Fallon O'Malley just outside the fairgrounds?" Mitzi broke in. She turned back to her audience. "As many of our viewers know, Ms. O'Malley was the manager of the popular Irish band Peat, and her death is now under investigation by the Shamrock PD in conjunction with the County District Attorney's office. The band was recently invited by Mayor Flanagan to perform at the fair. Ms. O'Malley, from Dublin, was also the fiancée of lead singer Ian Forde."

Side-by-side photos of Fallon and Ian flashed up on the screen.

And here we go. I glanced toward the bowling area. I hoped Maeve and Bliz weren't hearing this.

Luckily, my daughters were busy trying to arrange unwieldy bumpers into their lane and had no interest in the TV screens.

"Imani, what are you hearing about how this murder investigation might affect the fair?"

Unfortunately, the on-site reporter was also sidelined by the interruption treatment—from Mayor Flanagan. The town's most prolific politician appeared from nowhere and practically grabbed her microphone.

"Mitzi, I want to assure everyone out there that the Great Shamrock Fair is a go. One hundred percent on," the mayor said. "We have no plans to postpone or cancel any events, and certainly not the fair itself. So come one, come all to Shamrock this week and get your Irish on! Don't miss the exciting pre-fair events on Wednesday, when our two newly crowned Miss Shamrocks will help reveal this year's extra-spectacular butter sculpture." He winked. "Take it from me, folks—you're going to love this one!"

The WSCK live correspondent leaned back and brought the microphone closer to her again. "Thank you, Mr. Mayor." Then she turned to her left, where Shamrock's official chief of police, Bob Ryan, had been waiting for Mayor Flanagan to finish. Beside Chief Ryan stood Detective Captain Shirley Walker.

Surly Shirley wasn't exactly scowling. But she definitely looked as if she were itching to get back to work on the O'Malley investigation and away from annoying reporters.

I could understand that.

"Chief Ryan, can fairgoers feel safe attending the Great Shamrock Fair this year?" Imani asked. "What do you want to tell them?"

He glanced nervously back at the mayor, who nodded encouragingly. "The Shamrock PD, working in conjunction with the Cloverhill County DA's office, is making strong progress regarding the investigation into the death of Fallon O'Malley early this morning."

The chief's tone was as wooden as his posture. Beside him, Surly Shirley's expression dared anyone to ask another question.

I couldn't help but shiver. What if they knew someone out there had snatched up—and lost—a key piece of evidence for their investigation? A someone who happened to be related in multiple ways to local law enforcement?

The acid in my now-cold coffee wasn't the only reason I felt sick to my stomach.

Fortunately, my cell phone alarm cut short my thoughts. I caught the girls' attention and waved for them to finish up their round. From what I could tell, neither was ready to join the pro candlepin circuit, but they were laughing and having fun. On her last roll, Maeve tripped and fell on her butt. She sat on the polished floor for a second or two, covering her face in exaggerated embarrassment as Bliz tried to drag her up.

My smile at their antics quickly died. What would happen to all of our lives if I went to jail? And what kind of role model would I be for my daughters if they ever learned I'd tampered with possible evidence of a crime?

I wanted to head back to the Buckley House right now and turn the entire B&B upside down looking for that note. Just in case. Guests or no guests. But I couldn't let Bliz down. If anyone else found the note while we were at Little Miss Shamrock practice, well . . . I'd worry about that later.

Maybe they wouldn't connect the note to Fallon's murder at first, but it sure sounded ominous. And eventually the truth would come out.

I wished I'd never met Fallon O'Malley, to be honest. But I felt a responsibility to the dead young woman from Ireland, too. I renewed my resolve to help bring her killer to justice, even if I messed up along the way. And if Ian's name was cleared in the process, at least Maeve would know for sure her dad wasn't a cold-blooded murderer.

Maybe I needed to know that, too.

My hand shook as I put down my coffee cup. I needed to lay off the caffeine. "Let's go, girls!" I called. "I mean it!"

On to the next event in this crazy-awful day. And when I got a breather I'd move "quiet, safe environment" from the Shamrock side of my pro-and-con list to the Brooklyn column.

Chapter Twenty

As I'd expected, Angels Hall was once again a total zoo. After I'd dropped Bliz off with her group near the stage, I deposited myself on a metal folding chair in the back of the buzzing room. Now I finally had a chance to check that Miss Shamrock parents' email. Beside me, Maeve scrolled her phone as well.

First I had to text Siobhan to thank her again for her help with Rover. I also gave her a quickie update on everything else and promised to fill her in more later.

I didn't see the Murphy girls among Bliz's group. And my friend was nowhere in sight. I texted again.

@ Angels. You guys coming?

Siobhan replied instantly:

Nope. Too busy. Can't deal with LMS x 3, lol.

Paddy's Paws sponsoring Pet Pavilion @ fair. Just found out I'm also running it. Already signed Rover up. Sry gotta go.

I winced as I read that line about Rover. Another contest? For our dog? Nope nope nope.

"Hey Mom, why are they doing the Miss Shamrock practice here?" Maeve looked up from her phone. "I thought the contest was always outdoors. I remember we had our pictures taken at the gazebo on the Square."

I didn't want to worry my older daughter by telling her that the Miss Shamrock Committee—along with the PD and most of the parents—felt the parish hall would be safer for everyone. "You're right, honey," I said. "The final rounds are usually on the green if the weather is nice. I guess it was easier this year to have the practices and first rounds here. *Easier to secure.* They haven't decided for sure yet where the finals will be."

Or at all, I also declined to add. By Wednesday, the fair and all related events might be canceled. No matter what the mayor had said earlier today.

I'd noticed a few cops out in the parking lot, and another at the door. Considering that backstage at Angels Hall was where Colleen, Maeve, and I had found Deirdre's body, I hoped the extra security precautions would make a difference. In the meantime, here we were, trying our best to go on with life as usual.

Was that a good thing or a bad thing? Would people be safe at the fairgrounds this week, with a killer on the loose? I wasn't sure. Neither was the Shamrock PD, judging from Chief Ryan's awkward on-air performance.

Maybe none of us were safe anywhere in Shamrock.

I tuned back in to the practice. Bliz and the other younger girls were practicing walking across the stage as they were introduced. Then they stood on masking tape Xs to answer questions.

I couldn't remember much about the actual Miss Shamrock logistics. But from where I sat they didn't differ much from those in any other pageant-type event. Smile. Wave. Face the audience. Speak up into the microphone when asked a question.

"Did everyone bring their music, if you'll need it for the talent portion?" Colleen asked the girls. "Or are you using any props or presentation materials, like video? If so, please see Miss Moira after your group run-though is finished."

Moira waved from the side of the stage, looking entirely professional in a button-up blouse, long pencil skirt and big, green-framed glasses.

Music? Oh no. I'd been so distracted by the case that I hadn't even considered yet all the things Bliz would need. Or wear. The first rounds were tomorrow, for heaven's sake.

A tall girl with multiple braids pulled into one long pony raised her hand. "What about the essays?"

"The essays are for the final round only," Colleen said. "But you'll want to write them now, so you'll be ready just in case." She turned to address the parents watching from the seats. "Remember, each contestant writes her own essay. No helping."

Uh-oh. Bliz wasn't always a speed demon in completing any kind of homework, unless it involved art of some kind. She'd need to get started on the essay tonight, if she wasn't too exhausted when we got home. Or tomorrow morning, at the very latest.

"Colleen, don't forget the dresses." I could hear Moira's stage-whispered reminder all the way from the back.

Colleen nodded and addressed the audience again. "So this info is also in the email you should have gotten, but we've had a lot of questions about what the contestants should wear, and when."

I squeezed my eyes shut. Did we need to make some kind of costume, too? Wouldn't Colleen have mentioned it to me? I braced myself for the worst.

"Contestants can wear outfits of their choice for the initial round," my sister announced. "Whatever they're comfortable in. It doesn't have to be fancy. At the end of practice tonight, each girl will be given a small tiara and a blank sash that they can decorate at home. You know, with their first name in glitter or buttons or google eyes or whatever they want. Final round contestants will be asked to wear dresses, though. Ankle length if possible. The final round dresses are usually more on the formal side."

Murmurs ran through the room. I distinctly heard "Seriously?" and "No way" more than a few times.

"Formal dresses, especially for the older girls, are traditional for the Miss Shamrock contest," Colleen said. "But again, not a requirement. No contestant will be penalized for their outfit. It's all about poise and presentation, no matter what you're wearing. We've had plenty of past winners crowned in their Irish dance dresses."

Moira stepped forward, pushing up her glasses. "Also, we do have an entire collection of donated and gently used dresses downstairs in the costume room, which will be open directly following the practice tonight. After each group finishes, the girls can check out the available dresses."

"Wow, that's great, Moira. Thank you. And don't be piggies, ladies," Colleen said. "You may try on one dress at a time. That way everyone gets a chance to choose something special."

Moira nodded. "For any girls, parents or guardians who don't sew, free tailoring will be offered by volunteers from the Rosary Society," she said. "See or email me as soon as possible for that. Most importantly, contestants who need help with costs in any way related to the Miss Shamrock contests can contact Bernie Donnelly or Theresa Meaney, our new coadministrator of the Deirdre Donnelly Scholarship Fund."

Moira pointed toward the piano, where a large older woman in leopard print leggings and a black sweatshirt—emblazoned by a shamrock-surrounded skull—waved. "That's Theresa right there."

My head spun. This Miss Shamrock deal was a nightmare, on top of everything else going on. I tried to imagine where Bliz's First Communion afterparty dress might be in the basement at the Buckley House. Did it still fit?

Probably not. But Bliz had other nice clothes, for heaven's sake. We could wait to see if she made the final round before we bought anything new.

"So thank you again to Moira McShane Kelly, for stepping up and getting us organized," Colleen said. "And to all of our amazing volunteers. Let's give them a big hand!"

I clapped with the rest of the audience. Moira was doing a good job on the Miss Shamrock PR too. Signs were already popping up around town. And she seemed genuinely happy up there on the stage, soaking up the appreciation.

Maybe it was all she'd ever wanted. To be noticed in a good way, not a bad one.

Maeve frowned at her phone. "Mom, they're saying Dad might have killed Fallon," she whispered. "That's crazy."

"Who's they?" I leaned over to look at her screen.

"Just . . . everyone," she said. "It's all over social media. That's so unfair. They don't even know Dad. He'd never hurt anyone."

"You can't pay attention to what people say online, honey," I said. "You know that."

Maeve sighed. "Yeah. But it's hard not to see the bad stuff." She scrolled down further. "WSCK says the cops found a bunch of knives in the woods near the fairgrounds. One of them might be the murder weapon, but they won't know for a while."

I sat up straight. "Can I read that article?" When Maeve handed me her phone, I scrolled the lines quickly. Yes. A collection of sharp implements had been discovered by investigators wrapped in a cloth bag.

They had to be Athena's missing sculpting tools.

If one of them turned out to be the knife Fallon's killer had used, would Athena replace Ian as the main person of interest? Now I really wanted to get home to talk to Dad.

Fortunately, the Miss Shamrock practice for the younger girls ended on time at seven thirty. Bliz was disappointed she didn't get to go down with the girls from her group to look at the dresses.

"Honey, you already have a lovely party dress at home," I said, as we headed toward the door. "And if you make the final round and we can't find it in time, we'll go shopping. Let's save those other dresses for girls who might really need them."

Bliz's tiny pout disappeared. "OK, Mommy," she said. "I didn't mean to be a piggy, like Aunt Colleen said. I just wanted to see the costume closet and play dress up."

Maeve reached down to give her little sister a squeeze. "Tell you what, Blizzie. How about if we look for your First Communion party dress downstairs tonight? And I'll help you dress up Ciara before bed. We'll find a really cool outfit for her."

Bliz immediately pulled the fashion doll from the dance bag Colleen had brought to Angels Hall for her and held it out to Maeve. "Ciara's all ready."

Just then, Lulu Cavanagh-Barry stepped through the door with Cassandra. The teen kept her eyes down as we passed, but Lulu gave a friendly wave. "Hello and *slán*," she said to me as she passed.

Talk to you later.

Was that a good thing or a bad thing? I wondered as the girls and I stepped out into the warm summer night. On the grand scale of things I had to deal with right now, speaking with Lulu was on the lower disaster end.

"Is that Zoe coming up the sidewalk?" I asked Maeve as we crossed the parking lot. "I thought she wasn't entering the Miss Shamrock contest."

"Yeah, she hates the whole idea," Maeve said. "But everyone started saying Cassandra was going to win because she's from Ireland. That made Zoe really mad."

"Ah," I said. "It's not supposed to work that way."

"It's the dumbest contest ever."

"You and Zoe are entitled to your opinions, honey," I said. "But don't let your Aunt Colleen hear that. Or your little sister, OK?" Bliz was skipping ahead, happily flying Ciara like an airplane. But silently I had to agree with my older daughter.

* * *

When Maeve, Bliz, and I reached the Buckley House, I saw a familiar car parked a few houses up the street. "You girls go in and say hi to Gram," I said. "I'll be right there."

I continued down the sidewalk and rapped on the passenger side window. Garrett put down the window and leaned across the seat. He must have seen me approach. What was he doing parked so far from our house?

"Hey," I said. "What are you up to out here? Are you coming in?"

"Actually, no," Garrett said. "I'm working."

"In your own car?" I said, puzzled.

"Yup." He gestured toward the seat at a takeout bag from Charlie O'Chix. Grease was starting to collect at the bottom. "Just eating my dinner."

"I see that," I said. "Looks, uh, yummy. Garrett, are you mad about something?"

"Nope." He reached into the bag and pulled up a fry. "I'm not. Really."

"Well, you seem ticked off. You're acting kind of weird. If it's because I was with Ian at church, I—"

"Katie," he broke in. "I'm not mad at you. I promise."

"Colleen and I are going down to the Barleycorn tonight with the Chief to see the Limerick Lads," I said. "Do you want to meet us there when you're off work? The show is supposed to start at nine, but Irish time. Irish *band* time."

"Sorry," Garrett said, his mouth full of fries. He reached into the glove compartment for a handful of napkins. "I probably won't finish until pretty late."

"Oh. Well, OK. Talk to you later?"

Garrett nodded. "See you, Kate." He waved and put up the window.

Dismissed. He was mad, no matter what he said. What was he doing here on our street? Making some kind of point?

But really, how was I supposed to act as far as Ian was concerned?

Garrett had never been the jealous type. He knew Ian and I were completely done. But obviously something was really irking him.

Unfortunately, there wasn't much I could do about it at the moment. I had other things I had to deal with right now. I walked back to the Buckley House feeling completely out of sorts.

I freshened up and changed, then headed back downstairs to make sure the girls were set for the evening. Between having the hard conversation with Ian and the Chief and—if all went well—accompanying my dad to the Barleycorn later, I probably wouldn't be around to say good night.

Bliz and Maeve were in the kitchen helping Mom with her pies for the fair. Strawberries, blueberries, raspberries, sugar, and flour were strewn all over the kitchen. Bliz looked as if she'd been eating more berries than she was stirring in a large green bowl with a huge pile of sugar. Mom was showing Maeve how to trim dough.

"Quite an operation here," I said, as I took in the scene. The cleanup job alone might take days. "Mom, are you entering any of these in the pie judging? Or are they being auctioned off?"

"No contests." Mom wiped her hands on a flour sack towel. Her apron said, *When Irish Eyes are Smiling, They're Probably Up to Something.* "They'll be on the refreshment table for the butter sculpture unveiling, sold per slice."

"Did anyone feed Rover his dinner yet?" I asked, looking at my daughters.

"Nooooo," Maeve said, biting her lip.

"I'll get it for him." Bliz dropped her berry-streaked wooden spoon on the tablecloth and started toward the pantry, apron strings trailing behind her with more berries.

"That's OK," I said quickly. "I'll do it, sweetie. You two help Gram."

I turned my daughter around in the other direction and made my way to the laundry room. Rover looked up from his snooze on his towel bed and thumped his tail on the linoleum. But he didn't jump up when I opened the container of kibble. I soon realized why.

The floor near the plastic tub was littered with little scraps of waxed paper. One of them was printed with the hot pink and orange logo of a popular New England donut chain. Well, the remnants of a logo.

I sighed. What a mess. Could this day get any worse?

"Rover, did you eat any of those Munchkins?" Super-fried-and-sugared donut holes couldn't be good for him. "You must have a tummy ache, you naughty doggy. Where did you get them?"

Ohh. On our long drive to Shamrock from the city yesterday, the girls and I had stopped at a Dunkin Donuts. Me for iced coffee, Maeve for some scary pink energy drink, and Bliz for . . . Munchkins. She couldn't finish the little packet of four donut holes. I'd left the last one in its wax envelope, wrapped it in a napkin, and stuffed it in the inside pocket of my purse for later.

Except for her one rejected request for Rover upon his arrival, Bliz had forgotten about the leftover Munchkin. So had I. Even after I stuck the folded note from Fallon and Ian's Airbnb in the same pocket of my purse. I'd been focused on the fact that the note would be safe next to my wallet.

Rover watched from his towel as I searched around the laundry room floor on my hands and knees, picking up scraps of torn paper. How could there be so many from one little envelope? Then I realized that the crumpled pieces weren't all wax. Some of them were regular paper.

When I had gathered all the pieces I could, I sat cross-legged on the floor and sorted the pieces into wax and not-wax. Some of the regular scraps were plain white, but others had black markings on them. Letters.

Uh-oh. Heart pounding, I smoothed them out.

Some of the letters were blurry due to gross doggy saliva. But they definitely created words. One said "truth." Another piece held two words: "Just you."

The same note. My eyes filled with tears of joy. It would have to be put back together, and it wouldn't be exactly the same, but hopefully it would somehow help clear Ian in his fiancée's murder.

And maybe my dad and the investigators wouldn't be angry. Well, not *as* angry.

And I wouldn't go to jail.

I collapsed on my back in relief against the cool floor and stayed there without moving for at a minute or two. Eventually Rover lumbered over and tried to lick my face, which got me up in a hurry.

I hugged his big furry neck. "You are such a Buckley, you crazy dog," I told him. "You and I really messed up. But everything's going to turn out just fine."

Hopefully.

Chapter Twenty-One

Leaving Rover on his disheveled towel bed with an extra pat on the head, I texted my dad and Ian a heads-up. Then I headed straight to the Chief's office. I knocked at the closed door before I could lose my nerve.

"Come in," he called.

My dad sat behind his massive mahogany desk, a fan blowing behind him. Ian was already slumped in one of the leather visitor chairs. Both of them looked tired after a long afternoon of chatting. With each other. And the investigators.

I wish I knew exactly how things had gone. My dad would never tell me. I could get the story out of Ian later. Or at least part of it. Maybe.

I barely glanced at my ex as I took my seat in the other chair beside him. Probably easier that way.

In the short time it had taken me to make my way from the laundry room to the Chief's office, I had made my decision. I would give Ian and my dad the note at the same time. As is.

That meant Ian wouldn't have the chance to explain himself to me first. And no buying time to get his story straight before we told my dad. But this was the way it had to be.

If Ian was innocent, it wouldn't matter.

I had definitely learned my lesson. Jeopardizing an entire murder investigation by removing potential evidence from a secondary crime scene was a flirtation with disaster. And even a possible ticket straight to jail. I couldn't undo my actions. But there was no way I'd risk adding yet another layer of deceit.

Everything might turn on that note. If Ian wasn't Fallon's killer, which I believed with all my heart, then it wouldn't hurt his plea of innocence. If he was guilty, I'd have to let the chips—or scraps of paper—fall where they may. It was a defense attorney's job to make Ian's case in a court of law. Not mine.

Taking a deep breath, I reached into my pocketbook and closed my hand over the baggie I'd grabbed from the dispenser in the pantry. Then I leaned forward and carefully shook the contents out over the Chief's desk.

From the corner of my eye, I caught Ian's puzzled expression. He sighed very softly.

I'd betrayed him.

My dad frowned at the collection of paper scraps piled in front of him. "What in blazes are these?"

I gave him and Ian the nickel version of my story. The less I said, the better. At least to start, because the Chief would begin firing questions in three, two, one . . .

"Let me get this straight, Kathleen," he said. "You just happened to find these on the floor in Ian's hotel?"

"Well, yes." I cleared my throat. "But they were all one page at the time, crumpled into a ball. I thought it was a piece of trash."

The Chief selected a pencil from his leather desk organizer and twirled it upside down. Then he started pushing the scraps of paper into place with the eraser end. "So you removed this note from the premises why?"

"Um . . ." Even I didn't really know the answer to that. "The whole place just looked really clean, so I thought it was trash. I picked it up to throw in a bin somewhere. But I didn't see one, and then I read the note, and it sounded like it might be important. Ian was in the other room, and we were rushing to meet you, so I tossed it in my pocketbook to ask him about later. And give to you."

My explanation sounded lame. Even to me. I plunged ahead anyway. "I didn't forget about the note, exactly. I was going to tell you both, but I wanted Ian to have a chance to explain first. And then with Carmel hovering around at Farrell's and you two away all afternoon and so many things going on later, I just didn't have a chance. There were always so many other people around. And tonight after I got home with the girls from the Miss Shamrock practice I realized Rover had gone after the donut hole in my purse and—"

"The dog further compromised the evidence, then?" My dad quirked one brow.

"Pretty much, yes. But on the bright side, he didn't swallow any of the pieces, at least," I tried.

Now I'd sold out poor Rover.

Was the Chief buying my explanation? Hard to tell. He put the last of the scraps into place with the eraser. "Son, come on over here behind the desk," he said to Ian. "I need your help with this."

Ian threw me another look that said I'd thrown him under a bus. But he rose and went to stand beside my dad.

The Chief tapped the desk next to the completed note puzzle. "Some of these letters are a little blurry. My eyesight isn't the best, so maybe you could read this aloud for us?"

Ian read the note, his Irish accent a touch stronger than usual. All the words I remembered were there.

My dad leaned back in his wheelchair. "Were you the recipient of this note, son?"

Ian shook his head. "No sir."

"But you'd read it before just now, I take it."

"I had." Ian's voice was barely audible. "This morning."

"You didn't mention that when we met with the detectives."

"No."

"Why not?" I said. "It could help prove Fallon was with someone else this morning, too. And it explains why she was in the middle of a field at the crack of dawn. It might even lead us to the murderer."

My dad didn't correct me on the "us."

Ian stood there for a long moment or two. Finally, he shook his head. "I-I can't tell you why I didn't bring up the note. I'm not in my right mind today, I reckon."

The Chief waved him back to his seat. "Do you know when Fallon received that note? Did she mention any kind of appointment to you for this morning?"

"No. And no." Ian flushed. "I, em, found the note inside her day planner. After she left the apartment this morning."

"Was the six thirty appointment noted in the planner as well?"

"Not that I saw."

"And you haven't a clue who might have written the message." The Chief was doing the steeple thing with his fingers. "Think harder, lad. There's not a single soul who might have wanted to harm your fiancée?"

Ian shook his head. "I can't think of anyone, I swear. The note must have freaked Fallon out, but she went to meet the person anyway. That's why I followed her out to the fairgrounds this morning."

"What about her family back home?" I asked. "Any big disagreements? Like, over money or something? Or they just didn't get along?"

"Nothing that I know of," Ian said. "Fallon didn't talk about her family much. She had a mum and a sister. I don't think they were close. I've never even met them."

"We've notified them," the Chief said to me. "They were shocked and upset, of course They hadn't even been aware Fallon was here in the States. Couldn't give us much in the leads department. The mother is hard of hearing. We mostly spoke with Fallon's sister, who lives with her."

"The truth of it is, Fallon kept a lot of things to herself," Ian said. "Fallon was just like that. I'm not sure she had any real enemies. Not many friends, either. She never introduced me to anyone."

"Really?" I said.

"She had loads of business connections," Ian said. "That was it."

I hesitated. "No, um . . . old boyfriends or anything?" Fallon was smart, gorgeous, and successful. She'd had a serious relationship with Ian. There had to have been others before him.

"Don't really know. Maybe." Ian's face was unreadable. Was he lying? And if so, why?

"She was always out and about," my ex went on. "Working, like. Doing stuff for the band." He sighed. "I hardly saw her myself."

Well, I could believe that. My ex had never been particularly clingy. I'd chalked it up to an independent streak and his passion for music. It sounded as if Fallon had been the same way, except her passion was work. Maybe that was what he and Fallon had shared most in common. A drive toward their own separate but related goals.

Ian and I had lived parallel lives, too. Him with his music, me with the girls and family stuff. Our relationship had worked for a while. Until it didn't.

"Ian, why did you check Fallon's planner in the first place?" I asked. "What were you looking for?"

He shrugged. "One of her meetings from last week. A work deal. She told me and the band about it at the pub."

Something in his tone sounded off. "You mean, when Fallon went to meet with Johnny Myer in New York?" I asked.

He frowned. "How did you know about that?"

"Oh, just talk, I guess." I gave a little shrug, not wanting to rat Macker out.

"Who is this Johnny Myer fella?" The Chief had visibly perked up in his chair.

"Some big music executive." I turned back to Ian. "Right?" He nodded.

Now my dad's eyes literally gleamed. "Ah. I see. Fallon was steppin' out on you, was she, son? Kate, why don't you leave us alone for a bit so Ian and I can have more of a chat?"

"No! She wasn't stepping out, or whatever you want to call it. It wasn't like that. Would you ever both stop?" Ian threw up his hands. "Fallon wasn't seeing yer man. Not that way. She didn't even know him before a couple of days ago."

Whoa. I hadn't expected this sudden burst of energy from my ex. Judging from my dad's expression, he hadn't, either.

Ian sure seemed touchy about the idea of Fallon having an affair with Johnny Myer. Even if he insisted it wasn't true.

"Sorry." Ian looked away, nervously clenching and unclenching his fists. Weirdly, his gaze seemed fixed on a framed '90s-era photo of my dad with Marty and the original Limerick Lads. It had been taken at the famous Forty Foot on the tip of Dublin Bay. The popular swimming spot was as chilly as it was rocky, but the men seemed to be having a grand time in the pouring rain.

"Whatever Fallon was doing with Johnny Myer," my ex went on more quietly, "it was nothing personal. Just business. And, well, the band wasn't too happy about it when they found out."

"Including you, I take it?" the Chief said.

Ian shrugged. "Musicians and managers disagree all the time. It's part of the gig. No one gets murdered because they have different opinions."

Not true. My brain immediately clicked through a checklist of past music biz headlines proving otherwise. But it wasn't worth pointing out.

"Let's start over, son," the Chief said. "Walk us through exactly what happened today from the minute you woke up. The full story. Not the bollocks you gave the detectives this afternoon at the PD." My dad's words were carefully measured as he tapped with the pencil again. "Get it right this time."

"Right. Sorry." Ian visibly tried to gather his composure. "It was a late night, and I felt groggy this morning. I went into the kitchen for some water. Fallon was just leaving to do her running. All I saw was the door closing behind her. I don't think she noticed I was there." He looked at the floor. "I never said goodbye."

Well, that was sad. Had Fallon and Ian made up their differences from the pub? That wasn't any of my business, really. But if not, he had to feel even worse about her untimely passing.

"Anyway, I went back to the bedroom for a bit of a lie-in. I still had time before I needed to be at the fairgrounds for the stage setup. But I couldn't go back to sleep. I kept thinking about that deal with Johnny Myer Fallon told us about last night. Like, maybe she had actually spoken with him earlier than when she met him in New York or some such." He looked at the Chief. "About business."

My dad nodded. "Go on."

"So after I took a shower, I checked her day planner on the desk in the bedroom. That's when I found that note inside, and it freaked me out. I had no clue what it meant. Especially, you know, the part about 'the truth.' I didn't like the sound of it, or the idea of Fallon meeting whoever it was on her own. I decided I'd try to catch up with her. I threw on some clothes and took a green cab to the fairgrounds. Well, the field next to it."

"Did you get a receipt?" my dad asked.

"Em, no. But the driver will remember me. I told him to drive fast. He did."

"What did you do with the note?" I asked.

"Crumpled it up and stuffed it in my jacket pocket on my way out the door." He sighed. "The cab dropped me at the stone wall. I checked the whole field." He looked at the carpet. "Obviously, I was too late."

"The note said for Fallon to come alone," I said. "Do you think anyone saw you?"

"Dunno. I wasn't concerned about that at the time. If they did see the cab—or me—it was after, well . . . it happened."

"What time did you leave the field?" the Chief asked.

"Not long after I found Fallon. About half-seven, I reckon. I started jogging back along the wall. Past the fairgrounds a bit."

My dad frowned. "Why didn't you alert anyone at the fairgrounds?"

"I—I don't know. I just wanted to get away from there. I was half-blind."

"Is there anything else you can tell us? Anything you remember?" the Chief pressed.

Ian didn't answer. He was hunched over now, shading his eyes with one hand. But I saw his shoulders shake, however slightly.

My ex was crying.

I reached out to pat his back, feeling helpless. Nothing I could say would make things better. His fiancée was dead.

I looked at my dad. We weren't likely to get much more information out of Ian right now. It seemed wrong to try, even though Fallon's killer was out there in the wind somewhere.

"All right, son," the Chief said, his tone gentler than it had been all day. "You need to get some rest so you can think straight. I'll make a few calls, and we'll talk again tomorrow, shall we?" He paused. "Kate and I are headed to hear the Limerick Lads in town tonight. You're welcome to join us, if you'd like some company."

"Thanks, I might," Ian said. That meant no. "We may have a band practice. And I have a couple of things to take care of as well."

A band practice? Tonight? Didn't he want to take some time on his own to grieve Fallon? Maybe he wanted to distract himself, as the Chief had suggested with the Barleycorn excursion. But still.

My ex stood up from his chair, looking shaky. "Appreciate your help, sir. And Kate." He gave me the briefest flash of a smile.

I watched him go with a lump in my throat. He looked smaller, somehow.

My dad and I sat together in silence for a moment or two as the summer twilight continued to fall outside the window. "So what do you think, Dad?" I asked finally. "How bad is it for Ian?"

"Hard to tell," he said. "Yer man has a long road ahead."

"But besides this note"—I gestured toward the desk—"the detectives found a possible murder weapon. That might point to someone else as the murderer, right?"

My dad raised one brow. "How do you know that?"

So he'd been holding out on me.

"Maeve saw the news on her phone," I said.

The Chief shrugged. "We'll see what the ME's initial report says. And what else Forensics turns up. The results may take a while."

"But that was Athena Sweeney's bag of tools they found, right? Won't the investigators look at her now? I mean, she told Garrett and me they'd been stolen, but still—"

"Ms. Sweeney was seen in the vicinity of the butter sculpture building within the likely time frame of the murder," the Chief broke in. "By workers camping at the fairgrounds." He, too, pointed to the desk. "And if this note was sent by the killer, it further confirms the time frame."

"Well, doesn't that vicinity include Athena's studio, where the knives allegedly came from?" I said. "Plus the butter sculpture building is at the edge of the fairgrounds, nearest to the actual crime scene. Other than the caretaker's cottage."

"OK. Motive?"

My dad had me stumped there. "Not sure yet," I said. "But Athena definitely doesn't appreciate trespassers on her property. She made that clear to me and Garrett. And she's not the nicest person in general, to be honest."

Neither was Fallon.

The Chief turned back to the jigsaw message on his desk and pointed to the piece that contained the words "half 6."

Americans didn't often say "half six." Brits did. Along with people from countries like Australia, New Zealand, and parts of Canada.

And Ireland.

"Athena studied in Europe," I tried.

The Chief gave a small chuckle. Well, maybe he wasn't impressed with my reasoning, but I didn't give up that easily. I could totally see Athena adopting the non-American way of telling time. To add a dash of flair to her artistic persona, maybe. Like the cape.

I didn't want to bring up Marty, but I had no choice. "Dad, there might be someone else, too." I mentioned how his old friend had freaked out when he saw Fallon when she visited the Buckley House. And I told him about the literal blood on Marty's hands this morning.

My dad didn't respond right away. He just frowned at me.

I brushed at an invisible piece of lint on my dress. "I mean, Marty obviously hated Fallon," I said. "He called her 'the divil,' for heaven's sake. Did he ever tell you he couldn't stand her? And why?"

The Chief waved. "Marty overreacts sometimes. Always has. There are a lot of people he doesn't particularly care for. He's famous for holding a grudge."

"What about his bloody hand? I mean, he said he fell, but . . ."

My dad sighed. "Marty isn't in the shape he used to be. Doubt he'd be able to hold his own in a fight."

"Even if he had a knife?"

"It seems the victim put up a struggle," the Chief said. "Investigators noted defensive wounds at the scene. By the location of the most devastating thrust of the knife, the ME thinks she and the killer may have been of similar height."

"Ian's not short," I pointed out. "Athena isn't, either. But . . ." I hesitated. "Marty is."

"It wasn't an official finding," the Chief said. "The ME is still working. She's not entirely sure yet."

"Oh." Now I felt completely frustrated. So far, nothing about this case made any sense. My dad agreed, I could tell. He was frowning a little behind his eyes.

At least he was sharing info with me this time.

"What about Fallon's engagement ring?" I remembered suddenly. "Did the CSI team find it?"

"No."

"So the murder could still be related to a robbery."

"Possibly. But the note you found appears to make that less likely."

"What about Fallon's phone?" I pressed. "There must be something useful on it."

"Haven't been able to access it yet."

I slumped back in my seat as the Chief took a photo of the message with his own phone. This was probably the worst time to bring it up, but I had to ask. "Dad, about that note. I'm—"

He cut me off with a raised hand. "That's enough, Katie Margaret. You go see to the girls and get yourself ready to go out. I have calls to make. Run along, now."

I wasn't about to argue. I'd take the dismissal. It even sounded as if I might be off the hook for the whole note disaster. At least for now. Katie Margaret was a good sign. I jumped up to leave.

"Oh, and one more thing," the Chief said. "Detective Captain Walker will be out to the house in the morning at oh-eight-hundred. She has a few questions for you."

Chapter Twenty-Two

It didn't take long for me to get ready for my night out with Dad and Colleen. I already had my makeup on from church—including plenty of concealer for the growing black circles under my eyes—and my hair looked halfway decent for once. The Barleycorn had an outdoor patio, so I grabbed a thin black cardigan to go with my black sleeveless top and short, straight black skirt.

Not the most exciting outfit, I had to admit as I stepped into my black sandals. But it was a casual deal. We were going to hear the Limerick Lads. The evening would be social, of course, but I hoped to somehow gather intel for the case.

I had no doubt my dad was looking forward to the same.

Colleen passed me on the stairs, on her way to take a quick shower after the Miss Shamrock practice. "This week is insane," she called over her shoulder. "I can't catch a break." She paused to lean over the landing. "Bliz was adorable, by the way. Everyone loved her. She's a shoo-in for the finals, I think."

"She must be thrilled," I said, trying to sound genuinely enthusiastic. I still didn't feel comfortable about the whole contest thing. Years ago, when Maeve was involved in the festivities, I hadn't given a second thought to any possible downsides. It was just something girls *did* in Shamrock. A town and family tradition, all in good fun.

But everything felt different to me this year. What would my daughter—and all the girls—be judged on, exactly? And why did the kids need to be judged at all?

Maybe I was feeling particularly down on the Little Miss Shamrock contest this year because it was Colleen's thing. And Bliz, my sister's mini-me, was thrilled to follow in her footsteps.

But I couldn't stand in my younger daughter's way. Or Colleen's. The two of them were over the moon with excitement just talking about the contest. But what if Bliz didn't win? How would she feel if she was the only Buckley girl in recent memory not to wear a Little Miss Shamrock crown?

I'd never won, of course. I'd never even participated. A shy kid outside of my family, I'd been so nervous about the idea of throwing a tiara into the Little Miss Shamrock ring that I'd barricaded myself in the Nest and refused to come out. I think maybe my dad was a teensy bit disappointed. But Mom put her foot down and that was that. No tiara. The same thing happened a few years later when the prospect of the older girls' contest loomed.

Fortunately, when Colleen came along, her enthusiasm for pageantry more than made up for my semi-failure. And Maeve, with zero pressure from me either way, had agreed to participate in Little Miss Shamrock all on her own. It was the same year Colleen competed in the teen contest, so Maeve had a built-in support system. Plus my sister bribed her with plenty of ice cream.

Lost in my thoughts, I almost didn't see Lulu Cavanagh-Barry sitting on the hallway bench near the bottom of the stairs. The woman looked a little forlorn, all by herself with a bunch of bags beside her and Cassandra's dance bag at her feet.

"Oh, hi, Lulu," I said. "How did Cassandra's Miss Shamrock practice go?"

"Very well, thank you. I think I'm more knackered than she is." Lulu sighed. "She did seem to get on nicely with the other girls."

"That's wonderful," I said. "Making new friends is the best part of the contest."

As the words came out of my mouth, I realized they were true. I never really considered the positive aspects of Little Miss Shamrock. Bliz was still new in town. And she loved her new friends from Irish dance, like the Murphy girls. She was sure to make even more friends through the contest. And with school starting in just two months here in Shamrock, it would be nice for her to see friendly faces. *If* we decided to stay.

I couldn't think about that whole question right now. I had enough on my plate.

"Where is Cassandra now?" I asked Lulu.

"Eating sweets in there with your girls, can you believe it?" She nodded toward the kitchen. "Brownies, I believe. I try to see to it that Cassandra follows a strictly healthy diet. But all that sugar, and with such a big day coming up tomorrow . . ." Her forehead crinkled.

I had to feel sorry for her. Finally, I'd met someone who worried as much as I did. Possibly even more. It was our superpower. Which of us was worse? Hard to tell.

"Don't worry, Lulu," I said. "Our daughters will be just fine. And so will we moms. I promise."

"You're very kind," Lulu said.

I looked back through the kitchen doorway and grinned. "I'll snag us each a brownie."

* * *

"Gosh, where is everybody?" Colleen asked, as we waited for the hostess at the stone wall outside the Barleycorn patio. It looked especially festive tonight, dotted with green-and-white striped umbrellas set over glass-topped tables on the flagstone porch. The entire outdoor space was strung with little green shamrock lights.

I could smell the fresh wood from the newly constructed performance platform at the far end of the patio. A set of navy curtains stretched across the stage, with a navy and gold striped awning above it to protect the performers from any unexpected weather. The audience was out of luck, I guess.

My sister was right. The patio wasn't exactly crowded. Especially for a Limerick Lads appearance during fair week. Ordinarily an event like this would be a huge draw for tourists and locals alike. The Lads were at their best in informal settings, in my opinion. Especially impromptu sessions in pubs, when they invited local musicians to join them, and even those spontaneous jams in the Buckley House living room.

Usually the other guests were delighted. Until midnight or so, anyway.

"People will be along soon enough," the Chief said from his wheelchair beside me and Colleen. "They're probably finishing up their dinners inside or enjoying the *craic* at the bar. The Lads haven't arrived yet anyway."

Nope, they sure hadn't. And I couldn't help but suspect that the merry band might not show up for a while. The last we'd seen of the Lads, they were trying to load up their rental van at the curb outside the Buckley House. Without their de facto organizer, babysitter, and newest band member Noel.

"I can't believe Noel disappeared like that," Colleen said. "Maybe we shouldn't have left those guys to get here on their own. Do you think they'll make it? Like, before last call?"

"Sure they will," our dad said. "The Lads are old hands at this. Don't they play here in Shamrock every summer? They'll be fine."

I hoped so. But without their oarsman Noel, the Lads could be up the river. When we'd asked, none of them, including Marty, had a clue where he had gone.

At least Marty's injured hand didn't seem to be bothering him. I noticed he'd changed the bandage to a smaller one so he could play his fiddle more easily. A little clunky still, but the elderly musician was completely unfazed. He'd even made a joke about it.

I needed to get Marty alone so I could ask him about whatever his beef had been with Fallon O'Malley. And while I was at it, maybe his exact whereabouts early Sunday morning.

There had to be a good reason why Marty had disliked that young woman so intensely. Other than her personality in general. I didn't buy Noel's claim that it was "nothing."

But he'd also said it was "old business." I was willing to bet Marty had heard about the Johnny Myer meeting somehow. Did he know the record company executive was headed to Shamrock to see Peat live?

But that was new business.

"I'll text Mom to make sure the Lads are on their way," I said, pulling out my phone. "If not, Frank should be home by now. I could ask him to stop by and check up on things."

The Chief shook his head. "I'm telling you, Noel wouldn't forget. That lad has a good head on his shoulders."

There was another possibility. Noel and Ian might have buried the hatchet under the circumstances and gone off somewhere together. It wasn't a stretch to imagine kind-hearted Noel trying to support his former bandmate—and good friend—in the shock and pain of Fallon's death. The two of them had been so close once. And maybe they'd lost track of time.

Ian, maybe. But not Noel.

I hadn't seen Marty's son since last night. But from all reports Noel had been at the fairgrounds this morning for the stage setup. And according to Mom, he'd repaired the garden gate when he'd gotten back to the B&B. Our doorbell was working now, too.

Mr. Fix-it.

He'd always been a stand-up guy, even as a kid. Steady. Responsible. Nice to everyone.

Of course, I didn't really know Noel anymore. But as with Ian, it was impossible for me to imagine him as a murderer. If he shared his dad's feelings about Fallon, he hid them well.

But still. Thanks to Fallon O'Malley, and Marty's increasing frailty and unreliability, the Limerick Lads could lose their big contract for Crossroad Dreams. Just after Noel had given up his rising career with Peat to help out his dad's band.

I couldn't overlook the fact that anger and revenge would be a strong motive for killing his former manager.

The hostess, wearing a sparkly green sequin tube dress and lace-up ballerina flats, hurried up, hugging a set of menus to her chest. "Sorry for the delay, Chief Buckley," she said breathlessly. "And hey, Colleen. I just got called in to work. They want me to help inside as well as out here tonight."

"Hi, Jolie. Understaffed, huh?" Colleen said sympathetically. "What's up?"

The hostess lowered her voice. "We're not as busy as we'd expected, but some of the staff were freaked about that awful murder this morning and didn't show up. And my bosses just found out Mayor Flanagan is on his way with a large party."

"Are you worried about the murder, Jolie?" I asked.

She gave a weak smile. "Well, I feel safer now that the Chief is here. I live super close, but my boyfriend is picking me up after my shift. And I'm getting double overtime."

"Don't you worry, Jolie," the Chief said. "Everything will be fine."

His words were reassuring, but even as my dad spoke, his eyes darted around the patio.

Our hostess directed us to a table close to the stage but slightly to the side to better accommodate my dad's wheelchair. "Enjoy your evening," she told us. "The music should be starting soon."

I caught the flash of a worried frown across the hostess's forehead. Did she have any idea that the Limerick Lads might be no-shows? Hard to tell.

Once we were settled at our table with our menus, I glanced around the patio again. People were starting to trickle out from the inside bar and restaurant, but I didn't recognize any of them. Mostly tourists, I guessed. Several wore those "Butter Meet Me at the Great Shamrock Fair" T-shirts from Gifts of Gab.

Gabby herself was manning an auction sign-up table at the other end of the patio. I'd go over and chat with her as soon as we placed our order.

Just like me, the Chief was scanning the crowd again. No one seemed impatient or restless about the delayed entertainment. People were chatting and enjoying their late dinners and beverage rounds. The summer evening was perfect. Well, if you didn't count that it followed a long day kicked off by a murder.

I couldn't help but notice the large number of gray and white heads around the dining tables. Fallon had been right about that "mature demographic" of Limerick Lad fans. The only music enthusiast under sixty or so was a bored-looking guy sitting toward the back of the patio. Even in the heat, he wore a lightweight navy blazer, pressed jeans, and slip-on loafers with no socks. A pair of designer sunglasses were perched atop his dark, wavy hair. I did notice a few streaks of gray at the temples, though.

"Hey, you two." Colleen waved in front of our faces from her seat. "Helloooo? We're supposed to be having a fun evening out here. Mom's orders."

"We are," my dad and I said at the same time.

Colleen shook her head. "You're thinking about the investigation, I can tell," she said. "Both of you. This is supposed to be Daddy–Daughters Night."

"It is," I said.

"Absolutely," the Chief said.

"Fine, if you say so." Colleen sighed. "But no talking about the murder tonight, OK? Just for an hour or two?" When our dad and I nodded extra-convincingly, she picked up her menu. "I don't know about you guys, but I'm starving."

"Me too," I said. It felt like forever since I'd eaten with the girls at the Blarney Bowl.

Colleen twirled her hair as she surveyed the choices. "I'm having the mac and cheese with fried pickles," she said. "Anyone want to split onion rings with me? We can order dessert later."

"Yes to both," the Chief said. "That leprechaun pie sounds good."

Leprechaun pie? I checked the dessert section of the menu. It sounded suspiciously similar to grasshopper pie. Served with hot Cadbury chocolate sauce and a little gold leaf pot of Smarties on top. "Count me in," I said.

The minute our red-bearded server had taken our orders and bounded off like a leprechaun himself, Mayor Flanagan arrived on the patio, trailed by a gaggle of enthusiastic supporters.

Of course they all stopped at our table on their way to the front row. The mayor waved his companions to go ahead.

"Surprised to see you out tonight, Chief." The perspiring man in the green seersucker suit placed a pudgy hand on my dad's shoulder. Then he dropped into the remaining chair beside him, uninvited.

"And why is that, Ray?" The Chief was the only person in town other than Bernie Donnelly who called the mayor by his first name.

The mayor shrugged. "Well, after our little talk earlier, I might have expected you'd be out pounding the payment for the O'Malley case. All hands on deck, so to speak."

"Just out for a fine night of music with my daughters," the Chief said pleasantly. "I'm retired, you know."

"Ah. Right." Mayor Flanagan turned his attention to me and Colleen—mostly Colleen—and smiled. "You girls are looking lovely, as always."

Girls? Lovely? Ugh. I glared at him as politely as possible. Colleen's blue eyes squinted very slightly before she gave an equally fake smile back.

The guy gave off the exact vibes of a TV cartoon villain. More smarmy than evil. But Raymond F. Flanagan was the perfect caricature of a pompous politician.

"I hear the youngest one is in the running for Little Miss Shamrock. Mary Elizabeth, isn't it?" The mayor chuckled. "Another Buckley shoe-in. I'd take that to the bank."

He'd take anything to the bank. And was he talking to me or Colleen? Hard to tell. And I didn't care.

Where were those crazy Limerick Lads, for heaven's sake? With all their popularity, they could at least try to be more professional. Fair play to Noel for his efforts to steer his new bandmates in that direction. But this time he'd dropped the ball.

"Bliz will have some stiff competition," Colleen was saying to Mayor Flanagan as I tuned back in. "Every one of the contestants in her group is super talented and absolutely adorable. And the essays for the final round will be judged blindly, of course."

"Oh, absolutely." The mayor gave a half smile, half smirk. "A perfect topic for our young residents of Shamrock to write about, their heritage. Came up with that idea myself."

"Hello? Testing, one, two, three."

Jolie tapped on a standing microphone from the stage, looking a little nervous in her sparkly hostess dress. "Hi, everybody," she said. "Welcome, and we hope you're enjoying your evening at the Barleycorn."

The small but growing crowd clapped, and there was a whistle or two.

"We've got an update for all of you waiting to hear the Limerick Lads. Good news! We just spoke with Noel McCleary, Marty's son. The band was unavoidably delayed, but they wanted to let you know they're here in the house and will be ready to play for you very soon."

"Finally," Colleen muttered under her breath.

"In the meantime, please welcome Mary Ann Mawhinney and her magic fiddle to the stage. You're in for a treat, folks."

A woman with long, gray, curly hair wearing boots and a patchwork dress with a high-low hemline came out through the curtain to polite applause.

"And more good news," Jolie added. The microphone squeaked, startling all of us, especially her. "Your next drinks are on the house, courtesy of the Limerick Lads!"

Very loud applause. That would set the band back a fair penny.

My dad jerked his thumb toward a group of center tables near the front. "Ray, I think your entourage over there is eager for you to join them."

Sure enough, the assorted group of businesspeople, fundraisers, local politicians, and church ladies all waved to the mayor as Mary Ann Mawhinney launched into a shaky "Molly Malone."

"Ah. Can't keep them waiting. If you'll excuse me, then," Mayor Flanagan said. "Keep me posted on the investigation, Dermot," he added to my dad, with a heavy clap to the Chief's shoulder. "Remember, we have a fair to throw!"

Colleen shuddered as the mayor left. "How can you stand dealing with him all the time, Dad? He gives off all kinds of ick."

"Comes with the territory," the Chief said. "Mayors come and mayors go. This one has been around longer than I'd like."

Our server appeared with a tray bearing tall green glasses of ice water. After he distributed them to the three of us, he placed a folded piece of paper on the table between me and my sister. It had been taped shut.

"Someone left this on my tray," the server said. "Which one of you is Kate?"

Chapter Twenty-Three

For a moment I thought maybe Garrett had sent the note the server had just delivered to our table. A romantic gesture, since things seemed a little off between us lately. Ever since I'd found Fallon's body. And Ian had arrived in town.

No. Garrett would never send a note. Especially in front of my dad. He'd text.

And Ian sending a note? Please. Equally out of the question.

Our server had disappeared, so I couldn't ask him any questions. But there was no doubt the message was for me. My name was clearly printed on the outside.

Block letters, black ink.

"I'll open that, Kathleen." The Chief leaned forward and stuck his arm toward the center of the table, but his reach fell short from his wheelchair. He grimaced in annoyance.

"Daddy, it might be *private*." Colleen grabbed up the note. "Maybe Kate has a secret admirer."

My dad and I exchanged glances. We had just finished dealing with a different note. And it wasn't a friendly one.

"Colleen, give that to me, please." I held out my upturned palm.

She sighed and handed it over. "Fine. You are no fun."

"I've heard that before." I broke the tape and opened the note.

One line. Those same familiar block letters in black ink.

Mind your _______ business or you'll be sorry.

A colorful word had been inserted before "business."

I silently handed the note to my dad.

He briefly read the message, gave a sharp nod, and handed it back to me.

"So what does it say?" Colleen demanded. "Come on, don't tell me you're not going to show me. That's not fair."

I briefly turned the note toward her to read, leaving my sister speechless. Then I refolded the paper and tried to restick the tape, with limited success. This time I would not allow it out of my sight. Or within sniffing distance of any nosy dogs.

The second note looked as if it had been fashioned from the light green envelope of an extra-postage greeting card. The kind Gabby stocked in her gift shop.

"Kathleen," the Chief said quietly. "Why don't I take that, if you don't mind? It'll keep the chain of custody cleaner. We'll give both notes to Detective Walker when she comes out to the house in the morning."

I nodded and gave him the note without a word, my hand visibly shaking. I didn't feel like looking at it again, anyway.

Someone—likely Fallon's killer—had sent me a warning. No, a threat.

"What do you mean, *both* notes?" Colleen looked from me to our dad and back. "There was another one before this?"

I sighed. "Yes. Not sent to me, though. Fallon."

"Oh my gosh." Colleen leaned over the table. "That means the person knows Kate found Fallon's body," she said in a low voice. "And that she's snooping around. They're watching her. They must know about Ian staying with us, too."

"It's not a secret," the Chief said.

Thanks to our buddy Mitzi.

"But this note means Kate is in danger, right?" Colleen said. "All of us, really." She straightened in her seat and craned her neck, eyes darting around the patio. "The person has to be here somewhere."

I placed a hand on my sister's arm. "Colleen, stop being obvious. Please. Just act normal."

"How can we be normal?" Colleen said. "None of this is normal." She turned to the Chief. "Will there be fingerprints on the notes? Like, DNA?"

"Not likely." Our dad was no sugarcoater. "Muddled, at best. But Forensics may be able to gather some other kind of information from them. Hopefully."

I slung my pocketbook over my shoulder and rose from the table. "Excuse me, I'll be back in a few."

"Sit down, please, Kathleen," the Chief said. "You're not going anywhere. And certainly not asking questions with a possible perp in the vicinity."

"I'm going to the ladies' room," I protested.

"Just hold it," he said, and signaled for our server.

I parked my butt back in my seat, fuming. I knew he'd never buy the powder room deal. But I needed to find out who had sent that note. Hopefully while they were still around.

Red Beard delivered the plates on his tray to another table before he returned to us. He'd been rushing around so much, his huge plaid bow tie was askew, partly obscuring his nametag. "Everything OK, folks?"

"No, unfortunately," Colleen said. I nudged her knee with mine.

"That note you brought us a few minutes ago," I said. "Who gave that to you?"

"No idea," the guy said. "Someone just left it on my tray. Sorry."

Colleen peered at him closer. "It's Paul, isn't it?" she said, offering him a smile he couldn't refuse. "I think we met recently. Can't quite place where, but . . ."

"Oh, yeah, right." Our server looked delighted that Colleen had remembered him. "Sorry, I'm such an eejit. I can't recall exactly where it was either. But I remember *you,* of course."

My dad gave a small cough. He wasn't subtle about it, either.

Colleen ignored him and smiled at Paul again. "Well gosh, it's too bad you didn't see the note person. My big sister here was hoping to find out the identity of her secret admirer." She gave him a playful wink.

Only my sister could pull off an actual wink at a guy. Maybe it was more a brief flutter of her lashes. But it worked.

"I didn't catch a glimpse of him." Paul sounded truly regretful. "But hey, maybe someone else inside did. I'll go ask around, OK? Be right back."

"Awesome." Colleen toasted him with her drink glass, then took a dainty sip.

"Now I really am going to the ladies' room," I announced, as soon as the server was out of sight.

"I'm coming with you." Colleen shot up from her chair. "It's an emergency," she added, before our dad could object again. "We'll be fine."

The note sender was long gone by now. The Chief knew that. "Stay alert," he said, as an incoming text buzzed on his cell.

I finished his favorite phrase for him as I followed my sister toward the restaurant. *And no one gets hurt.*

* * *

"I really do have to use the loo," Colleen said as we stepped into the Barleycorn. "But I'm not letting you out of my sight. Who knows where that note person is?" She looked right and left in an obvious way.

"Come on, Colleen Queen," I said, taking my sister by the elbow. "Let's try the bartenders first. They notice everything."

Not in this case, as it turned out. None of the three had seen anything out of the ordinary.

"No customers allowed behind the rope," one told us. He pointed toward the end of the bar where drinks were placed for the servers to take away. "Food goes out directly from the kitchen."

I frowned as I checked out the crowded tables. "No one's eating inside now," I said to Colleen. "The bar is turning into a zoo."

As I spoke, a large guy with a black snake tattoo pushed past me to grab his drinks off the bar. He tossed down a couple of dollars tip and a half-hearted "sorry" to me as he reversed course. Two young women dressed in identical fair sweatshirts took his place.

"You're right," Colleen said, waving to someone she knew across the room. "Anyone in this crowd could have dropped a piece of paper onto Paul's tray as he walked by. He wouldn't even notice."

"Or he could have set his tray down for a minute to unload it." I glanced toward a far corner where a folding tray stand was parked.

Paul himself spotted us in the crowd and headed our way. "Hey," he said. "I've asked around the staff. No one saw who left that note. Really sorry," he added to me. "Best of luck with the guy."

"Thanks," I said.

"Hope I'll see you around, Paul." Colleen gently dismissed him with a smile.

"Count on it," he said, then disappeared toward the end of the bar to pick up his next drink orders.

My attention was drawn to the other far corner as my eyes adjusted to the dim light. "Are those the Limerick Lads over there at that table?" I asked my sister.

Colleen squinted. "Yup," she said. "There's Marty, talking to some lady. I don't see Noel, though. Looks like they're all having a few drinks."

"But why aren't the Lads outside already?" I said, over the growing cocktail chatter around us. "They're supposed to be onstage ASAP."

"Dunno," my sister said. "Doesn't look like they're in a hurry. We might as well get back to Dad. OK if we stop by the ladies' room first?"

I sighed. "Sure."

The lighting in the black-and-white tiled ladies' room seemed extra-bright after the dim main dining and bar area. Colleen glanced in the single long mirror over the sinks, placed strangely high. "Yikes. I look like death warmed over," she said, before stepping into a middle stall.

I entered the one next to it and struggled for a second or two with the sliding door latch. The hook to hang a jacket or purse was loose, too. With a frustrated huff, I detoured to another stall two doors down. Not the cleanest, but secure at least.

The Barleycorn's new outdoor performance space was great, but apparently they hadn't gotten around to renovating the ladies' room recently. Once one of Shamrock's oldest dive bars serving employees of the woolen mills, this establishment hadn't started allowing women customers until the 1970s.

"So who do you think sent that note?" my sister asked. "And shouldn't we give it to the cops tonight instead of waiting til tomorrow morning for Detective Walker? I mean, it sounds like a threat to me."

"It's just a few hours difference." I peered at the toilet paper dispenser. Was it *empty*? No. A few sheets left, thank goodness.

"But there's a *killer* out there, Kate. They already got to Fallon, but they could be after Ian now. Or you. They're definitely watching the house. I mean, what if—"

"Colleen, we can't just kick Ian out," I broke in. "He's safer with us. With people he knows. He's Maeve's dad, for heaven's sake."

"What if one of the guests killed Fallon?" Colleen said. "Then Ian could be a sitting duck."

"I hope not," I said. "But I've been thinking about Marty. He hated her. And he literally had blood on his hands this morning when he came back to the house."

"Blood? Oh my gosh. That's horrible." I heard a flush, then the sound of Colleen wrestling with her own door latch before stepping into the sink area. "Why didn't you tell me about that? And also . . . what about Noel?"

"Noel? Why him?" I flushed with my foot and reached for my pocketbook on the hook.

"I dunno. He's just so *nice*. But he could have been mad at Fallon, too. Like, for the same reason as his dad. Maybe they were working together."

I hated to admit I hadn't considered that scenario. Yet, anyway. Noel and Ian weren't friends anymore. They'd been pretty much avoiding each other, as far as I could tell. Ian probably wasn't happy Noel had left Peat. "Yeah, you're right," I said with a sigh. "That's a definite possibility."

I sure hoped Noel wasn't a cold-blooded killer. If so, his Mr. Nice Guy act would make him even more of a psychopath.

As I joined my sister at the sink and turned on a blast of cold water from the mislabeled faucet, I glimpsed the stalls behind us in the mirror.

Oh no. Planted on the floor of the furthest stall were two black Converse sneakers.

Someone had heard our entire conversation.

I nudged Colleen and silently jerked my head in the direction of the lurker. How could we have been stupid enough to talk about Fallon's killer in a public bathroom?

My sister stared at me, her brows sky-high and her freshly glossed lips forming an O. Then she grabbed her tiny clutch from the counter above the sink in preparation to flee. I'd be right beside her.

Too late. A sudden flush, and the stall door swung open. Out stepped Macker from Peat.

Of all people. And all my Irish luck.

Chapter Twenty-Four

Colleen gathered herself together first. "Oh, hey," she greeted our unexpected eavesdropper. "You scared us. We, um, didn't realize you were in here."

"Obviously." Macker headed toward the sinks.

"Sorry if you, um, overhead our conversation," I said, hoping against hope she hadn't. Macker was Ian's bandmate, after all—and a guest at the Buckley House.

Unfortunately, my sister and I had pretty much just lumped all the musician guests together as potential murder suspects.

Macker carefully washed her hands, then hit the air dryer with her elbow. "Yeah, I heard the whole thing," she said when it shut off. She glanced at us in the mirror rather than directly.

"Awkward, huh?" Colleen threw her a smile and tiny shrug that said, "you-got-us."

"No worries," Macker said. "It makes sense that you're nervous and wondering which of us at the B&B might have killed Fallon. I mean, we're the ones who knew her, right?"

Phew. She was being practical. She didn't sound insulted. Or mad. "Thanks for understanding." I reached out to draw

Colleen to me in a side hug. "My sister and I get a little carried away sometimes."

"You know," Colleen added. "Cop kids and all."

"Yeah, this one here really interrogated me earlier." Macker jerked her head in my direction. Was that a slight snicker? I might have imagined it.

I caught a faint whiff of eucalyptus oil as Macker turned from the sink. "Come here to me now, what was it you said about a note? Someone threatened you? Like, tonight, here at the Barleycorn?"

I stepped back slightly, nearly tripping on my sister's foot. I really didn't want to discuss the notes with Macker. Or any other details of the case. I wasn't sure I trusted her. "No big deal, really." I waved. "A prank, most likely."

To my surprise, Macker gazed down at the cracked tile floor. She looked a little guilty. "Actually, there's something I forgot to tell you, Kate," she said. "I didn't recall it until after we spoke back at the B&B. It may be nothing, but I thought you should know."

"Of course, no problem," I said, trying not to sound too eager. The last thing I wanted was to scare her off. "What is it?"

"I don't want to get him in any kind of trouble," Macker said. "And hey, I could be wrong about this. But I saw Noel follow Fallon out of Farrell's last night. You know, when she left early. He was sitting at another table across the room with the Lads. When she flounced off, he got up and took off after her."

I frowned. "You're saying Noel was the last person to see Fallon at the pub?" Beside me, I felt Colleen draw in her breath.

I hoped Farrell's had security cameras. Working ones.

It would be easy enough to find out from the Chief. Or Garrett. Or even my best buddy Carmel, if I bribed her.

But the cops had to have retraced Fallon's steps last night. And wouldn't the Chief have noticed Noel going after her? My dad had to have been sitting at the Lads' table, too.

And then Noel had shown up at the Buckley House. The two of us had sat and talked together in the parlor after everyone else had gone to bed.

But he'd gone out again. Back to the pub, he'd said.

"Did Noel go back into Farrell's after he talked to Fallon?" I asked Macker.

The Peat drummer frowned. "I don't think so. I don't remember."

"Maybe he returned an hour or so later?" I pressed.

"Couldn't tell you that," Macker said. "I didn't stay at Farrell's for long."

"Where did you go, then?" Colleen sounded a little impatient, as if she wasn't buying the petite woman's story. I wasn't sure whether I was, either.

"We all split up and went different places," Macker said with a shrug. "I don't even remember where, to be honest. You know, the jet lag. And the drink. I can't remember what I told the detective. Liam did most of the talking."

"Which detective?" I asked.

"Yer man. The good looking one."

Garrett. Sargeant Walker must have let him back on the case. Good news for him. And for me, because that had to mean there was no chance I was a suspect in Fallon's murder.

Well, almost no chance.

All of the Limerick Lads—including Marty—had gone back to the Buckley House. And the Chief had been with them. The seniors went straight to bed, and unless any of them snuck out again, only the members of Peat had been out and about in the hours before Fallon died.

And Noel.

"It was probably really innocent," Macker went on. "But they must have talked about something outside the pub, Fallon and Noel. Don't you think? I mean, they knew each other pretty well. Fallon was Noel's manager, too, when he was still with Peat."

"Did the two of them get along?" I asked.

"They did," Macker said. "Now that I think of it, Noel was probably the closest to Fallon of any of us. I mean, until he left the band like that, and she and Ian got together. For whatever reason."

"You never know with couples." My sister's tone was light.

"Sorry ladies, but I've got to go," Macker said, stepping past us. "Me and Liam and Jaymes are supposed to be setting up the stage for the Lads right now. We told Noel we would. Especially since Johnny Myer's here."

"Really?" Johnny had to be the guy in the blazer on the patio. The one with the sunglasses on top of his head.

But more importantly, Noel hadn't gone completely AWOL. Nothing had happened to him. That was a relief.

"Yeah, Noel's talking with Johnny right now," Macker said. "Probably trying to explain why the Lads are acting the maggots. I told him he should. It's better to be on the professional side with big executives like Johnny Myer."

"Where did Noel go earlier?" I said.

"No clue," Macker said. "He didn't say. He just stepped out and got caught up somewhere, I guess. Me and my band-mates helped him get the rest of the Lads here. Some problem with their rental van, they said. Plus Noel had a lot of trouble getting his dad and the twins moving in the same direction. The three of them, they're like wee lads. But old."

"Did they really have van trouble?" I asked. "Or was that just the story?"

"It was true enough," Macker said. "Their van is garbage. If you ask me, though, Marty did seem a bit off. Kind of tired and wobbly, like. I dunno, maybe too much of the drink."

I frowned. Would Marty be so irresponsible as to completely blow off a gig? I found that hard to believe. Especially with a newer, younger band nipping at the Limerick Lads' heels.

Case in point: Peat was here at the Barleycorn, ready to step in. Without Ian, I was pretty sure.

"Is your band playing tonight as well?" I asked Macker. "Did Ian come out after all?"

"No to both," Macker said. "Unless the Lads invite us to join them in a session or something. Ian's still holed up in his room. Last I knew, anyway."

"Well, who could blame him?" Colleen said. "His fiancée is dead. Why does everyone keep forgetting that?"

"Right," Macker said. "We talked him out of our band practice in the garage. That was a stupid idea anyway. I offered to stay in with Ian tonight, but he didn't want company." She sighed. "I even made up a tray—well, your Mom did—and brought it up to his room. He didn't answer, so I left it outside the door."

"Sleeping, maybe," Colleen said.

"I'll check on him as soon as we get home," I said.

"Oh, you don't need to bother yourself." Macker waved. "I told him I would, if he heard me. But hey, I've really gotta get my butt over to the stage. Liam and Jaymes will wonder where I went off to. "*Slán*," she tossed over her shoulder as she pushed through the ladies' room door.

Colleen blew out her breath once the Peat drummer was safely gone. "I'm telling you, that is one strange girl. I don't know why, exactly, but she really annoys me."

"Me too," I said. "And I think the feeling is mutual, in my case."

"I wouldn't lose any sleep over that. So what do you think about Noel running after Fallon last night?" my sister asked.

"It probably doesn't mean anything," I said. "Maybe he saw Fallon was upset, and he was just being nice. I could totally see him doing that. But I can ask him about it."

"Well, right now we'd better head back to the Chief," Colleen said. "He's probably wondering where we are."

"Tell him I'll be right there," I said as we headed down the hall toward the main room.

"I thought we were supposed to stick together." My sister frowned.

"I'll be fine," I said. "The note leaver is either long gone, or we're not going to find them. Even if they're still here at the Barleycorn, they could be practically any of these people here."

"So where are you going?"

"Out to the patio with you," I said. "I just want to stop by the auction table to talk to Gabby. You'll have me in sight the whole time."

"Fine," Colleen said. "But don't be too long, or the Chief will send me after you."

The crowd inside the restaurant had thinned by now, even at the bar. As we reached the open doors to the patio, I glanced back toward the Limerick Lads' far corner table. The members of the band, sans Noel, were gathering themselves to leave. Sort of. The twins each held one of Marty's arms as he rose to his feet. He looked a little dazed, as if he might have fallen asleep again.

What was wrong with Marty? I wondered. Was it some kind of health emergency? Should I run over there to help?

As the old man shook off his friends' assistance and clearly insisted he was fine, I told myself not to interfere. It was none of my business, really. But at this point, they'd be lucky if there were any fans left out on the patio. Not to mention Johnny Myer. Hopefully the musical ministrations of Mary Mawhinney had been enough to tide them over.

To be honest, I could see why Johnny Myer was losing interest in the Lads. Fallon O'Malley had been dead right. Even with the boost of Noel joining the band, the Limerick Lads were a growing liability for their record label.

And if I were even more honest? From the way they'd been carrying on lately, maybe they deserved a bit of a fall.

Chapter Twenty-Five

My first thought as I crossed the patio was that Gabby seemed a little glum. Surrounded by all the enticing items for bid on the silent auction tables, she gave off the vibe of a dejected kid in a toy store full of colorful playthings.

As soon as she spotted me, my old boss pretended to be diligently wrestling with a floppy gold ribbon atop one of the larger gift baskets. The bow slipped repeatedly off the clear plastic wrap bag holding the whole thing together.

"Hi Gabby," I said, reaching to assist. I caught the bow before it hit the ground, not quite making up for knocking down all her T-shirts yesterday. "How are things going?"

"Oh, everything's hunky-dory, Katie." She gave me a wavery smile. "Such a lovely night to hear the Limerick Lads. Are you here to place a bid?"

"I'm just browsing for now," I said. My eyes swept over the gift baskets and numerous other items displayed on the green satin tablecloths. Celtic crafts, sweets and jams, cheerful floral teapots, shamrock tote bags, and numbered bundles of knitwear, toys, and Irish music CDs. A collection of elaborately beaded Irish dance dresses hung from the wooden fence behind the tables that separated the Barleycorn property from

The Galway Glaze pottery store. Gold-legged easels displayed photos of special items for bid, and tiny woolen sheep dotted the green tablecloths. This year's bright yellow fair T-shirts were stacked high at both ends of the tables.

I stepped back slightly to avoid them.

"All these treasures," Gabby went on. "And not many bids so far, last time I checked, so your chances to win are good." She sighed. "Like I told you back at the store, I wish I could bid myself, but I'm not eligible to participate." She leaned forward to add, "It's nice to bid online, but it's much better to see the things in person, don't you think?"

"Definitely," I agreed.

"You could even win a trip to Ireland," she said, pointing to one of the easels. "Wouldn't that be fun?"

"You're such an amazing salesperson, Gabby," I said, with a laugh. "That minimum bid alone is out of my league. But I'm sure I'll find something. Hey, how are those cute Athena Sweeney gnomes doing?" I looked down at the tables again. "Are they here somewhere?"

"Goodness, no," Gabby said. "I couldn't transport all of those here tonight. But they're still being advertised in my store window, of course. And there's an easel with a photo of them somewhere, I think . . . Oh, yes, right here. The easel must have fallen over."

She retrieved the display card, half-hidden under a fuzzy green unicorn, and carefully repositioned it on a suspiciously empty easel. "Now where is my phone so I can check the bids? Oh dear."

Poor Gabby. I couldn't help but suspect she'd purposely tucked the gnome easel out of sight. She really, really didn't want anyone to bid on those twisted statues.

"That's OK, Gabby. Maybe I'll place a bid later, when I have more time." *And money.* I peered closer at the easel showing the group photo of Athena's gnomes. They looked as demonic as ever. "Do you have any idea what the hidden prize is?"

"Oh, I told you, I really don't know, dearie," Gabby said. "Believe me, I tried to find out. Athena said she'd been sworn to secrecy by the donor. And she isn't much of a chatter anyway, I'm afraid."

Very true. But I had to find out as much as I could about those sculptures. There was a reason why they'd caught Fallon's attention, if not her fancy. From what Gabby had said earlier, my ex's fiancée was desperate to buy up every single one of those ugly monsters. And she wasn't interested in commissioning duplicates.

What was so special about them?

"Does just one of the sculptures have a hidden compartment?" I pressed. "Or are all of them hollow?"

Gabby immediately looked as if she needed to beeline back to Father Declan's confessional STAT. "Well . . . I'll admit, I wondered that, too. I checked every one of them myself," she said. "Now that I think of it, I suppose that poor young woman was trying to do the same. You know, the customer who came into the shop before you and Colleen. So sad, what happened to her. I couldn't believe it. And just think, you were—"

No, I didn't want to think. Mercifully, the lights from the stage dimmed, and Gabby was interrupted by a sudden shriek from the sound system. The cables were plugged in, the stools and equipment set up, and a green spotlight appeared on the curtain.

The Limerick Lads were about to take the stage. About time. And I needed to get back to the Chief and Colleen pronto.

I quickly said good-bye to Gabby, and as I turned away I spotted Noel from the corner of my eye. He'd just jumped up from a table a few yards away, where he'd been sitting with Johnny Myer. Wow, he was cutting things close performance-wise.

Or was he purposely making a dramatic entrance?

Either way, Noel sprinted up the center of the patio and bounded onto the stage as the audience clapped and cheered. Macker handed him a mic and, after depositing a few bottles of water at center stage, exited to the side. Liam and Jaymes disappeared through the back curtain, passing the Limerick twins on their way out.

Wearing matching caps and suspenders, Timmy and Jimmy gathered up their instruments for the first song—one a flute and the other an accordion—and took their places on high stools across from each other.

Marty's face fleetingly appeared behind the break in the curtain. The band's elderly leader seemed to be fumbling with the billowy material.

Everyone laughed and applauded. A few audience members shouted good-humored encouragement.

"Is Marty doing that on purpose?" I whispered to my dad as I sat down. "To be funny, I mean?"

The Chief frowned. "I don't think so."

"Someone should help him," Colleen said. "Noel!" she called, waving, but Marty's son was adjusting his guitar strap and didn't notice. He probably thought the fans were cheering because the music was finally about to start.

"Hello, Shamrock!" he shouted. "Thanks very much for coming out tonight to see us on this lovely night. We apologize for the late hour, but we promise we'll make it up to you with fine tunes and good *craic*. How is everyone doing?"

No one in the crowd answered. Instead, everyone gasped as Marty headed toward the middle stool with his fiddle—and kept on walking.

Straight off the front of the stage.

Chapter Twenty-Six

My dad propelled himself and his wheelchair to Marty's side like a rocket. I raced in his wake, and we reached his old friend at the same time as Noel, who jumped from the Barleycorn stage.

My sister was right behind us, already on her cellphone to 911.

Marty lay face down, blood streaming from his head. His left leg looked oddly twisted.

He wasn't moving.

"Dad." I could tell that Noel was trying not to panic. "I'm here, Dad."

"Martin." My dad's voice was steady as he leaned down to touch his friend's shoulder. "You've had a bit of a bump on your head. A bus is on the way. You're going to be fine. Hang in there."

I realized the Chief couldn't reach far enough to check Marty's pulse from his chair. Quickly I knelt beside the injured musician and placed two fingers on Marty's neck. His skin felt like paper to my touch, and blood seeped onto my hand.

"I've got a pulse," I announced, as the group around Marty expanded to include the twins, the members of Peat, and a tearful Jolie.

Not a strong pulse, but it was steady.

"Get back, Everyone!" Colleen shouted to the rapidly gathering crowd. "He needs room. And quit with the freakin' cell phone videos. Any medical people here?"

"Doctor." The throng parted for a tall, silver-haired man who nodded me out of the way. "Has anyone moved him?"

"No," I said. "But he's breathing."

"What exactly happened?" the doctor asked, reaching to check Marty's pulse. "I didn't see the incident."

"Me neither, sir," Noel said. "I turned around and saw my dad fall straight off the stage. All on his own."

"He didn't seem himself," Macker said.

"Stumbling, like," Timmy added. Jimmy nodded.

A rush of guilt flooded my heart. I'd noticed that Marty was unsteady as he left the restaurant. The twins had helped him make his way to the stage. They hadn't seemed overly worried. But we all should have been.

"Was he drinking?" the doctor asked. "Is he on any medications? Any history of strokes or TIAs?"

"No drinks," Timmy said. "A Guinness this afternoon, maybe. He'd only had peppermint tea with honey since dinner. It's good for his singing voice."

I thought back to the Lads' table inside the restaurant. Two empty bar glasses, side by side. Most likely they belonged to the twins. And yup, a Barleycorn mug at Marty's place. It could have been tea.

"He takes metformin for high blood sugar," Noel said. "And something else for the blood pressure. Ramipril, I think. No strokes that I know of."

Sirens sounded from both ends of the street as emergency vehicles from Shamrock Hospital, PD and Fire all showed up at the same time.

So did Frank, wearing jeans and his black PD windbreaker. He pushed his way through the crowd, and Colleen filled him in on what had happened.

"I'm going with Marty to the hospital," my dad said, as the medical team went to work on Marty. They carefully turned him over and two paramedics brought a gurney and a spine board. I heard Marty moan slightly.

He was conscious now, at least. A hopeful sign.

"Dad, they won't let you ride in the ambulance with him," Colleen said. "Noel will. He's Marty's son."

She didn't mention there was no room for his chair, either. Especially in a medical emergency.

The Chief started to object, but my brother had already disengaged the chair's electric motor and was firmly wheeling him away from the scene. I scrambled after them as Colleen kept the lookie-loos at bay with Liam's help.

"What in the blazes are you doing?" my dad was shouting at Frank as I caught up with him and my brother. "I'm headed to Shamrock Hospital forthwith, and you are not about to stop me."

"I won't, Dad," Frank said. "You just can't go in the ambulance with Marty. I'll drive you myself, OK?"

"Fine." The Chief crossed his arms and let my brother know by the jut of his jaw that it wasn't.

"If you drive the van, Frank, I can take your car home," I offered. "I haven't had anything to drink tonight."

"Thanks." Frank nodded and tossed me the keys to his precious leased Lexus. I grabbed them out of the air with one hand. "Be careful," my brother added. "I've got the telematics system on. It tracks your speed and every move. It saves me money on insurance."

I stifled my annoyance. Frank was as blunt as he was cheap. "Got it," I said. "I have a perfect driving record, for your information."

"Uh-huh." Frank looked down at the Chief. "Where are you parked, Dad?"

The Chief pointed impatiently. "Down the block there."

"Everything will be OK, Dad," I said, as Frank started pushing the wheelchair again. "Marty's already talking. And they'll take great care of him at the hospital."

The Chief twisted toward me as I jogged just behind him and Frank. "Do a look-see around the Barleycorn for me, would you, Kathleen? On the down-low. See if you can find anything off. Something's not right. The old coot didn't take a dive off the stage for no reason. He's in fine health. Well, mostly fine. Other than needing to take the odd nap on occasion."

"I'll be discreet, Dad," I promised, a little out of breath. Frank was moving extra fast in a clear attempt to leave me in the dust.

"Remember, Kate, be careful," my brother threw over his shoulder as they reached the van.

Did he mean while I was checking out a possible crime scene, or driving his pet car baby? Probably both.

"Tell your mother what's going on," the Chief called. "And don't forget your meeting with Shirley in the morning," he added, his words starting to fade. "In case I'm not back in time."

Me, forget that fun upcoming chat with Detective Walker? Not likely.

I slowed to a stop and stood under a streetlight for a moment, watching my dad and brother disappear into the darkness. Then I gave the Lexus keys a toss in my hand and headed back to the Barleycorn.

Chapter Twenty-Seven

As I approached the patio, the flashing lights from the parked ambulance were practically blinding. The scene seemed surreal, somehow.

Marty was being loaded gingerly inside the ambulance by the emergency medical team. He wasn't his usual self, obviously, joking and talking up a green streak. But he was awake and alert, thank goodness, safely strapped to the spinal board.

Noel climbed into the ambulance beside his dad as two paramedics secured both the board and Marty onto a gurney for transport to the hospital. The Limerick twins, Macker, Jaymes, and Liam anxiously watched and offered encouragement to the injured musician before the ambulance doors were closed.

Colleen stood behind the group, nervously twisting a long blond curl with her head on Aidan's shoulder. She looked exhausted. Aidan had his arm around her. I wasn't sure when he'd shown up. Other than meeting up with my sister here at the Barleycorn, it made sense he would have wanted to attend the concert. He had a vested interest in the Limerick Lads. They were under contract to do the music for his show.

No sign of Johnny Myer. Maybe he'd already left.

"See you there, boyo!" Timmy called as the ambulance took off. A cheer rose from the other bystanders.

I approached the spot where the ambulance had been parked as the somber attendees of the canceled Limerick Lads concert filed onto the sidewalk and dispersed in all directions. "Sorry, what did I miss?" I asked my sister.

"Not a lot, really," Colleen said. "They think Marty will be OK. He may have a concussion, though, and his leg is really messed up. It might even be broken."

"What about the bleeding?" I asked.

"They got it stopped, fortunately," Aidan said. "Pretty much, anyway. The doctor told us even minor head wounds can bleed heavily. You never know, though, especially with older folks. They'll check Marty out thoroughly at the hospital."

"Speaking of blood." Colleen pointed.

"Oh. Right. Yikes, sorry." I quickly stuck my crimson-streaked fist behind my back to hide it from view—mine as well as everyone else's. I'd forgotten about the dripped blood from Marty's injury when I checked his pulse.

Then I realized I was still holding Frank's keys in my hand. I'd probably gotten them all sticky. Ugh. He was going to kill me.

Much worse, I suddenly remembered something else. The blood on Marty's own hand this morning. And the red drops on the clover when I found Fallon.

I gave an involuntary shudder, and Aidan frowned. "Kate, are you OK?"

"I'm fine," I assured him, forcing a smile.

Colleen raised her head from Aidan's shoulder. "You don't seem fine."

"It's been a long, tough day," I said. "We're all tired. Aidan, why don't you take Colleen back to the Buckley House? Frank gave me his keys. I just need to do a thing or two here for my dad. I'll be right behind you."

"We can't leave you here alone." Colleen frowned. "What about that note person out there? No way."

"There are a whole bunch of people still here," I said. "The employees need to close up. And it'll take me two seconds to get home. Go on now, both of you. Tomorrow's a big day. Scram." I grinned and made a shooing gesture.

They were still reluctant, but eventually I convinced them. Also, Colleen was practically asleep on her feet.

I was beyond exhausted too, but Marty's accident had given me another wind. Adrenaline, maybe.

As I stepped back onto the Barleycorn patio, I saw a pair of cops up near the stage, casually poking around. Probably for the insurance accident report. Hadn't everyone seen Marty stumble off the stage himself?

No sense in me playing Nancy Drew while the cops were there. I'd head inside first and see if the bartender had noticed anything out of the ordinary. Or Paul, our server. Anyone.

Everyone knew the Limerick Lads—or at least might recognize them. Someone had to have seen something.

Gabby's auction tables were bare, other than a lone green satin tablecloth on the one at the end. She must have cleared out fast and left it there by mistake. I'd grab it for her on my way out.

Inside the restaurant, I went straight to wash my hands—and wipe down Frank's keys as best I could with a paper towel from the automatic dispenser. Then I headed to the empty bar, where I found Jolie stuffing a tips envelope with her name on it into her cross-body bag.

The Barleycorn was definitely shutting down for the evening. Judging from all the glasses left on the bar and the semi-cleared tables in the restaurant, though, the employees might be there a while. Most of them were outside at the moment.

"Hi Jolie," I said. "Heading out?"

She turned and blinked at me from behind large, owl-framed glasses, which she hadn't worn during her hostess duties. Her hair was pulled back in a messy ponytail. Without the green sequins underneath her light sweater, I might not even have recognized her.

"Yeah, I'm leaving a little early," she said. "My boyfriend's here to pick me up. I can't wait to get out of here. The bar's closed, by the way."

"Oh, I know," I said. "And I'm sorry about the rough night. Pretty awful, what happened to Marty McCleary."

She nodded, and I added quickly, "Can I ask you a question?"

"Uh, sure. I don't have much time, though." She tried not to be obvious as she peeked for new texts on her phone.

"Do you know who was serving the Limerick Lads tonight? They were sitting back there at that corner table." I pointed.

"Sorry," Jolie said. "No one was waiting on them, as far as I know. Paul was supposed to be their server, but they didn't order any food. If you're just having drinks, you're supposed to order them at the bar. And the Lads' drinks were comped by the house anyway. Paul was kinda ticked off. He left already."

"Can't blame him." I glanced back at the table again. It obviously hadn't been cleared yet, but there was an empty folding tray table nearby. No way to know for certain if the Limerick Lads were the most recent customers who'd sat there, but it was a good bet. Not that much time had passed between Marty being helped away from the table by the twins and his accident.

"I'm pretty sure my sister stopped by the Lads' table to say hello," I said. "She just texted me, and she thinks she lost an earring. Could I go check around over there for a sec?"

Jolie shrugged. "I don't see why not. Sorry, I really gotta go. Tell Colleen to text me if you don't find the earring, I'll be on the lookout for it."

The barman was engrossed at his computer register. No point in bugging him right now. I headed to the Lads' table and made a subtle tour around it. Four near-empty pints of Guinness, two half-full waters, one Barleycorn mug with a tea bag resting on a Smithwick's coaster. A crumpled napkin lay beside it.

Two beers each for the twins, I was fairly sure. They'd been sitting next to each other. And the tea at the place across from them had to be Marty's.

I furtively glanced around to see whether anyone might be watching. The coast seemed clear. I leaned toward the drinks—the pint glasses were definitely Guinness. And the tea smelled strongly of peppermint and something sweet. Hadn't one of the twins mentioned that Marty had drunk peppermint tea for his voice? With honey.

And there was definitely something sticky in that gummed-up napkin. I wasn't about to touch it. Or take the napkin, either. I'd learned my lesson.

All in all, everything seemed to add up at the Lads' table. To nothing.

I returned to the bar, but the barman had disappeared and turned off the fake-Tiffany overheard lights. I'd hoped to ask him about any receipts, but if the drinks were comped and the bar had been busy enough, maybe they didn't exist.

I set my investigative sights back on the patio. Specifically, the stage.

The cops had left while I was inside the Barleycorn. No crime tape. Other than the Lads' instruments, which had been packed up and removed, it seemed everything else was left as-is: the stools, a few cables running under taped-down rubber mats. Had Marty tripped over one of those mats?

I also noted a few bottles of water, all unopened except for one. That bottle, a third or so empty and missing its cap, had rolled under the stool Marty had stumbled past.

Could there have been a slippery wet spot in his path?

I bent to touch the wooden platform floor. Yup. Slightly damp. But would it have been enough to throw Marty off balance?

Maybe. But doubtful.

The string lights surrounding the patio suddenly turned off. "Hey, over by the stage!" someone called. "Sorry, patio's closed."

Fair enough. I had no idea how late it was at this point, but all at once I could hardly keep my eyes open. I felt as if I'd been run over by one of those huge trucks unloading at the fairgrounds.

I took Frank's keys out from my pocketbook and tossed the paper towel from the ladies' room I'd wrapped around them into a nearby bin, disguised as a whiskey barrel. After retrieving Gabby's tablecloth, I kept the keys hidden in my fist as I continued on my way to my brother's Lexus.

One key pointed out the way Chief had taught me back in high school.

Just in case.

Chapter Twenty-Eight

The Buckley House was dark and still as I entered the foyer. Except for a faint rosy light from the parlor to my left.

And a few familiar snores.

I tiptoed to the doorway of the parlor and peeked inside.

I didn't see them at first.

Maeve, curled the length of the satin-covered loveseat in a black cami and PJ shorts, a velvet pillow under her head. One arm hung off the edge, her cell phone still clutched in her hand.

Ian, head drooped to his chest, wearing another Peat T-shirt and light gray joggers as he snored away in the large armchair.

And Bliz, nestled in the crook of his arm in her little pink rosebud nightie and lavender unicorn slippers. Between her and my ex was a giant book of cartoon movie princesses. Her current favorite bedtime read.

I stood for a moment, taking in the unexpected scene. The three of them seemed so . . . peaceful. As if all was well within the dim glow of the B&B's cozy parlor—and beyond. No murders. No suspicions. No divorce. No doubt.

Time had stopped in a perfect place.

I hated to awaken my little still-family and bring them back to reality, but they'd sleep a lot better in their beds. If Bliz woke up in an unfamiliar place, even within the Buckley House, she'd be terrified.

"Ian," I whispered, placing a gentle hand on his shoulder. "Ian, wake up."

In the pale rose light, his eyelids flickered, then opened. Weirdly, he didn't seem startled. "It's me, Kate," I said. "You all fell asleep down here."

"I know," he said. "The girls were hot up in the Nest, even with the AC. And so knackered they dozed off in the middle of"—he pointed to the book in his lap—"whatever this is. Bliz wanted me to read it to her. I think Maeve was listening, too. She said I used to read it to her."

I smiled. Ian had never been big on princess stories. But I knew he remembered. And Maeve remembered, too.

"Here, I'll take Bliz upstairs." I held out my arms.

"That's OK, I've got her. She's heavier than she looks." Ian handed me the book and carefully stood up from the chair. Then he walked slowly toward the stairs in the foyer with Bliz still cradled to his chest.

I gently awakened Maeve, then helped her sit up and get her bearings for a minute. "Did you have a nice nap, honey?" I asked. "Time to go up to the Nest. It should be cooler now. Your dad has Bliz."

"OK." She still looked confused. "Why didn't you just let me sleep?"

"You'll be glad I didn't in the morning, when you're feeling nice and rested." I guided her off the loveseat and toward the door.

Then I remembered I hadn't turned off the lamp. We always turned all of them off at night to save on the electric bill. "Hold on, sweetie," I said, leaving her by the nightlight near the front desk.

I ran back into the parlor, but as I switched off the little lamp another light filled the room.

A car was pulling away from the curb out front. Were Dad and Frank back already?

I'd pulled the Lexus into the driveway, and Frank would want to park the van there. Oops. Should I get out and move his car? I needed to give my brother his keys back anyway.

I went to the window and pulled back the filmy white curtain between the drapes.

Not the Chief's van. But I recognized the vehicle, all right.

It belonged to one Garrett McGavin.

What was he doing hanging out on our street again? In the dark, no less. Without saying anything to me, his not-girlfriend. I hadn't even seen him when I came in.

Of course not. He was well-versed in undercover surveillance. What exactly did he think he would see here? Me and Ian making out in the front room of the Buckley House?

I watched, fuming, as the car continued down Galway Court. Not too fast, not too slow.

Well, I had more important things to do than worry about Garrett right now. Like get Maeve back to the Nest and tucked in beside her little sister.

Now the parlor was completely dark, with only the nightlight at the foot of the stairs—and years of childhood memories—to guide me toward the stairs. But as I moved past the coffee table, I caught a distinct whiff of mint.

I stopped to peer closer. Yup, an abandoned mug of peppermint tea. Marty must have been drinking it before he left with the other musicians for the Barleycorn.

I couldn't leave the dirty mug there for any early rising guests to find. Mom would have a complete fit. I'd dump it in the kitchen across the hall. Annoyed, I grabbed the handle in a jerking motion, splashing a bit of cold tea on Bliz's precious princess book. Aargh. I dabbed at the liquid as best I could with the sleeve of my cardigan in the dim glow of the nightlight.

Maeve hadn't waited for me. I looked up and saw she was already at the top of the stairs.

Once again, I felt the sudden weight of this long, horrible, exhausting day. I was too tired to even drag myself into the kitchen now. The princess book and the stupid mug felt like high-intensity CrossFit weights as I followed after my daughter, the tiredness increasing with every step.

Behind me the grandfather clock launched into the Westminster Chimes. A single chime after the familiar melody—1 AM.

Tomorrow was sure to be another tough day. And it was already here.

Chapter Twenty-Nine

I awoke to gray clouds through the round window and the brush of a furry cat tail across my face. Banshee. I swatted at air, then rolled onto my side on the braided carpet.

Round window? Braided carpet? The rug in Colleen's room—that we currently shared—was pink shag. The windows were not round. For some reason, I was in the Nest. On the floor.

I sat up, rubbing my arm. I'd slept on it wrong.

Maeve and Bliz were both asleep under the quilt of the iron double bed. The princess book and Marty's tea mug were set on a small table across the room. I must have dozed off here somehow.

No sign of Ian. He'd left down the Nest's ladder after tucking in both girls. Or had I dreamed that?

I knew I'd had some strange dreams, but I couldn't remember them right now. Just the general feel of them. Not nightmares, exactly, but dark and stressful.

Reaching for my cell phone beside me on the rug, I checked the time: 7:58 AM. Oh no.

One of the dreams swiftly came into focus in my brain. Fallon. Flashing lights. Detective Walker.

I jumped to my feet and slid into my shoes, which I'd fortunately removed before conking out. Dad had said my interview with Surly Shirley was at oh-eight-hundred. That was in exactly two minutes.

No time for a shower. Or to brush my teeth, unless I got Mom to stall Surly Shirley for me. She was always prompt.

I borrowed Maeve's hairbrush from the dresser, running it quickly through my hair, and found a brand-new deodorant sticking out of her backpack. We'd bought it at a rest stop convenience store yesterday, along with a few bottles of water and a pack of peppermint gum.

Perfect.

I shrugged off my lightweight cardigan to apply the roll-on and took a swig from the water bottle. I squeezed out enough water into my palm to freshen up my face and make me feel more awake. I really tried to smooth my outfit from last night—the black sleeveless top and skirt—enough that I wouldn't look as if I'd done the walk of shame home.

I tied the cardigan around my waist to hide some of the wrinkles. Ugh. One of the cuffs was sticky from Marty's tea mug. Gross. Hopefully the sharp-eyed Detective Walker wouldn't notice.

Finally I took a stick of gum from the pack, popped it in my mouth, and snuck as quietly as possible down the ladder of the Nest. I hadn't even folded it up last night before I fell asleep. Any of us could have fallen through the open door in the floor if we weren't careful.

Mom met me at the bottom of the main stairs. "Good morning, and Shirley is here," she said, nodding toward the kitchen. "I'm sorry I didn't wake you earlier, but when I checked your room neither you nor Colleen was there." She lowered her voice. "I'm not sure your sister came home last night. And your father certainly didn't."

"Oh. Sorry, Mom. Dad asked me to tell you, but I didn't want to wake you either."

"No harm. Frank called me. He and your father are still at the hospital. They should be back soon."

"How is Marty?" I asked.

My mom sighed. "The poor man had to have emergency surgery on his broken leg. But he's doing as well as can be expected, the doctors said. He has a concussion and a broken rib or two on top of the leg. I'm afraid he'll be laid up for a while."

"That's terrible," I said. "But I'm glad it wasn't even worse."

Mom nodded. "I'll visit him this morning, but I need to make sure the guests are sorted first. Hopefully your sister will show up soon."

"I can take you to see Marty," I said. "I should pay him a visit as well." *And maybe ask him some questions.* "We'll take him some of your cookies."

Mom smiled. "He does love sweets. Anyway, I've set Shirley up in the kitchen with a cup of coffee and a blueberry scone. There's some for you, too. The guests can take their breakfasts in the living room while you have your conversation. Not a peep out of any of them so far. Even Lulu and Cassandra."

"Thanks, Mom," I said. "Does, um, Detective Walker seem like she's in a good mood?"

Mom pursed her lips. "Hard to tell. Though she did seem pleased with her pastry. She looks tired. As do you."

"It was a late night," I said. *After the longest day ever.*

"Oh, and just so you know, Bliz was sneezing quite a bit before bed," Mom said. "She didn't have a fever, so I don't think she's sick. I gave her a bit of that allergy syrup in the bathroom, which she doesn't care for one bit. But she did all that digging around in the garden yesterday." She paused. "And that dog is a walking carpet of fur."

I nodded. "Maeve is already signed up for grooming detail today. She'll give Rover his breakfast, too. We put up a chore chart in the laundry room."

"Good idea," Mom said. "And one more thing before you go. The Miss Shamrock first rounds are still on tonight, but the Donnelly School dance practice for the fair is off. Some of the parents were worried about security downtown, after what happened with Marty at the Barleycorn, even though the police say it was an accident. Bernie called first thing this morning to let us know."

"Is the actual dance event canceled?" I asked. This whole scenario was shaping up to be a deja-vu from St. Paddy's week.

"Not yet," Mom said. "Just the Limerick Lads concert. Peat is still scheduled, and they've added someone named Mary Ann Mawhinney. But the town council is meeting today about the fair itself. There are rumblings about canceling the whole thing. Mayor Flanagan is still optimistic, Bernie said. He's holding firm that the show must go on, and it's his call."

"What a mess." I gave a heavy sigh. "I'm with the council, I think. Maybe the town should just skip the fair this year, at this point."

"Skip the fair?" Mom looked horrified. "But honey, it's such a wonderful tradition. From before the Green Wave. And our local businesses need traffic, especially after the Saint Patrick's week debacle."

"We still have Banshee Fest coming up at Halloween," I pointed out. *Had I said "we"?* "And Twelve Days of Celtic Christmas."

"Let's not think about any of that now, honey." Mom gave me a hug, then spun me in the direction of the kitchen. "Everything will turn out as it should. Keep the faith. And for heaven's sake, go talk to Shirley."

As I entered the kitchen, I saw that Detective Walker was almost done with her scone. Either she was a fast eater, or she'd arrived early. My bet was on the second.

Mom had started making the scones herself more often, instead of Colleen buying them from Kilpatrick's' bakery section. It saved us money, as well as any unnecessary run-ins with Una McShane. The mix was imported from Ireland, but still.

"Good morning, Detective," I said in a cheery tone. "Sorry I'm late." I glanced at Mom's rooster clock. Twelve minutes late. "Not as hot today, is it? Thank heavens."

I had no idea whether it was warm or not, since I hadn't been outside yet. But it was a good guess due to the clouds.

"Mmhm." Detective Walker drummed her fingers on the table as I poured a quick coffee for myself and snagged a scone from the tin. "Would you like another one of these?" I asked. "Mom made plenty. How about more coffee?"

"I might take half a scone," she said. "And it's an affirmative on the java refill." She gave me what almost passed as a smile. For her, anyway.

Surly Shirley wasn't much on small talk. After I carefully poured her coffee and placed the scone on her plate with tongs, I took the seat across from the person most likely to haul my ex into jail. The county DA's lead detective wasn't wearing her usual trench due to summer. But she did have the next best thing: a tan blazer over her tan T-shirt. I had to say, though, the outfit looked nice with her dark skin and short salt and pepper curls.

"I'll get straight to the point, Ms. Buckley," Detective Walker said.

"Please, call me Kate."

She gave a sharp nod. "I'm here to find out whatever you can tell me regarding the O'Malley homicide," she said. "You've already made a statement to the investigators on the scene and answered questions. But I have a few more for you."

"Of course," I said. "But before we get started, I'm just wondering. Is my former husband an official person of interest in Fallon's murder? I mean, I know she was his fiancée, and cops always look at the people closest to the victim first, but I can assure you, Ian would never—"

Detective Walker held up one hand to cut me off. She must have picked that up from my dad. "Ms. Buckley—Kate—you know I can't discuss the specifics of a case with you. We're looking at *anyone* who might have had motive, method, and opportunity." She paused for an extra second or two, looking straight at me.

Oh. Right. Point taken.

"I've been speaking with your father, per usual, as a matter of professional courtesy," Surly Shirley went on. "And he's shared the most recent updates from your end. But I'd really like to hear more from you, Ms. Buckley, about that note you happened to find in the victim's hotel. And you personally received a similar one last night. Is that correct?"

The interview went downhill from there. I'm not sure how long it lasted, but it was uncomfortable to say the least. And then it got worse.

"One thing that continues to strike me, Ms. Buckley—Kate," she corrected with that seemingly painful smile, "is how involved you somehow continue to be in the homicide investigations of the Shamrock PD. Despite continued warnings from law enforcement personnel, you keep popping up like a bad penny." She pushed aside her crumb-filled plate to lean across the table. "Not only do your actions risk jeopardizing the cases themselves. You're also creating further inconvenience. As in, depleting the available pool of local officers and"—she cleared her throat for emphasis—"detectives otherwise eligible to work the investigations."

As in my brother. And Garrett. I squirmed in my seat. "Detective Walker, it's not as if I get involved on purpose," I tried to defend myself. "Everything just . . . I don't know, happens. And then I need to fix things."

"No, Ms. Buckley, you do not." The detective tapped her empty coffee mug. "You are not a member of the Shamrock PD. I appreciate your enthusiasm as a private citizen. And I'll allow that you made significant contributions to the Donnelly case last spring. Mostly lucky ones."

Lucky? I steeled myself against the temptation to correct her.

"But you are neither trained nor professionally certified to participate in criminal investigations," Detective Walker went on. "And by doing so, you're risking both your own safety and the welfare of others. Including your family. Am I making myself clear?"

"Very." I sighed. Was she referring just to me or to my dad as well? Chief Ryan welcomed his contributions.

"If you'd wanted to be a detective, especially considering your family's history with the department, you should have done things the right way. Say, by studying criminal justice rather than music or accounting." Detective Walker added. "Maybe you need to consider your personal goals."

Was she giving advice or just slamming my life choices? Hard to tell.

She smiled and pushed her coffee mug slightly toward me. "Another shot, if you don't mind?"

"Sure." I jumped up to fulfill her request, glad for the chance to hide my flaming face. Fortunately I needed to make another whole pot of coffee.

Surly Shirley was right, I told myself as I hunted for a new box of filters. I had no business poking around in police matters. Technically my dad didn't either, as a retired member of the force. But stubbornness and denial ran in the Buckley family. Along with a certain stick-to-itiveness.

What the Chief and I shared was a love for puzzles, where every piece needed to fit so the big picture became clear. It bugged us both when things were out of place—like, a stray piece of paper on the floor. Raise the stakes—to homicide, for example—and our interest was even stronger.

I could never let go of a problem until it was solved. Even if I really, really wanted to. Closure was an obsession for me, I'd realized lately. And so far, trying to find answers in a murder investigation seemed a lot easier than in my personal life.

And I had to admit, the pursuit of justice for those who'd been wronged—or wrongly accused—brought a tiny bit of excitement to my life. But what if the truths I uncovered weren't what I'd hoped or expected?

There was also the possibility of too much adrenaline. Last night someone had sent me a threatening note. And they meant business. The last person they'd threatened had turned up dead.

As I pressed the button on the coffee maker, Colleen swept into the kitchen. She, too, wore the same outfit she'd had on last night. For an entirely different reason. "Ooo, caffeine," she said. "I'm in. Dad and Frank and Noel just got back, too. Oh, hey, Detective Walker. Great to see you. Dad really wants to talk to you."

Detective Walker pushed away from the table and hoisted herself up from her chair. "Forget about that refill, thanks, Kate. I think I have all the info I need from you. For now."

Chapter Thirty

I had hoped to talk to Noel after Detective Walker was safely gone, but he went straight up to bed after arriving back at the Buckley House. Poor guy. He'd had a long night with his dad at the hospital.

As Colleen scrubbed at stubborn stains on the stovetop, I took inventory in the pantry for our rapidly growing grocery list and the girls ate their highly nutritious breakfasts. Mom's crispy rashers with in-season blueberries. Plus a cinnamon toaster tart for Maeve and strawberry for Bliz. Neither of my girls liked scones. Maeve insisted she'd break her braces on them.

As I made my list, I couldn't help trying to organize the spices and boxes of rice and canned goods and spaghetti jars and flour and peanut butter. Just a quick job for now. With all the stuff in there, it was hard to tell what we needed. And groceries were already costing us a bundle.

Marty and Noel, I suspected, would have a much longer stay with us than we'd expected. Dad would be delighted. Mom and me, the Buckley House accountant, less so.

My older daughter was reading the toaster tart variety-pack box. "Ew," she said, throwing down her pastry. "These are expired."

I went over to check the box. "Just by a month," I said. "They're fine."

Colleen turned around from the stove. "Kate, did you find that dress for Bliz? And what did we decide on her outfit for tonight?"

I took a deep breath. "No dress downstairs. And nothing yet for tonight. We were going to pick something out after breakfast."

"I need to figure out a costume for Rover at the Pet Pavilion show," Maeve said. "Mom, can I have money to get something at Paddy's Paws?"

"Twenty bucks," I said. "After that, you can use your allowance, OK?" Ordinarily I would say she needed to make the costume herself, but at this point convenience was everything. Plus it would help support Siobhan's business.

"So Kate, I had an idea for Bliz's outfit," Colleen said. "What about my old Little Miss Shamrock dance dress? Mom kept it in the cedar closet. It's still in great shape, and really cute."

"Ooo, I want to see it!" Bliz clasped her hands. "Mommy, can I wear Aunt Colleen's dress?"

"Sure, sweetie." I smiled at her excitement, ignoring the tiny, now-familiar twinge in my heart. She looked so much like Colleen at her age, it would be like a trip back in time.

"I can do her hair and makeup and everything," my sister said. "You know, like we do for dance shows."

Mom stuck her head into the kitchen. "Kate, when you go out, would you mind dropping off those pies on the counter to the gazebo on the Square? The Rosary Society wants to get the baked goods together early, so they can see what they have. They're all ready to go."

"No problem," I said, before Mom added, "and oh, don't forget those cookies for Marty in the green and gold tin. It's on top of the fridge. I didn't want Frank to find them."

"Got it," I said. Shamrock Hospital was the first stop on my itinerary. Hopefully Marty would feel well enough to answer a few questions. I'd have to be careful, though. I didn't want to upset him during his recovery.

"Mommy, what does 'heritage' mean?" Bliz's mouth was covered in frosted crumbs. "Maeve and I looked on the computer, but I don't get it."

I had to agree it was a tough concept for little kids to grasp—not to mention write 150 words about. Mayor Flanagan probably didn't know any almost-eight-year-olds. They didn't vote.

"I told you, Blizzie. It means what all the old people in your family leave you after they're dead," Maeve said. "Like, recipes and traditions and stories about where they came from and stuff."

"But I don't want anyone to die." Bliz frowned. "Like Deirdre and Dad's friend who wasn't very nice."

I went over and knelt by her chair. "Sweetie, listen to me. No one in our family is going to die. Not for a long, long time." *Hopefully*. "It's nothing for you to worry about. Maeve meant people in our family from way back when the Buckleys and Nolans lived in Ireland."

"And Spain. And France and somewhere in the Middle East," Colleen put in. "I gave Mom and Dad that ancestry kit for Christmas a couple of years ago," she added, when we all turned to her in surprise.

"Cool. Guess they can hunt for serial killers through our genes, then," Maeve said helpfully.

Bliz looked stricken. "Just kidding, Blizzie," her sister added quickly.

I turned to Colleen. "Now would be the perfect time to show Bliz your old dress, don't you think?"

Half an hour later I was showered and ready to go to town. Right after I dropped a breakfast tray outside Ian's room. As far as I knew, he hadn't eaten in forever.

Balancing the tray with one hand, I tucked a strand of my still-wet hair behind my ear and smoothed the bright yellow sundress I'd borrowed from Colleen's closet. She'd never miss it.

I knocked on my ex's door. "Ian?" I called. "It's me. I've got breakfast for you. Tea and blueberry scones and Mom's rashers. Extra-fried."

Macker, wearing a short, skull-print bathrobe and carrying a toiletry bag, walked by me in the hall. She must have been using the shower in the Chief's private wing. "Don't bother," she said, without looking back. "He won't answer. I already tried."

I didn't answer her, either. She didn't seem like much of a morning person. "Ian," I tried again, after the Peat drummer disappeared. "I know you love rashers."

The door cracked open. "Thanks very much," he said, taking the tray. "I'm famished. I just didn't want to deal with Macker right now. She's driving me loo-lah with all her helping."

"I bet," I said, with a grin. "Listen, I'm off to town. But did you hear about Marty?"

"No." Ian frowned and opened the door wider. The room was dark with the curtains drawn and his hair was wildly spiked. "Is he OK?"

I filled my ex in on the Barleycorn disaster. "Noel was at the hospital all night," I finished. "He's really been having a hard time lately with his dad."

"I'm sorry for it," Ian said. "I'll talk to him when I come down."

"Oh, and also, Bliz has her Little Miss Shamrock first round at Angels Hall tonight. Well, at five. No one's expecting you or anything. Just giving you a heads-up."

He nodded. "Thanks," he called as I pushed the button for the Chief's private elevator.

I turned. My ex gave me a little wave and disappeared inside his room.

* * *

I was loading the last of Mom's pies into the Subaru for the trip downtown when a bloodcurdling scream sounded from the backyard.

Maeve.

I dropped the strawberry pie on top of the pistachio cream and charged up the driveway. I may have rebroken the newly repaired gate in my hurry to enter the yard.

My older daughter stood in the middle of the lawn with both hands to her face as Rover danced around her with something in his mouth.

"I'm here, honey," I said, rushing over and pushing Maeve behind me. "What is it? A snake? Probably a garden snake. They aren't poisonous."

"Not a snake," Maeve said. "He dug it up from over there somewhere." She pointed to a far back corner of the yard, where a huge pile of dirt had flattened one of Mom's antique rosebushes. "I tried to get him to quit it, but he wouldn't."

Rover stopped his frenzied whirls for a moment, wagging his tail. Whatever it was, our new dog was clearly proud of his prize.

I slowly stepped forward, careful not to spook him. "It's some kind of rusty old garden tool."

My daughter shook her head. "I don't think so."

That darned dog started prancing around again. He thought this was the best game ever. But I had had enough.

"Rover, sit!" I commanded sharply. To my shock, he obeyed. "Drop it," I directed.

He did. A miracle. Or his previous owner had actually trained him.

"Stay," I said.

At this point I suddenly became aware that everyone who'd been inside the Buckley House was now outside. Or most of them were, anyway. Ian and Noel stood right behind me. Mom frowned from the patio with Colleen next to her holding Bliz's hand. Dad had zoomed down the back porch ramp and was navigating the soft grass. Lulu's mouth hung open as she stood with her arms protectively around Cassandra. The Limerick twins, wearing matching bathrobes, watched from further back with Macker, Liam, and Jaymes.

And Mrs. Sheehan, of course. Our next-door neighbor was practically falling out of her window.

The Chief came up with a squeal of brakes and peered toward the ground.

"It's a knife," I said to him softly. "A very rusty one." Long, narrow, and scary-looking.

"That's not rust," Garrett said beside me. "It's dried blood."

Garrett? What was he doing here?

"Bag it," the Chief said tersely.

No one said a word as my sort-of boyfriend snapped on a pair of disposable gloves from his back packet. Then he disappeared through the gate and down the driveway. He had to have a car somewhere on the street.

OK, fine. I'd think about Garrett's unannounced appearance later. At the moment I was focused on the certainty that Rover had dug up the weapon used to murder Fallon O'Malley. Which I had no doubt her killer selected straight from Athena Sweeney's filched bag of sculpting tools.

And deliberately buried in the Buckley House backyard.

But why had the killer brought it here?

* * *

In the Shamrock Hospital parking lot I shut off the ignition and sat in the Subaru for a couple of minutes, trying to get myself together. I felt completely drained. I couldn't remember anything about driving here.

Except that I'd thought about the case the whole way.

Whoever buried the knife in our yard had to be the killer. And that killer had to be one of our Buckley House guests. No surprise, really. Most of the possible suspects on my list were guests: Marty, Ian, and now Noel. That left Athena and—in a real stretch—Gabby. As far as I knew, neither of the women had been by the house. Lately, or even ever.

It was a long list, for sure. But it was clear that the rivalry between the Limerick Lads and Peat was key to solving this case. And those evil stone gnomes had to be involved somehow.

Yikes. Not *involved*, exactly. *Connected.* They were ugly statues, not actual living creatures. Other than in Gabby's mind, maybe. And now mine.

Time to get some answers from Marty, before I officially lost it. I needed to do it fast, or Mom's pies in the cooler on the back seat would be mush.

I took a last swig from my water bottle and crumpled the wrapper from the—expired—power bar I'd grabbed in my rush out of the house. It had taken me a while, even with Mom's and Colleen's help, to get the girls back on track and set up for the next couple of hours.

To my surprise, Ian had come through with a guitar for Maeve. She was thrilled, even though she'd never seemed interested before in playing an instrument. She'd taken piano lessons in the city, but practicing on a plastic keyboard wasn't the same. Maybe she'd try my old piano in the Buckley House living room.

I left the two of them in the sitting room, where my ex was showing our daughter how to play a few basic chords.

Bliz was happily getting her hair and nails done at Spa Colleen.

Everyone was fine. Time to go see Marty.

Bearing Mom's cookie tin, I checked in at the visitors' center, where I was handed a pass to the fifth floor. I cooled my heels in a small green waiting room near the nurses' station, staring at green carnation arrangements and a sign that spelled "Welcome" with leprechauns forming the letters. Then I watched the hands of an old-school IBM wall clock as they moved agonizingly slowly. Just like the ones in my student days at Our Lady of Angels and Holy Innocents.

Would I even be allowed to visit Marty? I wasn't a family member, and I had no idea if he was feeling well enough for visitors. Even ones with cookies.

Finally a smiling young nurse poked her head in the door. "Kate Buckley?" she asked. "You father mentioned you'd be stopping by. You can see Mr. McCleary now."

I followed her to a shared room at the far end of the hall. The door was slightly ajar. "He's doing well after his surgery last night. He may be a little groggy from the painkillers, though," the nurse warned as she left me.

Marty's bed was the closest to the door. Unfortunately, he was more than groggy. He was completely zonked out.

The elderly musician was hooked up to all kinds of tubes and monitors. One leg was in traction and that cut on his head was heavily bandaged. A tiny, still-steaming cup of hospital tea was set on the overbed table. Poor Marty.

I'd wait a few minutes to see if he woke up. If he didn't, at least he'd have the cookies. But I wouldn't have my answers.

I perched on one of the two plastic visitor chairs and took my cell phone from my pocketbook. As soon as I tapped in my password, my screen was bombarded with breaking WSCK news headlines.

The Limerick Lads concert was canceled. The butter sculpture could be in jeopardy due to a refrigeration problem. The fair committee met. The town council met. Both voted to cancel this year's Great Shamrock Fair in light of recent unfortunate events. The mayor vetoed all closure recommendations.

The fair was officially on, come heck or high water. And dollars.

"I don't know, Baba," I heard a deep female voice say. "Everything is such a mess. I've really screwed up. I'm so sorry. Taking on those fair projects was a massive mistake. Especially that crazy butter sculpture. I've let you down. I've let the business down."

"No, Athena," an older man's voice answered. "This could be a wonderful opportunity for you. You need to keep a positive attitude, my doll."

What a stroke of Irish luck. Finally. Marty's roommate was the sculptor Nicholas Sweeney. And he was speaking with his daughter. About the fair.

Then came the crisis of conscience. Should I announce my presence with a discreet cough? Stick my head around the divider and say hello to Athena? Or stay quiet and see if there was anything important I could learn for the case?

I chose the silent option. Even though I'd been embarrassed and annoyed when Macker eavesdropped on me and Colleen in the Barleycorn ladies' room.

This was different. The faster I found Fallon's killer, the sooner the Great Shamrock Fair and everyone in town would be safe.

Especially my family.

Chapter Thirty-One

Between the constantly beeping monitors and Marty's loud snoring, I was having trouble hearing Athena and her father on the other side of the hospital room divider. With each mighty snore, I quietly scooted my visitor chair closer to the curtain.

"Things can't be that bad for the fair, Athena. Always my dramatic child."

"I hate him," Athena said. "He won't let me work in peace. He wants to come by the butter sculpture building. Baba, every day he asks when he can see his masterpiece."

"*His* masterpiece?" Nick chuckled. "The Mayor is such a funny little man."

"He approved all of your original sketches. He loved them. Because you made him look handsome and heroic. But he doesn't look that way now. At all."

"What is the problem?" Nick asked.

Athena sighed. "I finished building the framework you started, exactly to your specifications. And I proportioned the butter mixture just like you told me."

"Not too much Irish butter?" Nick asked. "You don't want too much fat, or it will melt faster. Use more American butter.

The cheaper, the better. You can add in some food coloring to make it more yellow."

"And then my sculpting tools were stolen. My favorite ones I brought home from Europe."

"With the knife that may have been used in a terrible crime?"

"Yes, Baba. Thanks for bringing *that* up. Another problem for me. Mayor Flanagan on one side, cops on the other. But anyway, the butter sculpture keeps melting way too fast. And it's making the mayor's face look worse and worse. There's something wrong with the refrigeration in the building, I think."

"Ah. That happens every year. The mayor likes to keep the electrical bills low. You need to tell him about the melting, so the thermostats in the building can be adjusted. He'll try to talk down your concern. But he wants a magnificent final product, to go with this year's Prosperity and Progress theme. Featuring him. Hold your ground. But nicely."

"I don't want to be nice," Athena grumbled. "I want to create gorgeous, unique art."

"Art is a business, my dear," her father said. "It always has been, starting with the great artists supported by their patrons. They may not talk about it much in your fancy art schools, but creators need to eat."

I slunk in my chair. I was listening to a private conversation between a father and daughter. What if someone eavesdropped on me and the Chief? I would be so upset. And possibly mortified. But I'd heard enough to convince me that Athena hadn't stabbed Fallon in a field with her sculpting knife for trespassing around her studio. She sounded like a completely different person when she wasn't showing off to the public. I needed to leave right away without Athena ever knowing I'd been here. I'd try to talk to Marty again later.

"There's something else, Baba."

I quickly sat back down.

"You know those fanciful gnomes I spent way too much time on? For my Samhain fantasy project? Well, people hate them. Except for one person and she seems a little . . . obsessed. Not a single person has placed a bid on them for the fair auction. I guess I set the minimum too high."

"Then lower it, my sweet girl," Nick said. "It's not too late. Again, it's business. You have to gauge correct demand. And you said you have one big fan. That's important, too. You are not creating for everyone. You're bringing art from stone for those who share and appreciate your vision."

"Yeah, but I sold out. I agreed to add a special mystery promotion inside one of the gnomes for the auction. I told myself I was paying things forward for a fellow artist. But I thought the promo would get tons of attention."

"Wasn't it featured on WSCK, my sweet?"

"Baba, please." I could practically see Athena rolling her eyes. "So far, the promo isn't upping the interest in my work. People are making fun of the gnomes. And I don't know if the promo will help the other artist, either, once the secret item is revealed."

"But you say it's a blind promotion? People want to know what they're bidding on, my daughter. Money is tight these days. Perhaps you should have fully partnered with this artist, if you were both looking for higher bids and greater visibility."

"I'm not sure that was what he was going for," Athena said. "The artist is a musician, from Ireland. He's trying to launch a solo career for the future. He said he was taking a big risk, but it would be worth it. Professionally and personally. He's a passionate guy. And maybe less of a businessperson." She sighed. "Like me."

Noel, I realized. *It has to be Noel.* And some kind of music, something special he wanted to call attention to. But why would he secretly put his work inside a hideous stone creature?

"Well, my pet, you can fix the situation," Nick said. "You are young and still learning. We all make mistakes. Even when we are older. Now go. I've enjoyed our visit, but you need to get to work."

"Yes, Baba." I heard Athena gathering her things and hit the floor behind one of the Marty's beeping monitors. "Thanks. I love you." She emerged from around the divider and swept out of the room.

"Remember, be nice!" Nick called. "You catch the flies with the honey."

Well. That was an earful. And a lot to think about. I got up and back onto my chair before a nurse or someone came in and saw me hiding amongst the medical equipment. But it was time for me to go, too.

When I leaned over to say goodbye to Marty, his cycs fluttered. "Marty," I said gently. "It's me, Kate Buckley. I've brought you cookies. They're right here on your overbed table. Don't eat them all at once."

"Thanks, darlin,'" he said weakly. "Give my regards to your dad and ma. And tell my son I'm keeping well."

Marty was fading again.

I'd ask him what I wanted to know. Maybe he wouldn't remember when the drugs wore off. "Marty," I whispered.

"Why did you call Fallon a 'divil'? Why were you so angry at her? Because of what she did with the Lads and Crossroad Dreams and Emerald Records?"

"Fallon O'Malley?" To my horror, Marty's eyes flew open, and he tried to sit up. The nurse would kill me.

"It's OK, Marty," I said soothingly. "Never mind. Go back to sleep."

He started snoring again, and I tiptoed toward the door.

"She hurt my son," I heard him say.

* * *

Mom's pies were not looking good in the cooler on the backseat. I turned on the Subaru's AC pronto. It would take a while until cold air started blowing through the vents. Right now the inside of the car felt like Mississippi in July.

I needed to get to the Square pronto.

As I wove through traffic—were the tourists returning after all?—a call came through on the car phone. I pushed the button. "Hey, Gabby."

My old boss was sobbing. *Oh no.*

"Kate, I need your help," she said. "I've been robbed!"

"What?" I almost drove straight through a rotary. "Are you OK? Where are you? Did you call 911?"

"Noooo," she said. "I don't know what to do. It was very strange."

"Gabby," I said. "Listen to me carefully. I need you to stay very, very calm. Lock up the store and go somewhere safe. How about the police station?"

"That's so far," Gabby said.

"Well, then, somewhere else. With lots of people around who can help you. I'm on my way to the Square right now.

There will be cops there, too. Meet me at the Rosary Society table, OK?"

"I guess so," Gabby agreed. "But I'd rather stay in my store."

I didn't bother trying to follow her reasoning. I hit the gas harder.

There was no sign of my old boss when I showed up at the baked goods table under the green and white canopy tent, lugging my cooler. There were plenty of people on the Square today, many setting up tents and chairs. The Miss Shamrock finals and the butter sculpture unveiling would take place on a temporary platform near the gazebo.

"Here, let me help you," one of the Rosary Society ladies said, reaching into the cooler. "Oh my. These are Eileen Buckley's pies, aren't they? I can always tell, they look so nice. And they're delicious."

"Thanks," I said. "That's my mom. I'll be sure to tell her."

Gabby still hadn't arrived. I bet she'd stayed at Gifts of Gab after all. I needed to check on her. I hoped she wasn't in trouble.

As I reached the gift shop door, I sidestepped to check the window. Yup, the malicious gremlins were still on display. I leaned closer to the glass and shaded my eyes. Nothing seemed out of place inside.

But as much as I wanted to help Gabby, I hesitated. Every now and then it had briefly crossed my mind that my old boss might be, well, losing her marbles. What if she had somehow had something to do with Fallon's death? She was definitely involved with Athena and in charge of the auction bidding. And she couldn't afford to have dupes made of her precious gnomes.

What if all of this had to do with money? Financial gain was a common motive for killers. And if Gabby wasn't in her right mind, based on her obsession with those crazy statues . . .

She didn't want to call 911. Or meet me in public.

Nope, I wasn't going inside Gifts of Gab alone. There were plenty of sharp objects in there.

I knocked on the door. She cracked it open, then released the chain. "Oh, come in dearie," she said. "I knew you'd come here. I just didn't want to go to the Square. What if the robber comes back?"

Then you don't want to be here, I wanted to say. Instead, I went with, "Hey, I have one of your green tablecloths from the Barleycorn last night. I couldn't juggle it with my pies, but it's still in my car. Want to walk over with me to get it?"

"Oh, I don't think so. It's much too hot." Gabby fanned her face with her hand. "The AC is heavenly in here."

This was ridiculous. "Gabby, I'm sorry, but I'm not going inside the store if you didn't call the cops. Do you have any customers right now, or can you come out and speak with me? Just for a minute?"

She hesitated, then stepped out onto the sidewalk. "Tell me what got stolen," I said. "Was it cash? Merchandise? Did you see the person? Was there more than one? Did they break in through a window? Hold you up at gunpoint?"

Gabby looked genuinely frazzled. "Oh, my, that's so many questions. Why don't I just give you the story?"

When I nodded, trying not to be impatient, she said, "I didn't call 911 because he was such a nice guy. Tall, handsome. From Ireland, I think. He had a lovely voice. He walked in like a regular customer. He wore all black, and he had a ball cap pulled over most of his face. Like he didn't want to be recognized. Because he was going to rob me."

Noel. "What did he want?" I asked.

Gabby pouted. "An Athena Sweeney gnome. My favorite one. The young man said he'd pay for it. But he only wanted that particular one."

"Did you explain to him about the auction bidding, like you did with Fallon O'Malley?"

She nodded emphatically. "Oh yes." Her face fell. "But I ended up selling him the statue he wanted because no one has bid on the gnomes yet. I figured no one would mind because it's a whole group of statues, and what's one less? And there'd be some money going to charity, at least. I figured it was a win-win."

"Absolutely," I agreed. Thank goodness Gabby hadn't actually been robbed. And Noel hadn't committed a crime. As far as I knew.

"But after he was gone I realized he'd taken the gnome with the extra-value surprise inside." Her voice dropped to a whisper. "I shook every one of them and weighed the different sizes, so I figured it out."

Oh wow. Poor Gabby really was losing it.

"No one knows what the prize is except Athena. It could be incredibly valuable. Maybe I didn't charge the young man enough. And now it's gone!" She burst into tears. "The Auction Committee will be so angry with me. And the mayor won't be happy."

"No, Gabby," I said, giving her a hug. "You didn't do anything wrong. And you know what? Things could turn out even better in the end."

Completely true. Now Noel had his item back, and Athena wouldn't need to worry about unartistic commercialism. Gabby might need to edit the auction blurb, but it didn't sound as if many people would even notice there was no longer a prize.

After assuring my old boss that she hadn't really been robbed, since she sold the gnome to the customer, and that no one would be mad at her, I said goodbye and headed back to the car. The groceries could wait for now. My pantry inventory this morning had shown Mom we had enough to get us through another couple of days.

I needed to talk to Noel. Hopefully, he'd returned straight to the B&B with his creepy purchase.

To my surprise, I ran into Noel in the parking lot, getting into his mini rental car. He must have stopped at Time for a Lime, because he'd placed a fresh-squeezed limeade on the hood while he buckled the gnome into the passenger seat.

"Planning a trip through an HOV lane?" I asked.

He flashed a quick grin. "Not a bad idea."

I shaded my eyes. The sun was coming out. Finally, some good news for the fair. "Just stopped to see your dad," I said. "He wanted me to tell you he's doing well. I think he was a little sleepy."

He nodded. "Good. He needs to rest."

"Noel," I said. "We need to talk." I nodded toward the gnome. "I know what's inside your little buddy there. Well, sort of."

He visibly froze for a split second. "What's that again?"

"Some kind of new music, right? It was nice of you to donate it to the auction. Was the winning bidder going to hear it first, or something? Why did you change your mind and buy it back?"

He sighed and leaned back against the car. "Please tell me, Noel. You've always been straight with me. I've known you forever, and you're a great guy. You've always been Ian's best friend."

"I was." Noel looked at the ground. "And maybe I'm not such a good guy. I'm a terrible friend."

"Why?" I asked. "And I don't believe that, by the way."

"The song was for Fallon," he said, briefly squeezing his eyes shut. The guy was clearly in pain. "She and I were . . . a couple, before her and Ian. We kept it a secret because Fallon thought it would look unprofessional. You know, because we were working together. But we talked about getting married someday. Maybe even start a family."

Noel? And *Fallon*?

Macker had said Noel had an unknown girlfriend who broke up with him. No wonder she'd been a secret.

But I just couldn't see those two together. At all.

Now I sounded like Macker, judging couples' compatibility. Had Macker known Noel and Fallon were in love?

I must have done a terrible job of hiding my reaction, because Noel gave a sad smile. "I can read your mind," he said. "Fallon was a great girl. She was just . . . misunderstood. We got on amazingly well." Now his eyes filled with tears.

"I'm so sorry," I said gently. "About everything that happened. I can't imagine how hard it must be on you. But . . . what about Ian? He and Fallon were engaged. Or at least, Ian thought they were."

Noel took a deep breath. "It's a long story," he said. "But here's the penny version. Fallon was raging when I quit Peat to join my dad's band. So was Ian. But Fallon, uh, wasn't as understanding. She said I'd thrown my whole music career away and ruined our plans. She broke up with me when I left in March and took up with Ian. Just like that."

"Wow." I shook my head.

"We were together for three years, and she gets engaged to my friend in less than three months. I couldn't believe it." Noel smiled faintly. "I'm not sure Ian knew what hit him either, to be honest."

"But when Fallon wanted something, she got it, right?" I said. How many times had Macker told me that?

Noel chuckled. "That's about right, yeah. It almost killed me when she showed around that fancy ring at the pub the other night. I followed her out when she left, and we had a row on the sidewalk. She said if I wanted her back, I'd need to rejoin the band." He shook his head. "She was so mad she threw that ring at me."

"Really? She picked it up, right?"

"No," Noel said. "I did, after she went off in the green cab. That rock had to have set Ian and her back a pretty penny. I went to their Airbnb that night after she texted me to apologize—I was talking with you in the parlor at the B&B when I got her messages. But when I showed up at the Airbnb, Ian was already there. I reckoned I'd give the ring to her in private when I saw her next. But I never did."

"That's so sad," I said softly.

"Yeah." He looked away. "When I learned Fallon was . . . gone . . . I planned to leave that crazy ring in Ian's room or something. Maybe not right away. I put it in my guitar case for safekeeping—I always have it on me—but someone stole it from right under my nose. I had the ring with me at the Barleycorn. It's bad luck, I tell you."

"Any idea who took it?"

Noel shook his head. "None. And now I owe Ian a fortune for losing it."

"He may not see it that I way," I said. "Ian doesn't care about money."

"I couldn't help thinking Fallon got engaged to Ian to make me jealous," he said. "It sure seemed that way. And now I'll never know."

"So it worked."

"Oh, yeah. I was jealous, all right." Noel looked away again. "I wrote that song, the one inside my little passenger guy here—because I wanted to let her know how much I still loved her. Maybe change Fallon's mind." He teared up again. "But she never got to hear it."

There was silence between us for a long moment. "I knew it was the best song I'd ever written," Noel said finally. "And I'll admit, I had this idea it might be a breakout hit for me. You know, to launch a solo career. I thought Fallon would come back to me. Maybe even be impressed by both the song and that I took initiative by doing my own publicity." He sighed. "None of that matters anymore."

"Did you tell Fallon anything at all about the gnome part?" I asked. "To give her a heads-up, or a chance to keep things between you?"

Noel shrugged. "Not exactly. I may have given a hint or two, but I really didn't think she'd guess. We saw each other in town on the down-low before Ian and Peat arrived in Shamrock. I pointed out the gnomes in the gift shop window display." He gave a small smile. "She hated them."

"And you took the CD back from the auction because you didn't want Ian to hear Fallon's song," I said slowly.

"It's on a jump drive, actually," Noel said. "But yeah, with luck he'll never even know it existed. You won't tell him, will you?" His eyes were pleading.

"No," I said. "But maybe you should. He might be upset at first, but the truth is always best. In the end, he'll appreciate it, I think. And maybe you can repair your friendship."

"Maybe," Noel said. But I wasn't sure he was convinced.

Chapter Thirty-Two

Noel and I took separate ways home, him with his ugly little gnome friend and me with an empty pie cooler. I took the long route near the lake so I could have some time to myself to think. Specifically, about Fallon's killer.

I'd been finding it extra hard to connect all the puzzle pieces and see the clear picture. So many things had happened since the girls and I arrived in Shamrock. Some good, mostly bad. All those people coming and going. Multiple events, responsibilities, case threads, pets. I couldn't help feeling overwhelmed.

But today several larger pieces had fallen into place. With the car windows down, my playlist cranked, and my hair blowing freely in the breeze, I felt lighter and freer than I had in a while. Supermom, Dutiful Daughter, Fixer Sister, and Sort-of Girlfriend were riding in the back. Illegal Detective had claimed the passenger seat.

It would be a while before all the forensic findings were in. But unless new and/or improved evidence turned up, I'd eliminated multiple suspects from my list: Marty, Athena, Noel, Gabby. And, of course, Ian. I wasn't sure Detective Surly

Shirley would agree with me, but that didn't matter. I'd figure out this case—from a parallel universe.

For Fallon. For Ian. And maybe for me.

The car phone rang, and I stabbed at the screen. Please, not another crisis.

"Hi big sis," Colleen said. "I'm at PJ Scoops with Mom and the girls. Don't worry, we had a good lunch first."

"Great," I said. My daughters would have high blood sugar like Marty soon, if they didn't already. "Is everyone else home?"

"Dad and the twins went to see Marty again. Ian's band is rehearsing in the garage. Noel just pulled in as we were leaving. Lulu and Cassandra are shopping, I think." My sister paused. "Yeah, extra whipped cream," she said to someone else. "Anyway, Mom wanted me to ask if you'd pick up more allergy syrup at Emerald Rx. Bliz is still sneezing."

"She can't have another dose until tonight. It's every twenty-four hours."

"Yeah, that's what Mom said. But we'll have it on hand, anyway. The bottle is completely empty, and I could swear I just bought it. They only had the peppermint flavor. Bliz wants bubble gum this time if they have it."

"Will do." I was getting pretty sick of peppermint myself. I'd have to hand-wash my sticky-minty sweater. As well as Marty's tea mug. I'd forgotten to bring it down with me when I left the Nest in such a hurry this morning.

Holy shamrocks. I drove straight past the turn for downtown as I had a Waterford-crystal-clear epiphany.

Marty and his peppermint tea. He'd complained that the American version wasn't up to snuff. Even with a zillion beehives worth of honey added to it.

He'd been dozing off lately. Stumbling around. He'd fallen on his walk the morning Fallon died and straight off the Barleycorn stage last night.

True, Marty's physical health had been declining of late, but nothing as dramatic as this. What if someone had added that awful peppermint-flavored allergy syrup to his peppermint tea? Not all at once, but a bit at a time? Those doses added up—to haziness and a lack of motor function. The box warned not to combine the medicine with alcohol, drive, or operate heavy machinery.

Or, presumably, take multiple doses with tea and honey and perform onstage.

Marty could have taken the allergy syrup himself. But I'd only noticed one guest at the Buckley House with puffy, red eyes. In the parlor, when I'd met with Fallon's mourners on the morning of her death. I'd assumed the person was overcome with emotion. But they'd told me they had allergies.

I didn't bother turning around to hit the Emerald Rx. That errand could wait. Instead I hit the gas hard for home.

I'd just added a new person to my Most Likely to Be the Killer list. And there was no time to lose.

* * *

Peat was rocking the garage as I squealed into the driveway. I couldn't hear the actual music that well, but the garage was literally shaking.

Good. Macker McWilliams would be occupied long enough for me to do a bit of snooping.

I stopped to grab the household cleaning caddy and guest room master keychain from the laundry room closet. Another pit stop at the linen closet, and I was off to the races toward Macker's room.

The first thing I did when I walked in, other than pulling on disposable rubber gloves, was to close the drapes. Just in case. This was the smallest guest room the Buckley House offered, and darker to boot due to the eaves. I had to move fast and finish before the rehearsal ended.

At least I had a cover, in case Macker or anyone else returned: housekeeping duties. Tidying the rooms was usually Colleen's job, with help from Mom. The job was supposed to be done by noon, but that rarely happened.

Case in point: Macker's room was a mess. Bed still unmade, wastebasket full, clothes thrown all over the place. Luckily, she didn't have much stuff.

I started with the drawers. Mostly empty other than underwear and socks. I tossed the contents anyway, not really sure what I was looking for. Anything that might point to Macker targeting Marty. Or Fallon.

I wasn't sure why the drummer would want to injure Marty, or worse. It had to have something to do with the rivalry between Peat and the Lads. Maybe she wanted to get rid of Peat's competition for the Crossroads contract by bumping off each and every member. But why would she have murdered Fallon, who'd gotten Peat the shiny new opportunity with Johnny Myer? Macker hadn't seemed that angry that Fallon had gone behind the band members' backs.

She'd seemed more ticked off that Fallon could make anyone do what she wanted. But plenty of people—like my sister—had that skill. Was it enough reason to kill Fallon?

I moved on to the closet, checking pairs of sneakers and boots and beat-up shower shoes. I rummaged through the pockets of the bathrobe I'd seen Macker wearing earlier. Nada.

I spent a longer time rummaging through Macker's knapsack. Some Irish-brand Chapstick, a comb, key, folded sheet music. Laptop and accessories. I pulled open the desk drawers, one by one. Completely empty. Next, the nightstand.

Bingo.

Beside the Holy Bible provided for every guest room lay a single black marker. No paper, just the marker. That made sense, because the person who'd sent the notes to Fallon and me had made do with whatever they could find. A piece of printer paper. A greeting card envelope. Both could have been extracted from the Buckley House trash.

I didn't touch the marker. I took a photo with my cell.

I was done. For now. No way would I actually clean Macker's room. I was about to pull off my gloves when I tried one more place. The bed.

I lifted the twin mattress, being careful not to dislodge the tucked linens near the end so I wouldn't have to readjust them. Then I took a quick look under the pillow.

Two faces stared back at me from a well-worn photo. Ian and Macker in a pop-up photo booth. Probably taken at some Peat promotional event. Ian's expression said, "This is lame." But Macker was actually smiling, her head almost—but not quite—resting on Ian's shoulder.

I snapped another photo and dropped the pillow back in place. I'd already noticed that Macker worshipped my ex. She'd called him a genius, turned down a load of money by siding with him on the Crossroads contract, pretended at first she hadn't known I was his ex-wife, and made a pest of herself trying to "help" Ian after Fallon's death. So far he'd rejected her overtures. That had to sting.

I stood motionless beside the bed in the darkened room, feeling nauseated. Macker was in love with Ian. The feeling was not reciprocated, and she knew it. But with Fallon out of the way, she could hope that, with time, he'd have a change of heart.

Macker must have been more surprised than anyone when Ian and Fallon became engaged. And with the way she closely observed the two of them, there was a good chance she knew there was something off in their relationship. From what Noel had told me in the parking lot, Fallon was lying to Ian. Pretending to be in love with him to make Noel jealous.

What would make a lovesick, rejected—or worse, unnoticed—just-band-buddy more furious?

But why would Macker target Marty? Then I remembered the elderly musician's only words to me in the hospital: *She hurt my son.*

Marty knew about Fallon and Noel's relationship. Maybe in Macker's twisted, jealous mind, she needed to destroy the Fallon–Noel connection—and anyone who knew about it. That way, once he got over the brief pain of his fiancée's death, Ian would be open to fall in love with the super-supportive bandmate who'd been there for him all along. And he'd never know the truth.

Macker could have told Ian he was being used by Fallon, and that his best friend had betrayed him. That would be the easiest option. But maybe Ian wouldn't believe her. No one paid much attention to Macker.

It was just a feeling, but a strong one. Noel's name was next on Macker's list. Right beside mine.

I jumped at the turn of a key in the lock. Macker was back.

She stepped into the room and frowned. "What are you doing in here?"

I pointed to the cleaning caddy on the floor beside my feet. "Housekeeping. We're a little late today, sorry."

The look alone she gave me could kill. "Yeah? No one's cleaned this room since I've been here."

"It's, um, every three days," I lied. "Thought I'd start a little early."

She didn't look convinced. "Why are the curtains closed? I left them open."

"I can see the dirt better," I said. When she raised her eyebrows, I added, "We have one of those vacuums with a light on it. The darkness . . . gives more contrast."

"Uh-huh," she said, clearly not buying it. "I'll leave you to it, then."

"Is your band practice over?" I asked, as she turned to go.

She grunted without looking back and exited to the hall, closing the door behind her.

I looked down at the cleaning caddy and sighed. Now I'd have to clean this pigsty of a room for real.

* * *

It only took me half an hour to finish cleaning Macker's room, because I did a terrible job. As soon as I was done, I headed outside and slipped into the garage through the side door.

I looked around, inhaling the familiar childhood scents of wood, fertilizer, spilled oil, and damp cardboard. Mixed with the more recent odors of sweat and beer. And a tinge of pizza.

No time to lose. I needed to find the one piece of evidence that would prove the case for Macker being the cold-blooded killer of Fallon O'Malley.

My ex's fiancée's engagement ring.

Noel had said someone stole it from him, and I believed him. I'd found Macker's treasured photo of her and Ian under her pillow. Where would she keep the ring she hoped she would someday wear herself?

Somewhere that meant something to her, but no one would ever look. A tough order in someone else's garage.

Macker's instruments were set up in the far corner, near the automatic garage door. My eyes flicked over her keyboard. She'd covered it in one of Mom's good sheets from the linen closet to protect it from dust. I dismissed that choice and headed straight to the rental drum kit.

The bass drum seemed promising. A beach towel rolled like a croissant was visible through the porthole on one side of the drum face. Drummers often used towels or T-shirts to dampen the sound for less echo and a more controlled tone.

I knelt before the kick, fiddling with the adjustable legs that held it off the ground.

Carefully, I moved the drum back and forth.

The towel was taped to the inside of the drum, but the movement was enough to shake out the object Macker had hidden in the folds of the towel.

A still-brilliant diamond engagement ring.

My breath caught. I could reach through the porthole and grab it. But as with the marker in Macker's nightstand, I didn't dare. Detective Walker would kill me, if my dad didn't get to around to it first.

Carefully I set the drum back exactly as I'd found it and reached for the cell phone in my back pocket. Before I could extract it, I felt a sudden rush of air and landed flat on my face on the cement floor.

I wanted to scream, but my lungs were empty. I'd had the wind knocked straight out of me.

Someone with small fingers roughly stuffed a large piece of cloth in my mouth, then wound my wrists behind my back with scratchy rope. I gagged and twisted and tried to shout for help, but my voice was as muffled as the bass drum with the towel. I could hardly breathe.

I made another attempt to scream.

"Shut up." Macker leaned close to my left ear. She yanked the cloth—Rover's still-furry, oversized bandanna, ugh—partway out of my mouth and tied the ends tightly behind my head. Then she held something sharp and pointy to my neck. "Move and I kill you right now. Don't move and you can live another five minutes."

She'd been lurking in the garage, hiding somewhere in the shadows. How could I have been so stupid as to come in here by myself? I'd felt safe here at my childhood home, with people I knew inside.

Oh, and a killer.

I should have called 911 earlier. Or at least someone on the force. Garret. Frank. My dad. I was an eejit. Hadn't I scolded Ian for not calling the cops? I was cooked.

If my wrists weren't tied, and I didn't have whatever that sharp thing was at my neck, I could take her. She was wiry, but I outweighed her. And I bet I was stronger. I did Pilates. Sometimes.

I had to go for it.

In one quick motion, I rolled onto my side, curled my knees to my chest and kicked upward with all my might.

I must have caught her by surprise. I knocked her off balance, and she dropped a pair of pruning shears. I rolled onto my back over the shears so she couldn't grab them and kept on kicking whenever she tried.

"You thought you were smarter than me." Macker drew back and made some kind of hissing noise between her teeth. "That pathetic detective boyfriend of yours who's been pining away in his car watching you and Ian and your rat hole of a B&B wasn't enough for you, was it? You wanted Ian back, too."

What? Beatrice McWilliams was crazier than I'd thought.

I swiftly jerked my head to one side and lifted my chin. The filthy bandanna slipped slightly. Not enough for me to make much noise, but it was something.

I gasped for air. "You murdered Fallon," I said, between short breaths. "You won't get away with it. And if you kill me here, this will be a crime scene. Your DNA's all over it."

"Oh, that won't be a problem." Macker leaned closer, smiling into my face before I kicked at her again. She leaned away. "I've already thought that out."

The petite drummer sat back on her heels with an even more devious expression. "But if it's any comfort, you won't die alone. Noel is next. And no worries, I'll get another shot at his artifact of a dad."

"Why would you do that, *Beatrice*?" I asked, stalling for time. Someone had to come into the garage. Where was St. Jude, the patron saint of lost causes, when I needed him?

No, St. Anthony, the patron saint of lost things. He'd helped Colleen find Bliz's doll. *Show Ian where the ring is,* I prayed. *Right now.*

Fallon's ring.

Our ring.

"It was Fallon you wanted." I tried to keep my voice even. "You knew she didn't love Ian. But *you* did. And Ian didn't love you back. He didn't even notice you, did he?"

Macker's pale face flashed practically purple. "Would you ever shut up?" she said again. "He's going to fall in love with me. When it's just us. You others are in the way. Especially you."

"That engagement ring will never be yours," I said. "Not for real. You stole it from Noel's guitar case. But you can't steal Ian's heart."

She scowled. "Fallon did. Easy-peasy. What did it take her, three months? But she didn't want anyone's heart but Noel's. I saw those two rowing outside Farrell's. The bleeping wagon threw that ring away. It's mine already."

"Macker, it doesn't work that way. Killing more people won't help. Turn yourself in now before things get worse for you. You can get help."

"If Ian is never going to love me, like you said, I've got nothing to lose."

She jumped to her feet and aimed a kick at my head, but I blocked it with one leg. That surprised Macker as much as me. "Ow!" she said. "You freaking witch."

Those weren't her exact words.

Soon she'd find another weapon to threaten me with. The garage was full of them, hung neatly from hooks on the walls. I prayed she wouldn't spot the chainsaw stored on a high shelf.

No one would hear us, thanks to the extra soundproofing. Maybe they'd feel the vibrations of a freaking chainsaw from inside the house.

I tried not to shiver. But thinking of possible handy weapons made me remember something else. "Why did you bring Athena Sweeney's fettling knife back to the Buckley House after you stabbed poor Fallon?" I asked, still trying to buy time. "Why didn't you just put it back in Athena's studio, where you found it? Or throw it in the woods?"

"You really are dense." Macker frowned. "Didn't you just mention DNA? I needed to clean the thing off. But I didn't have a chance with so many people around this place. Luckily, your stupid dog had already made a mess of your backyard. There was dirt everywhere, so before everyone woke up on Saturday morning I dropped the knife into a hole and covered it up with branches. I planned to go back for it later. I didn't realize that hairy nuisance hound would go and dig it up."

Obviously she knew nothing about dogs. But good on Rover.

"You know what? I've had enough of all your questions," Macker went on. "You're dead now, nosy American witch." Her eyes lit up as they darted to the Wall of Every Torture Implement Known to Man. But instead she scurried toward the container of gas near the side door to the house.

Hopefully she wouldn't find the lighters for the grill. None of us but Mom ever could.

Make that Mom and Macker. The petite psycho immediately plucked a lighter from the corner shelf. Then she lugged it with the gas container over to me. "Say your prayers," she said, twisting the gas cap. "And say a nice good-bye to the future Mrs. Forde, too. I won't be here to see you die."

The side door suddenly opened. "What the—?"

Ian.

I turned my head toward my ex's voice. He stood open-mouthed as he took in the scene, a water bottle and a page of sheet music in his hand. Noel was right behind him, guitar case on his shoulder, looking equally shocked. But only for a second.

Both of them charged Macker, who had shriveled into a tiny, miserable shadow of herself. They had her hog-tied in less than a minute with bungee cords from a clear plastic tub beside the chainsaw. The young woman's cruel bravado was suddenly gone, leaving a pale, shaking, terrified girl.

Who was likely to be found guilty by a court of law for the ruthless murder of Fallon O'Malley. And maybe also the attempted murder of Kathleen Margaret Buckley.

"I'm so sorry, Kate," Ian said in a shaky voice. His face had almost less color than the still-silent Macker. "This is all my fault."

"No," Noel said quietly. "It's mine."

"Thanks, but can someone please untie my wrists and help me up?" I asked. I'd managed to sit up, without spearing myself with the shears, but that was about it.

As soon as I was on my feet and free from the rope that had skinned my wrists raw, I pushed the automatic door opener. I needed fresh air so I could breathe again.

As the door rose, grinding and groaning as usual, I was relieved to see the outside world—and Garrett, running up the driveway with his hand on his gun. The driver's side door of his car was open at the curb.

This really was my lucky day. A win for me. And St. Anthony.

Chapter Thirty-Three

"Do you think Bliz will be OK up there?" I asked Ian as we stood under the brightly lit Ferris wheel. "This is the first year I haven't gone with her." I shaded my eyes against the LED points of green, white, and orange, scanning the bucket seats for this year's Little Miss Shamrock.

Ian looked up, too. He didn't need to protect his eyes because he wore dark shades. At night, so no one would recognize him as the lead singer of Peat. Or so he figured. He also had on an old Shamrock PD hoodie of Frank's, and he'd tucked his hair under his ballcap. "Ah, she's delighted with herself," he said. "See, she's laughing with her friends. She's waving to us now."

I finally spotted Bliz, and Ian and I both waved back. She did seem to be having a ball as she sat wedged behind the safety bar between Zoe and Cassandra. All three wore sparkly tiaras and sashes. To everyone's surprise, the two older girls had been crowned co-Miss Shamrocks on Wednesday night. A tie. First time in town history.

I caught my breath as the royals started kicking their feet to swing the bucket. "I wish they wouldn't do that," I said.

"You're up to ninety now, Kate," Ian said. "Relax. They'll be fine. Want to get a jig-away sundae? There's a cart over there."

A crème-de-menthe sundae in a stale waffle cone did sound heavenly. But I was starving. And the enticing aroma from the chicken barbecue tent behind us overwhelmed the ones of kettle corn, cotton candy, and fried dough.

Plus the chicken was unlikely to be dyed green.

A few minutes later, Ian and I sat at the end of an empty picnic table behind heaping plates of chicken, salt potatoes with melted butter and parsley, and knock-off Parker House rolls. Ian's green plastic cup held Guinness, mine Sam Summer. A true New England Irish-fair meal.

We had the table to ourselves because the previous party had spilled a pitcher of sticky green punch—a Shamrock special—across the white plastic tablecloth.

Ian cocked his head thoughtfully as he chewed. "The spuds always taste different here in America," he said. "Or in Shamrock, anyway."

"Better, right?" I teased.

He shrugged. "Not bad." He put his fork down and reached into the pocket of his hoodie. Then he placed an envelope on the section of dry tablecloth between us. "For you," he said.

I stared at the white, legal-sized envelope. It was blank, other than the "Emerald Records" address in the left top corner. "What is this?"

"It's official," Ian said. "Peat and the Limerick Lads are joining forces. Well, Noel anyway, with occasional guest artist appearances by Marty. He'll be on the Crossroad Dreams studio soundtrack as well. The twins are retiring. Anyway,

I've had papers drawn up. You and the girls will get a cut of my portion of the profits."

"Ian, I—I don't know what to say." It was true. I didn't.

"We should have the advance in time to pay the girls' school fees." Ian glanced around before continuing, "I'm sorry, Kate. For everything. I know this won't make up for the way I've acted since we split. No, before we split."

"Don't apologize. It's OK."

"It isn't, though. I promise, I'll try to be better in future. I was selfish. And stupid."

My gaze met his. "Well, I appreciate that. But really, it wasn't all your fault. I—"

"No," Ian broke in, shaking his head. "You know what the dumbest thing I ever did was? Leaving you and Maeve. And Bliz." He looked down at his now-cold potatoes. The butter was starting to congeal. "I'm an eejit with relationships. I don't know how things went as far as they did so fast with Fallon. I was lonely, maybe. I can't be a rocker forever. Life on the road is starting to get old. And so am I."

"I think we both have a few miles left." I smiled.

"Garrett's a good man," Ian said. "I was wrong about him. And hey, if he makes you happy—"

I felt myself flush. Garrett was here on the fairgrounds somewhere, working security. To be honest, I hadn't completely forgiven him yet for his secret surveillance of my ex—and me. The Chief's idea, I'd learned, as a security precaution for all of us. But Garrett could at least have told me.

Nothing had prepared me for the way this conversation with Ian had turned. So many feelings were spinning in my head. Good. Bad. Neither.

I was saved from responding when a blur of gold and Kelly green whirled into the tent, followed by Maeve in hot pursuit.

Rover, dressed in some kind of jockey-style green satin costume with shamrock-topped feelers from Paddy's Paws, ran straight to me and skittered to a stop, a string of bangers dangling from his mouth. He looked from me to the leftover chicken on my plate, clearly torn, as everyone else in the tent stared at us. And laughed.

"Sorry, Mom." Maeve grabbed the end of his leash from the grass. "He got away from me. I don't think they're going to let him back in the Pet Pavilion."

Chapter Thirty-Four

Later that night, I sat alone in the backyard porch swing, sipping a cool glass of blueberry lemonade as I viewed the post-fair-night action in the Buckley House backyard.

It felt as if I were watching a movie where I was part of the scene, but also the viewer in the theater. My emotions might be running particularly high due to the crazy-extreme events of the past few days, but the love I felt right then for every person on the lawn was nearly overwhelming.

Still wearing her tiara and her former First Communion dress—Mom had tucked it away in the cedar closet with Colleen's first Irish dance dress—Bliz shrieked with glee as she played tag with the Murphy girls. Her main official duty earlier today as Little Miss Shamrock had been to help finally unveil the much-anticipated butter sculpture at the fair.

Unfortunately, the heat had been so intense on Wednesday that the butter dripped all over the gazebo before the dairy-version likeness of Mayor Raymond F. Flanagan could be revealed. Athena deemed it beyond repair—apparently the statue's melted face bore an even greater resemblance to one of her twisted gnomes than she'd told her father. A delay in the unveiling was decreed and Athena's masterpiece was whisked off to a nearby farm to be converted into renewable energy in the farm's methane digester.

The mayor graciously took it all in stride. Athena offered to create a whole new sculpture in less than forty-eight hours by plastering the auction gnomes with butter to replace the butter mayor monster on the pedestal. No one had bid on them so far anyway, so everything worked out well. Especially for Gabby. After being slathered with butter, they were unsellable, so back to the Gifts of Gab display window they would return after the fair.

Along with the remaining gnome Noel had already given back to her.

Ian and Noel were chatting with Moira McShane Kelly at the picnic table. I never thought I'd see Moira in our backyard, but as long as her great-aunts didn't show up with her, she was welcome. Colleen happened to mention Moira's PR and management skills to Ian, and it looked as if Moira might have a new job with Peat.

Marty would be in the hospital for a while, but despite his injuries he was enjoying the life of Reilly. He'd become fast friends with his roommate Nick Sweeney, and at this very moment they were playing Irish Poker with Jimmy and Timmy. The twins would head back across the pond after the weekend.

The Chief was delighted that Marty would be sticking around in Shamrock beyond his recovery, to work with Peat on the music for Crossroad Dreams. Mom was possibly less delighted, but she was happy for Dad. Plus, Noel and Frank had promised to set up the new Buckley House security system ASAP. She wouldn't have to listen to his grumbling anymore.

My dad was also pleased as Shamrock punch, I think, that I'd helped crack the O'Malley case. I was Detective Katie Margaret now.

Colleen sat on the porch steps with Aidan. The two were deep in conversation. Had she gotten wind that we were planning a surprise birthday party for her on Sunday night after the fair closed? Hopefully Bliz hadn't blabbed. My sister was a Fourth of July baby, but I had a feeling Ms. Independence's relationship with Aidan was getting more serious. I'd never ask, and she'd never tell. But I had a hunch we'd find out soon.

Maeve sat cross-legged on the grass with Zoe and Conor Murphy. Rover's head was in her lap as he looked up at her adoringly. Cassandra had left directly from the fair tonight with her mom and all their bags and boxes and suitcases. They'd stay at a hotel in Boston and fly home to Ireland tomorrow, but they promised to be back next year. Lulu had already booked the Connemara Suite.

As I watched my older daughter with her friends, I couldn't help but notice she seemed the happiest she'd been in a long time. Maybe I hadn't fully realized how angry and hurt she'd been about the situation between her and her dad. In just a few days, the two seemed to be on the road to a closer relationship, and Maeve was already making progress on the guitar. Ian had told me he planned to spend a lot of time between New York and Shamrock, and not just for band business. He and Noel had had some long talks, and he'd accepted the truth about his best friend and his fiancée. Ian admitted the news was a shock, but maybe if he'd been more tuned in, he would have realized it himself.

Garrett was manning the grill while Siobhan passed out plates and kept the food orders straight. He looked up and grinned at me after flipping a burger and catching it on his spatula to impress me. To be honest, I had no idea whether my not-boyfriend and I would end up in a real relationship. Especially after the turbulent events of the past six days. If I decided to stay in Shamrock, I guess we'd find out.

And Macker? Fallon's alleged killer was denied bail and still in custody at the Cloverhill County Jail. I'd have to face her in a courtroom down the road, but I was ready.

* * *

"Mommy, why do I have to go to bed so early in the summer?" Bliz flopped back against her pillows and pulled the quilt up under her chin.

Through the round open window of the Nest, laughter, voices, and music floated up from Colleen's birthday party. Things were just getting started.

"It's not early," I said. "And tomorrow is another big day. I thought you wanted to eat fried pickles and see the pigs and go on more rides at the fair. Plus you'll get to wear your crown again."

Bliz immediately sat up. "Can you read my princess book? Please?"

"How about if I tell you a princess story instead?"

"OK," my daughter said. "Make it a really good one, please. With a big, beautiful castle."

I smiled and stretched out next to her. Banshee jumped up on the bed and curled between us, making Bliz sneeze again. "Once upon a time there was a beautiful princess just your age, with long blond curls," I began. "And she was a very good dancer."

"Like me."

I nodded. "And the princess's mother, the queen, loved her very much. But guess what? The queen's sister, who lived in a different castle, loved the princess, too. The two queens loved the princess so much, they decided they would both be her mothers."

"That's nice," Bliz said. "Did they all come to live in the same castle? And have lots of adventures? With a cat like Banshee? And a big dog and the princess's sister and their grandparents?"

"They did," I said. "And you know what?"

Bliz's Buckley dimple deepened. "They all lived happily ever after."

"That's exactly right," I said.

Acknowledgments

For this return to the world of the Buckley Family in Shamrock, Massachusetts, I'd again like to thank the people close to me who helped bring *Buried in Shamrocks* to life. Without them I'd be up the River Liffey without a paddle: my kids Kimberly, Stephanie, and Rory; the littles (and not-so-littles) Alison, Eleanor, Fionn, and Margaux; my sister Robin and my entire extended family, both Irish-American and Irish.

Many thanks as well to my fabulous agent, Stephany Evans, and the amazing folks at Crooked Lane Books (especially Thaisheemarie Perez); my blogmates at Chicks on the Case: Ellen Byron, Jennifer J. Chow, Marla Cooper, Vickie Fee, Leslie Karst, Cynthia Kuhn, and Patricia Sargeant. Much love and appreciation as well to the other members of my Fearless Foursome writers' group: Gigi Pandian, Ellen Byron again, and Diane Vallere. And I'd probably still be floating in the water without Dru Ann Love, Mary Monnin, Lori Roberts Herbst, Tammy Barker, and Ruth Koeppel.

Special added thanks to awesome author and dear friend Cleo Coyle, as well as Samantha Gallo, our intrepid librarian at the Fuller Public Library in Hillsborough, New Hampshire.

And last but also first, I can't express enough love and appreciation to my husband, Saint Rich.

Thank you to my readers who love the Buckleys as I do, and may the pages rise to meet you all.

Sláinte!